MATT JENSEN:
THE LAST MOUNTAIN MAN
DEADLY
TRAIL

William W. Johnstone
with J. A. Johnstone

PINNACLE BOOKS
Kensington Publishing Corp.

www.kensingtonbooks.com

PINNACLE BOOKS are published by

Kensington Publishing Corp.
850 Third Avenue
New York, NY 10022

PUBLISHER'S NOTE
Following the death of William W. Johnstone, the Johnstone family is working with a carefully selected writer to organize and complete Mr. Johnstone's outlines and many unfinished manuscripts to create additional novels in all of his series like The Last Gunfighter, Mountain Man, and Eagles, among others. This novel was inspired by Mr. Johnstone's superb storytelling.

All Kensington titles, imprints, and distributed lines are available at special quantity discounts for bulk purchases for sales promotions, premiums, fundraising, educational, or institutional use. Special book excerpts or customized printings can also be created to fit specific needs. For details, write or phone the office of the Kensington special sales manager: Kensington Publishing Corp., 850 Third Avenue, New York, NY 10022, attn: Special Sales Department; phone 1-800-221-2647.

PINNACLE BOOKS and the Pinnacle logo are Reg. U.S. Pat. & TM Off.

ISBN-13: 978-0-7860-1867-3
ISBN 10: 0-7860-1867-4

First printing: April 2008

10 9 8 7 6 5 4

Printed in the United States of America

Prologue

"Here ye, hear ye, hear ye! The sentencing is about to be announced. All rise for the Honorable Felix J. Crane presidin'," the bailiff shouted. "Everybody stand respectful."

The Honorable Felix J. Crane came out of a back room. After taking his seat at the bench, he adjusted the glasses on the end of his nose, then cleared his throat.

"Would the bailiff please bring the accused before the bench?"

The bailiff, who was leaning against the side wall, spit a quid of tobacco into the brass spittoon, then walked over to the table where the defendants, Clyde Payson and Garvey Laird, sat next to their court-appointed lawyer.

"Get up, you two," he growled. "Present yourself before the judge."

Payson and Garvey were handcuffed, and had shackles on their ankles. They limped up to stand, as best they could on busted knees, in front of the judge.

"You two have been tried by a jury of your peers, and

found guilty of the murders of Miss Margaret Miller, a beloved teacher of our children, as well as little Holly McGee, one of her students. For these two murders, you are sentenced to hang by your neck until you are dead," Judge Crane said. He cleared his throat, then looked over at Matt Jensen, who was present in the courtroom.

"Mr. Jensen, I regret that we could not find these two despicable creatures guilty of the murder of your family. While I have no doubt of your veracity, the court has only your account of the incident, and that account is your memory from when you were ten years old. However, though we could not find them guilty for that particular crime, I hope you can find some comfort in knowing that these two men will hang. And they will hang because you have brought them to justice."

"I am satisfied, Your Honor," Matt said. He looked at Payson and Garvey. "You two will be dead," he said. "And dead is dead."

"You go to hell, Matt Jensen!" Payson shouted. "Do you hear me? You go to hell!"

"Silence that man!" Judge Crane said, banging his gavel.

The bailiff signaled two deputies, and they stepped up quickly to gag Payson.

"It is interesting that you would mention hell, Mr. Payson," Judge Crane said. "Because, although I do not have the power to sentence you to hell, I will soon be passing you on to a higher judge who does have that power. And there is no doubt in my mind but that you will suffer eternal torment for the misery you have caused others during your stay on earth.

"This court is adjourned."*

---

*Excerpt from *Matt Jensen—The Last Mountain Man*

* * *

The sentence was carried out within two days, and nearly the entire town of Cedar Creek had turned out to watch. Some were there because they felt a need to see justice done. Many were there because of the morbid attraction of watching someone hang.

One of the witnesses to the execution had walked up to Clyde Payson just a few minutes before they took him up onto the scaffold. Payson had not yet had the hood put over his head, so he could still see everyone in the crowd. When he saw the person staring at him so intently, he made a face.

"What the hell are you looking at?" Payson demanded. "Who are you?"

"Quiet Stream," the man said.

"What? Your name is Quiet Stream?"

"You son of a bitch. You don't even recognize the name, do you?"

"Who is Quiet Stream?" Payson asked.

"Do you not remember her?"

"Never heard of her."

"She is an Indian woman that you once raped."

"Haw! I've raped a passel of women in my day, white and Injun. I've even had me a few coloreds, but I never bothered to learn their names."

The witness stared into Payson's eyes until the prisoner was taken up onto the scaffold and the hood was drawn over the outlaw's face. Then, just before the trapdoor lever was pulled, he called up to the prisoner.

"Quiet Stream was my mother, you son of a bitch. I am your son."

"What? What did you . . . *uhhn!*"

Payson's last words were cut short as he dropped through the trapdoor and his neck was broken.

Chapter One

Two years later,
Walkback Ranch, near Cuchara, Colorado

The single lantern put out enough light to illuminate the bunkhouse, showing not only the sleeping accommodations in four sets of double-stack bunk beds, but also the walls, which were covered with newspapers and decorated with photographs and advertising posters.

There were three men in the cabin, two sitting at a table playing cards, and a third who was cooking something in a pot that sat on top of a little wood-burning, potbellied stove.

Pete, one of the men at the table, looked over at the man who was cooking their supper. Making a face, he waved his hand in the front of his nose. "What the hell is that you're a'cookin' over there, anyhow, Dumey? It smells like skunk."

"You don't have to eat it if you don't want to," Dumey replied as he stirred the pot. "You can always rustle up your own grub."

"Hell, I didn't say I wasn't goin' to eat it," Pete said.

"There didn't nobody figure you wasn't going to eat it," Shorty said. Shorty was the other man at the table. "You bitch about the food, but when the time comes, you're always the first one there."

"Well, it's better'n starvin' to death," Pete said.

Dumey laughed. "They's a lot of ways you might die, Pete, but from the looks of you, starvin' to death ain't one of 'em."

Pete and Shorty laughed at Dumey's observation.

"But it makes you wonder why Matt Jensen always finds some reason to go into town whenever it's your turn to cook," Pete said.

"He don't always go into town whenver I'm cookin'," Dumey replied.

"Really? Well, it seems like he does."

"Do you fellas know who Matt Jensen is?" Shorty asked.

"What do you mean do we know who Matt Jensen is? Are you saying he ain't Matt Jensen?" Dumey asked.

"No, that's exactly what I am tellin' you," Shorty said. "He is Matt Jensen."

"I swear, Shorty, you ain't makin' one lick of sense. First you say do we know who Matt Jensen is, then you say he is Matt Jensen," Dumey said.

"Yes," Shorty said. "He is Matt Jensen. The real Matt Jensen, the gunfighter."

Dumey laughed. "No, he ain't. He may have the same name and all, but there ain't no way he's the one that's been wrote about in them dime novels."

"Yes, he is," Shorty insisted.

"Now, you tell me why Matt Jensen, I mean *the* Matt Jensen, would be workin' as a ranch hand for twenty and found," Dumey said.

"I don't know," Shorty said. "I just know it's the same one, that's all."

"What the hell, Shorty. Are you goin' to gab all night, or are you going to play cards?" Pete asked. "Are you in, or out?"

"I'm in, I reckon, but I can't bet more'n one match," Shorty said. He slid a match into the little pile in the middle of the table.

"Whoa! One whole match!" Pete teased. "Well, I'll just raise you five matches."

"Damn, what are you doin', buyin' the pot?" Shorty asked, throwing in his cards.

"It's called smart poker," Pete said, taking the match and adding it to the stack of matches that were already in front of him.

"What are you plannin' on doin' with all them matches anyway?" Shorty asked.

"Hell, I thought ever'body knew that already," Pete answered. "What I aim to do is win all the matches in the whole bunkhouse so's Dumey can't cook no more. Then we won't have to worry none about being poisoned."

"Ha! Like you're worried," Shorty said. "Don't you pay him no never mind, Dumey," he said over his shoulder to the cook. "You know him. He'd eat the north end of a southbound mule while it was still walkin'."

"Well, I hope he would," Dumey said. "'Cause that's just what I'm cookin'."

Dumey's comment drew a laugh from both Pete and Shorty.

Outside the bunkhouse, a rider stopped on a little hill overlooking the ranch and ground–tied his mount, then moved about thirty yards forward to the edge of the hill. Crouching, he looked down toward the bunkhouse. He could see three men through the window, two sitting at a table and another one standing close by.

From this distance, he couldn't tell which one was Matt Jensen, but it didn't matter. He would kill them all.

The rider raised his rifle and took slow, careful aim. The targets were well illuminated by the lantern that burned brightly inside the bunkhouse.

Squeezing the trigger, he sent out the first bullet.

Shorty heard the tinkle of glass, as if something had been tossed through the window, and he looked up in surprise and curiosity. Behind him, Dumey let out a little grunt of pain, spun around once, then fell to the floor.

"What the hell you doin' Dumey?" Pete asked. "Did you taste some of your own food?" Pete laughed at what he thought was a joke.

"Boys, I been shot!" Dumey gasped.

The laughter died in Pete's throat as another bullet crashed through the glass window, smashed some crockery, then careened off the iron stove, projecting lead splinters and shards of glass like miniature bursts of shrapnel.

"My God! My God! What is it! What's happening?" Shorty shouted.

Pete rolled off his chair, dropped to the floor, then crawled over to the window while yet another bullet crashed through the little shack. When he looked out the window, he saw the muzzle flash.

"Somebody's shootin' at us!" Pete yelled, but there was no one left to hear him, for when he looked back inside, he saw that the other two were already dead.

Pete knew he had to get out of there, or he would be dead too. The walls of the bunkhouse were so thin that they couldn't stop the bullets. The only protection they could offer would be to mask Pete's movement. Using that to his advantage, Pete managed to tear out a couple of boards from the floor. As soon as the hole was big enough, he crawled through it to get to the ground below the cabin. He felt the dank coolness of the dirt, smelled its odor, and breathed a small prayer of thanks that he had come this far without being hit. Whoever was shooting at the cabin did not realize that Pete had slipped away, for the bullets continued to crash through the cabin overhead.

Lifting up his head just enough to see where he was going, Pete slithered on his belly to the back of the bunkhouse, opened the door, then rolled down into a small depression that allowed him to move, undetected, several feet away. There, he was able to let himself down into gully that was deep enough for him to stand. And standing, he started running without looking back.

Matt Jensen was on his way back to the ranch when he heard the shooting. Because of the effect of echoes, however, he couldn't be sure of the direction from which the shooting was coming. He climbed to the top of a large rock outcropping while the firing was still going on to see if he could find out. Then, far to the west, he saw the muzzle flashes. He knew that it was at the Walkback Ranch, but he didn't know who it was, or why they were shooting.

Matt remounted and started toward the ranch. Within a minute, he met Pete, who was running in the opposite direction.

"Pete, hold up! What's going on?"

"Don't go to the ranch!" Pete called back. "Some madman is shooting up the place. He's already killed Dumey and Shorty."

Matt slapped his legs against the side his horse, then urged him into a full gallop, which was dangerous on this ground and in the dark. But he knew that Spirit was an exceptionally agile horse, and he counted on the animal to negotiate the trail without incident.

By the time Matt reached the ranch, the shooting had stopped. He swung down from his horse in front of the big house.

"Mr. Kincaid!" Matt called. "Mr. Kincaid, it's Matt Jensen! Are you in there?"

"Is the shooter gone?" a voice called from the darkness of the house.

"Yes, sir, I believe he is," Matt said. "Is anyone hurt in there?"

The front door opened and a tall, thin man with white hair and beard stepped out onto the porch.

"We're all right in here," Kincaid said. "For some reason, all the shooting was directed at the bunkhouse."

Drawing his pistol, Matt moved through the shadows of the towering aspen trees, alongside the barn, and finally to the bunkhouse, which was nearly one hundred yards away from the main house.

Matt approached cautiously, dashing across the last open area, then pressing himself up against the side of the bunkhouse. The windows facing the tree line were all shot out, and there were bullet holes in the wall. Because of that, it was easy to determine that the shooting had come from the hill beyond the corral.

"Shorty, Dumey?" Matt called. "It's me, Matt. Anyone alive in there?"

When Matt didn't get a response, he moved to the door, but didn't go inside. Instead, he looked through the door and saw both Shorty and Dumey lying on the floor.

The interior of the cabin was still illuminated by the lantern and, using the light thus provided, Matt was able to make a thorough inspection of the cabin, making certain no one was lying in wait for him.

After satisfying himself that that was the case. Matt stepped inside the cabin, where he moved quickly to check on the two cowboys. He knew, even before he reached them, though, that both Shorty and Dumey were dead.

To Matt's surprise both men, in addition to the wounds in their body, had very precise wounds in their forehead, as if the shooter had come into the cabin purposely to finish them off.

That was when he saw a single .50-caliber bullet on the table, in the middle of a spread of cards and a pile of matches. Wrapped around the .50-caliber bullet was a piece of paper, held in place by a strip of rawhide. Matt untied the rawhide and opened the piece of paper. The paper had a name, and a strange symbol.

MATT JENSEN

Shorty Caldwell and Chris Dumey were being buried in a plot at the Walkback Ranch. Neither one of them had family that anyone knew about, and when Dwight Kincaid had asked the other cowboys what they thought about the idea of burying the two men at Walkback, they'd all agreed that Shorty and Dumey would probably appreciate being buried on the ranch where they'd worked and had friends.

Cowboys and friends of the two men had come from adjacent ranches as well as the nearest town to attend the funeral. Everyone was wearing his finest clothes for the funeral, and they all were now standing alongside the two open graves, heads bowed, hats in their hands. They were waiting for Matt and Mr. Kincaid to join them.

Matt was alone in the bunkhouse because all the others were outside. He sat on the edge of his bunk and just stared, morosely, at the floor.

At the other end of the bunkhouse, the door opened and Kincaid came in.

"Is it true you're planning on leaving us?" Kincaid asked.

Matt nodded.

"There's no need for you to do that, you know."

"Shorty and Dumey are dead because someone came after me," Matt said. "I have no right to put others in danger like that."

"You don't know that the shooter was after you," Kincaid said.

"My name was only name the shooter left."

"Do you have any idea who it might be?"

"No," Matt said.

"I'll be honest with you, Matt. When you first came here, I went into town to ask the sheriff about you. He said you have a sterling reputation—that you have never killed anyone who didn't need killin'."

"That's right," Matt said. "But it turns out that those people all seem to have brothers, or cousins, or fathers, or sons who want revenge. I have no idea who this was, but I suspect it is someone bent on revenge. And people like that don't always care who gets in the way. No, sir, I think it would be better if I moved on."

Kincaid nodded. "All right," he finally said. "I hate to see you go, but I can see your point." He reached out to shake Matt's hand. "You're a good man, Matt," he said. "As fine a man as I've ever known."

"I appreciate that, Mr. Kincaid. Now, I reckon it's time to go say good-bye to my friends, living and dead."

Kincaid nodded. Then the two men left the bunkhouse and walked back to the cemetery plot where the burial party was waiting.

After the burying, Matt said good-bye to Pete and the others. Then he mounted Spirit and rode off. He was about ready to leave the ranch anyway, though he would have preferred to leave under different circumstances.

Matt never stayed anywhere very long. He was a lone wolf who had worn a deputy's badge in Abilene, ridden shotgun for a stagecoach out of Lordsburg, scouted for the army in the McDowell Mountains of Arizona, and panned for gold in Idaho. A banker's daughter in Cheyenne once thought she could make him settle down—a soiled dove in the Territories knew that she couldn't, but took what he offered.

He was a wanderer, always wondering what was beyond the next line of hills, just over the horizon. He traveled light, with a bowie knife, a .44 double-action Colt, a Winchester .44-40 rifle, a rain slicker, an overcoat, two blankets, and a spare shirt, spare socks, spare trousers, and spare underwear.

It had been two weeks since Matt left Walkback Ranch, and since he had no particular place to go, and no need to be there, he was enjoying going nowhere. He killed a rabbit and spitted it over an open flame to cook for his supper. Then, during supper, he realized he was being watched. Slowly, showing no sign that he even knew that anyone was out there, Matt threw sand on the fire to extinguish it. Then, with the fire out, he spread his bedroll as if he were about to go to bed, being careful to place his boots at the foot of the bedroll and his hat at the top.

Walking a few steps away from the bedroll, Matt relieved himself, then returned to the bedroll and crawled down into the blanket. He lay there for a moment, then, in the darkness, silently rolled away and slid down into a small gulley that ran nearby. Pulling his pistol, he cocked it as quietly as he could and inched back up to the top of the gulley to stare through the darkness toward the bedroll, using a technique of night vision he had learned from his mentor, Smoke Jensen.

"Don't stare right at what you are trying to see," Smoke had told him. "There's always a dark spot right in the middle of your eyes when you try to see something at night. But if you will look just to the side of it, you'll find that you can see it."

From here, and using the trick Smoke had taught him, Matt could see that with his boots and hat in position, it looked exactly as if someone were in the blankets, sound asleep. Matt was satisfied. If his campsite looked that way to him, it would look that way to whoever was dogging him.

He waited.

Out on the prairie, a coyote howled.

An owl hooted.

A falling star flashed across the dark sky. A soft, evening breeze moaned through the mesquite.

And still he waited.

It was almost a full hour after Matt had "gone to bed" before the night was lit up by the great flame-pattern produced by the discharge of a shotgun. The roar of the shotgun boomed loudly, and Matt saw dust and bits of cloth fly up from his bedroll where a charge of buckshot tore into it. Had he been there, the impact debris would have been bone and flesh rather than dust and cloth, and he would be a dead man.

Instantly thereafter, Matt snapped a shot off toward the muzzle flash, though he was just guessing that was where his adversary was as he had no real target.

"Oh, you son of a bitch! You're a smart one, you are," a voice shouted, almost jovially. The voice was not near the muzzle flash, and Matt knew that his would-be assailant must have fired and moved. Whoever this was, he was no amateur and as Matt thought about it, he realized that the assailant could use the flame pattern from his own pistol as a target.

Matt threw himself to the right, just as the shotgun roared a second time. Though none of the pellets hit him, they dug into the earth where he had been but an instant earlier and sent a spray of stinging sand into his face. Matt fired again, again aiming at the muzzle blast, though by now he knew there would be no one there. A moment later, he heard the sound of retreating hoof-beats and he knew that his attacker was riding away.

Who was it? Who was after him?

Matt moved his bedroll for the remainder of the night, but the next morning he returned to his original campsite, then took a look around to see what he could find.

He found where the assailant had waited, and saw two expended twelve-gauge shotgun shells.

Then he found something that he had seen before. It was a .50-caliber bullet, around which was wrapped a piece of paper, held in place by a strip of rawhide. Opening the paper, Matt again found the symbol and his name.

MATT JENSEN

"I'll give you this," Matt said as he held the bullet and paper in his hand. "You are a persistent bastard, aren't you?"

Putting the bullet in his pocket, Matt walked back over to Spirit, remounted, and continued on his way. Coming to a road, he saw a little sign pointing to the east. The sign read CUCHARA.

"Cuchara," Matt said aloud. "What do you think, Spirit?"

Matt sometimes talked to his horse, just to hear a human voice—even if it was his own. And somehow, talking to a horse seemed a little saner than talking to himself.

"It might be good for us to live in town for a while," he said.

Spirit accommodated him with a whinny and a dip of his head.

Chapter Two

Matt Jensen had been in town for almost two months now, staying in a rented room at Emma Foley's Boarding House. When Mrs. Foley learned who he was, she was concerned at first, but as she told the Reverend Nathan Sharkey, pastor of the Cuchara Baptist Church, she couldn't ask for a better guest.

"He is quiet, never disturbs anyone, and pays his bills on time," Mrs. Foley said about her famous guest. "And he is always willing to lend a helping hand around the house, even without my asking. I also don't mind telling you that, though I was sometimes frightened around him at first, now I find it comforting to have someone of his reputation staying with us. I know that nobody would dare to break into the house, not with a man like Matt Jensen around."

Matt, who was a tall, broad-shouldered man with ash-blond hair and piercing blue eyes, was well known for his acumen with a gun. What many did not know was that he had learned his deadly skills from the legendary Smoke Jensen, a man whose exploits had been celebrated from coast to coast.

* * *

"How many do you think are faster than I am?" Matt had asked Smoke when Smoke declared that his young protégé had mastered the skills of drawing and shooting a pistol.

"It doesn't matter how many are faster," Smoke answered.

Matt looked confused. "What do you mean, it doesn't matter how many are faster?"

"It doesn't matter," Smoke repeated. "There may be some who are faster; there probably are some who are faster. But you have now reached the point where neither the speed of your draw nor your accuracy in shooting is a consideration."

"What is?"

Smoke sighed, and ran his hand through his hair before he answered.

"I've held this for last, Matt. What I'm about to tell you is the final secret of the gunfighter. And, I'm sorry to say, it is a terrible secret."

"What is the secret?"

"At this level, being fast or accurate is not the differing factor. At this level, everyone is fast and everyone is accurate. But not everyone is willing to kill."

"What?"

"The average man will pause—hesitate for just a heartbeat—before he pulls the trigger for the shot that he knows is going to kill," Smoke explained. "In a situation like that, the victory goes to the man who will not hesitate."

"Yes," Matt said. "Yes, I see what you mean."

"I hope you do see," Smoke said. "Because being able to see and understand that will keep you alive."

"How do you overcome it?"

"You will have to think about it every day. I want you to know that if you have to do it, you can kill a man without a second thought."

"All right," Matt agreed.

"There's one more thing I want you to remember," Smoke said.

"What is that?"

"Matt, you now have an awesome power. You have the power of life and death. Only God, and the righteous, should ever have such power.

"You aren't God, so that means you must be righteous. Be a knight, Matt. Never abuse this power you now have."

"I won't."

"Swear to me, Matt," Smoke said. "Swear on the graves of your ma and pa that you will be a knight."

"I swear to you, Smoke. I will be a knight," Matt promised.

It had been a long time now since Matt had that conversation with Smoke. But the essence of it had stayed with him all through the years. Not once, in the many deadly gunfights in which he had engaged, had he been the aggressor. Every man who had fallen before Matt Jensen's gun had precipitated the event.

At this moment, Matt was lying on the bed in his room at Mrs. Foley's Boarding House, with his hands laced behind his head. Then, realizing that it was about supper time, Matt got up from bed, poured water from a pitcher into a basin, washed his face and hands, then went downstairs to the dining room.

The other guests were just coming into the dining

room as well: Mr. and Mrs. Simmons and their eleven year-old boy, Kevin; Clarence Poole, who worked in the dry-goods store; and Amon Withers, a druggist in the town's only apothecary.

Mrs. Foley came into the room then, carrying a large platter of biscuits.

"I hope you folks have an appetite tonight," she said. "I seem to have gotten carried away. I cooked way more than I should have."

"Mrs. Foley, it is impossible to be around anything you cook and not have an appetite," Matt suggested.

Mrs. Foley laughed. "You do know how to flatter a woman," she said as she put the tray of biscuits on the table.

"Those certainly look good, Mrs. Foley," Withers said.

"Thank you," Mrs. Foley replied. "Oh, by the way, Mr. Withers, I got a letter from my son in San Francisco today. He told me to give you his best. He still says he is a doctor because of you."

"Nonsense," Withers said, though it was obvious he was pleased by the comment. "Dr. Foley is a wonderful physician, and would be whether or not he had ever met me."

"Still, I think being around all the wonderful medicines, potions, and nostrums that you keep in your store had a great influence on him."

"Mr. Jensen, can I ask you a question?" young Kevin Simmons asked.

"It's 'may I,' dear," Mrs. Simmons corrected.

"May I?"

"Yes, of course," Matt replied.

"Is it true you killed your first man when you were my age?"

"Kevin!" Mrs. Simmons gasped. "What a terrible thing for you to say to Mr. Jensen!"

"That's all right, Mrs. Simmons, I'll answer him," Matt said. "No, Kevin, it isn't true."

"Oh."

When Matt went to bed that night, he thought about the question Kevin had asked him. Matt wasn't eleven when he killed his first man.

He was ten.

It was just after the Civil War and Matt, who at the time was only ten years old, had gone West, by wagon, with his father, mother, and older sister. They encountered six men on the trail. When it became evident that the six men intended to rob them, Matt's father told them to move on.

"What if we don't want to ride on?" the leader of the group asked.

"Then I'd be obliged to make you," Matt's father, who was named Martin, said.

"How you goin' to do that? There's only one of you and there are six of us."

"You seem to be the one in charge," Martin said easily. "So you are the one I'll kill."

The leader of the outlaws, a man named Payson, threw his duster to one side and raised a double-barrel shotgun. Matt's father snaked his own pistol from his holster in a lightning-fast draw. Before Payson could shoot, Matt's father pulled the trigger. But the hammer made a distinct clicking noise as it misfired.

Payson pulled the trigger on his shotgun and the blast, at nearly point-blank range, opened up Martin's chest, cutting his heart to shreds. He fell off the wagons seat, dead before he hit the ground.

"Martin!" Matt's mother screamed.

"Get them two women down here!" Payson ordered. "If they ain't got no money, then we may as well have us some fun with 'em."

"Matt, run!" his mother shouted.

Earlier, Matt had moved his father's rifle closer to the edge of the wagon. Now he grabbed the rifle and darted into the rocks alongside the wagon trail.

"What about the boy?" one of the men shouted.

"You can have 'im if your taste runs to boys," Payson said with an evil chortle. "But for me, I'm goin' to have me one of these women."

The others laughed at Payson's comment. Then they grabbed Matt's mother and sister and jerked them down from the wagon seat. Mother and daughter fought hard, biting and scratching.

"Damn you!" Payson said, jerking back from the woman. "Be still!"

Matt's mother and sister continued to struggle, putting up such a fight that Payson and the half-eared man, who had taken first dibs, couldn't get the job done.

"To hell with it!" Payson said. He took a knife from his belt, then slashed it across the mother's throat. She began gurgling as blood spilled onto the dirt.

"Mama!" Matt's sister shouted.

"Cut the bitch, Garvey!" Payson said, and the half-eared man silenced the girl.

Payson stood up then, and looked down at the bodies of the mother and her daughter.

"Damn," he said. "Why'd they make us do that? Hell, I don't want 'em now."

"I'll do it," one of the other men said.

"What are you talkin' about, you'll do it? They're both dead," Payson said.

"What difference does that make? Hell, all I want is a poke. She don't have to be alive for me to get a poke. Wasn't aimin' to make her fall in love with me."

The others laughed nervously.

"Anyone else goin' to join in the fun?" the man asked as he began unbuttoning his pants.

By the time Matt found a place in the rocks that would let him see what was going on, his mother and sister were already dead. Matt was less than twenty-five yards away from the six men who were standing around his mother and sister. He aimed the rifle at the head of the man who was standing over his sister, and pulled the trigger.

The sudden gunshot startled everyone.

"What the hell?" Payson shouted, spinning around. Behind him, the man Matt shot was pitching back with blood and brain matter oozing from the top of his head.

The moment Matt shot, he pulled back from the rock where he had been, and slipped into a very narrow fissure between two large rocks. As a result, Payson didn't see Matt, but he did see a wisp of gun smoke hanging in the air from where Matt had fired.

"It's the kid!" someone shouted. "Somehow he's got hold of a rifle."

"Get him!" Payson ordered.

"He went in between them rocks."

"Lucas, you the smallest one of us. Poke your head through there and see if you can get in and pull him out," Payson ordered one of his men.

Nodding, Lucas ran over to the two rocks, then started squeezing through the narrow opening between them.

"Can you get through?" Payson called.

"Yeah, it's tight but I can do it," Lucas called back as he struggled to work through.

From his position behind another rock, about ten yards beyond the fissure, Matt watched Lucas working hard to squeeze through. Lucas was in a very contorted position when Matt noticed that, while both arms were through, his waist, and consequently his gun, was not.

Matt stood up then and stared pointedly at Lucas.

"Ha!" Lucas called. "Payson, come on! We've got his ass now."

"No," Matt said as he raised the rifle to his shoulder. "I've got yours."

Matt killed Lucas that very day, then managed to get away, but not before making a vow that he would avenge the murder of his family. Years later, Matt did just that.

Sangre de Cristo Mountains

It was cold, and the campfire they had used to cook their food and make their coffee was also providing warmth. Seven men were sitting around the fire, eating their supper of beans and staring into the dancing flames. A trapped bubble of gas in one of the burning pieces of wood burst, making a loud popping sound and sending up a shower of sparks.

Using his hat as a heat pad, Boone Parker reached out over the fire to take the coffeepot from its perch on a little metal frame. He poured himself a cup, put the pot back, then took a swallow.

He spit the first swallow out. "What the hell!" he sputtered. "What did you make this coffee with, Taylor?"

"I got the water from a pond back a'ways," Billy Taylor said. "It might be a little brackish."

"Brackish? It tastes like horse piss," Boone said, even as he took another swallow.

"Damn, Boone, you've drunk a lot of horse piss, have you?" Marcus Strayhorn asked, and the others laughed.

"Very funny," Boone replied. "Now, let's get back to business. Do any of you have any questions?" he asked.

"We're going to rob the bank in Cuchara," Al Hennessey replied. "What's there to question?"

"I just want to make certain that everyone understands what they are supposed to do," Boone said.

"Come on, Boone, it ain't like we're plannin' some battle or somethin'," Ed Coleman said.

"Yes, it is," Boone insisted. "It's exactly like plannin' a battle, and don't you forget it. Now, you, Strayhorn, Hennessey, and I will go inside the bank. Taylor, you, Teech, and Clay will stay outside, holding the horses."

"The hell you say," Clay replied. "You brought me into this because of my gun." Rufus Clay was the youngest of the group. He tossed a twig into the fire, then looked up at Boone. "I don't plan to be no horse holder."

Boone sighed. "Use your head, Clay. If there's goin' to be any shootin', it's more'n likely goin' to take place outside. If someone gets word of what's goin' on, we could have the whole town turnin' out on us before you know it. You've heard about what happened back in Northfield, Minnesota, when the Jameses and the Youngers tried to hold up their bank."

"That ain't goin' to happen here," Clay said.

"I know it isn't," Boone said. "And I'm countin' on you to see that it don't happen."

"What about Matt Jensen?" Strayhorn asked.

"Matt Jensen?" Clay said. "What about him?"

"I heard he was livin' in Cuchara right now. What if he gets word of what's goin' on?"

"Don't you be worryin' none about Matt Jensen," Clay said. He stood up and in a lightning draw, had his pistol in his hand. He fired three quick shots at an empty bean can, knocking the can into the air with his first shot, then shooting and hitting it two more times while the can was in the air. The sounds of his shots echoed and reechoed back from the surrounding hills. The horses, tied nearby, were startled by the unexpected gunfire, and they whinnied and reared back against their ties.

Getting up quickly, Hennessey hurried over to calm them.

"Goddamnit, Clay, what do you want to do? Put us afoot out here?" Boone asked angrily.

"I was just givin' you a demonstration as to why you don't have to worry none about Matt Jensen," Clay said. "I'd welcome the opportunity to go up against him."

"Would you now?" Strayhorn asked.

"Yeah, I would. You seen what I did with that tin can, didn't you?" Clay said.

"Yeah, I seen," Strayhorn said. "But what I didn't see was that can shootin' back."

"Maybe you want to take me on," Clay challenged.

Strayhorn, who was squatting alongside the fire, drinking coffee, stood up and poured his coffee out.

"No," he said. "I don't want to take you on. As a matter of fact, I don't want anything to do with any of this. If I'm going to take a risk in robbing a bank somewhere, then the bank is going to have to be big enough to make it worthwhile. I doubt there's more'n five thousand dollars in this bank."

"Five thousand dollars is a lot of money," Hennessey said.

"It ain't a lot of money if you're dead."

"Look," Boone said. "If you don't want to be a part of this, why don't you just ride on out of here."

"Yeah," Clay said. "We don't need no cowards ridin' with us."

Strayhorn glared at Clay for a long moment before he spoke. "All right, I'll just get my gear and ride on out of here," he said.

Clay turned to look at the others, and he laughed out loud. "I thought Strayhorn was a big brave outlaw. Did you see how I—*ummph!!*"

Clay suddenly went down on his face. Standing behind him was Marcus Strayhorn, holding a good-sized club in his hands. When Clay tried to get up, Strayhorn hit him again, and this time Clay went down and out.

"Did you kill him?" Coleman asked.

"If I didn't, I will," Strayhorn said, drawing the club back for another blow.

There was the sound of a pistol being cocked and, looking up, Strayhorn saw that Boone had a gun in his hand, pointing at him.

"I don't want him killed," Boone said. "I may need him."

"If you are having to depend on him, all I can say is you are in bad shape," Strayhorn said. He tossed the club into the fire, where it stirred up smoke and sparks before the flames began licking around it.

"I expect you had better get on then," Boone said.

"Don't worry. I don't want no part of this," Strayhorn said. He looked at the others. "Are any of you going with me?"

"Yeah," Teech said. "I'll go with you."

Strayhorn looked down at Clay. "I won't kill the son of a bitch," he said. "But I'll expect you to keep him from comin' after us."

"He won't be comin' after you," Boone said. "Not till after we pull this job, anyway."

Strayhorn nodded. "Fair enough. Come on, Teech, let's go."

In silence, the two men saddled their horses, then rode off into the night. Clay regained consciousness about the time they were leaving, but he was still too groggy to do anything. After a moment, when the fuzziness went away and he realized what happened, he stood up.

"That son of a bitch hit me from behind, didn't he?" Clay said angrily.

"Yes," Boone answered.

"Why that . . . ," Clay reached for his gun, but his holster was empty. "What the hell? Where is my gun?"

"I've got it," Boone said.

"Give it back to me."

"Not yet. Not until they are far enough away that I know you won't be going after them. We're going to rob a bank, and you're going to make certain that Matt Jensen don't interfere. After that, if you're still alive, you can go after Strayhorn all you want."

Hennessey chuckled. "If you're still alive," he repeated. "That's pretty good."

"Don't you be worryin' none about that," Clay said. "I tell you true, if I ever get a chance to go up against Matt Jensen, he'll be the one that is dead."

"Let's get back to talkin' about the bank," Taylor said. "When do we hit it?"

"Not for a couple of days. I want to go into town and

check it out first," Boone said. "I figure I'll do that tomorrow."

"Good. I'd like to go into town and get myself somethin' to eat other'n beans; maybe even have a pretty girl serve me a whiskey," Hennessey said.

"I'm afraid you're goin' to have to put that off for a while, Hennessey," Boone said.

"What do you mean? I thought you said we was a'goin' into town tomorrow."

"Not all of us," Boone said. "If we all ride in together tomorrow, then ride in again together the next day, some folks might find that a little strange. I'm only goin' to take one person with me tomorrow."

"Well, then, take me," Hennessey said.

"No, I'm takin' Clay," Boone said. "I need him to get a good look at the lay of the town. If folks do get wind of what's goin' on and come after us, I want Clay to know where they would most likely be."

"Can I have my gun back now?" Clay asked.

Boone handed the pistol back to Clay. "Clay, I want you to pay particular attention to anywhere they might be able to set up an ambush," Boone said.

Clay replaced the cartridges he had expended when he shot at the tin can. Then he stuck the pistol back in his holster.

"You don't have to tell me how to do my job," he said pointedly.

Chapter Three

The next evening Matt walked from the boardinghouse down to the saloon to have an after-dinner beer and see if he could find a card game that would hold his interest. He stepped up to the bar, and slapped a silver coin down in front of him. The sound of the coin made the saloon-keeper look around.

"Hello, Matt. How are you this evening?" the bartender asked.

"Doing fine, thank you, Paul," Matt replied. "Any good card games going?"

"One back there in the corner," Paul said as he drew a mug of beer then set it in front of Matt. "No opening right now, but I think I heard Kevin say he was about to leave. Kevin," Paul called. "Mr. Jensen is looking for a chair in a game. Let him know when you leave, will you?"

"I'm in no hurry," Matt offered quickly.

"No problem. Just a few more hands and I'm going to have to leave. I promised the missus."

"And believe me, she has him on a leash. If he don't leave, why she'll just jerk him out of here," one of the other players said, and the others around the table laughed.

Matt laughed with them, then picked up his beer, blew off some of the foamy head, and took a drink. It was now twilight, and as daylight disappeared, flickering kerosene lanterns combined with the smoke of cigars, pipes, and self-rolled cigarettes to make the room seem even hazier.

"I thought you were going hunting," Paul said.

"I'm going out first thing in the morning," Matt replied.

"Is Mrs. Foley going to take care of the deer if you get one?"

"*If* he gets one?" one of the others in the bar said with a chuckle. "You ever know Matt Jensen to go after deer and not get one?"

Paul laughed. "Well, you are right there," he said. "What will you do with it, Matt?"

"I've got a deal with Jason Cumbee over at the Mountain View Café," Matt said. "I kill it and dress it; he'll store it and cook it."

"You can't beat that."

At the opposite end of the bar stood a slender young man with dark hair and dark eyes. There was a gracefulness and economy of motion about the way he walked and moved.

The man had been watching Matt in the mirror, thinking that he had the luxury of studying Matt without himself being studied. In fact, quite the opposite was true. For although Matt had not looked directly at him, he already knew a lot about him. He knew that the man was wearing a quick-draw holster that hung low on the right side of a bullet-studded belt. In the holster was a Colt .44. And he knew, with the intuition of a survivor, that this man meant trouble.

The man tossed his drink down, wiped the back of his

hand across his mouth, then took a deep breath and turned to look at Matt.

"Hey, you."

Matt didn't turn toward him.

"I'm talkin' to you, mister."

Matt looked around. The man at the other end of the bar was wearing a low-crown black hat with a silver hatband. The expression on his face was one of pure evil, but Matt had seen such expressions before, and this one neither surprised nor frightened him. He raised his beer mug toward the man in a silent salute. He did that, all the while knowing that the man was not addressing him by way of a simple greeting. On the contrary, there was challenge in the tone of his voice.

"I heard you were here in Cuchara. That's why I came here," the man said.

"Really? Do we know each other?"

"No. We don't know each other."

"I see," Matt said. "So, you just wanted to meet me, is that it?"

"In a matter of speaking that's it. Though, truth to tell, there ain't goin' to be time for us to have what you might call a real friendship."

"What is your name?" Matt asked.

"Rufus Clay," the man said. He smiled a wide, toothy smile, but the smile did little to alter the evil look on his face. "But you've probably heard of me as Ruthless Clay."

Matt shook his head. "No, I can't say as I have," he said.

The expression on Clay's face grew even more evil as he frowned in wounded anger.

"You're lyin'," he said. "I know damn well you've heard of Ruthless Clay. Anyone who has ever read a paper knows about Ruthless Clay."

"Now that you remind me of it, perhaps I have heard of you," Matt said.

Clay nodded, his smile actually broadening in appreciation of the recognition.

"Well, I'm glad you have heard of me because I've got a bone to pick with you, Mr. Matt Jensen—Mr. Famous Gunfighter." He set the last words apart from the rest of the sentence, and said it with a sneer.

"Mr. Clay, I have a feeling we are getting off on the wrong foot here. Why don't you let me buy you a drink?" Matt offered.

"Huh-uh, buyin' me a drink ain't goin' to do it," Clay replied. By now, everyone in the saloon had picked up on the tension developing between Matt Jensen and Ruthless Clay, and all conversation had stilled as the patrons began following what was playing out at the bar.

Clay, sensing the audience, spoke louder, playing not to Matt but to the saloon.

"You'd like for me to just have a drink and go away, wouldn't you? You'd like me to just"—Clay stopped, then shook dramatically to emphasize a point—"quake in my boots because I am in the presence of the great Matt Jensen."

Matt put the beer down with a tired sigh and turned to face his tormentor. "What is it, mister?" he asked. "Where are you going with this?"

"You know where this is going," Clay replied.

Matt didn't answer.

"You haven't really heard of me, have you?" Clay asked.

"No, I haven't," Matt said.

Clay nodded. "That's what I thought. Everyone has heard of Matt Jensen, but nobody has heard of Ruthless Clay. Well, I intend to change that."

"How, by getting yourself killed?" Matt asked.

Clay's smile quickly turned to an angry snarl. "Draw, Jensen!" he shouted, going for his own gun even before he issued the challenge.

Clay was quick, quicker than just about anyone in the saloon had ever seen. But midway through his draw, Clay realized he wasn't quick enough. The arrogant confidence in his eyes was replaced by fear, then the acceptance of the fact that he was about to be killed.

The two pistols discharged almost simultaneously, but Matt had been able to bring his gun to bear and his bullet plunged deep into Clay's chest. The bullet from Clay's gun smashed the glass that held Matt's drink, sending up a shower of beer and tiny shards of glass.

Looking down at himself, Clay put his hand over his wound, then pulled it away and examined the blood that had pooled in his palm. When he looked back at Matt, his smile had become almost whimsical.

"Damn," he said. "You're good. I thought I could beat you. I really thought . . ." His sentence ended with a cough. Then he fell back against the bar, making an attempt to grab onto the bar to keep himself erect. The attempt was unsuccessful, and Clay fell on his back, his right arm stretched out beside him, his finger still in the trigger guard of his pistol. The black hat, with its silver band, had rolled across the floor and now rested against a half-filled spittoon. The eye-burning, acrid smoke of the two discharges hung in a gray-blue cloud just below the ceiling.

Matt turned back to the bar where pieces of broken glass and a small puddle of beer marked the spot of his drink.

"Looks like I'm going to need a refill, Paul," Matt said.

"Here you go," Paul said, putting another beer in front of Matt. "No charge, the house is buying the beer in celebration."

Matt looked up sharply. "Celebration?" he said. He looked over at Clay's body, now surrounded by the morbidly curious. Matt shook his head. "Thank you, but no," he said. "I don't celebrate a killing that was absolutely unnecessary."

Matt put another coin on the bar, then took his beer over to a table in the corner. If there were those who wanted to congratulate him, or bask in his presence, he showed by his demeanor that he wanted none of it. As a result, no one came to bother him, and he was able to sit alone.

Nobody even noticed when Boone Parker left the saloon. He knew now that it was a mistake to bring Clay into town. All Clay had been able to talk about was his hope that he would have the opportunity to go up against Matt Jensen. Well, the fool got his chance, and he got himself killed.

Boone had brought Clay into the group because Clay was very good with a gun. He knew it was a risk, even from the beginning, because Clay was also an arrogant and exceptionally vain man. His arrogance was predicated entirely upon his skill with the gun, though, because in Boone's mind, there wasn't anyone in his group who wasn't a superior man.

The irony was Matt Jensen was not going to even be a problem. Boone had heard Jensen say that he would be leaving on a hunting trip at first light in the morning. That meant that Boone and his men could come into town, rob the bank, and be gone without worrying about any interference from Matt Jensen. He wouldn't even have needed Rufus Clay.

Boone chuckled. The more he thought about it, the more he realized that Matt Jensen had actually done him a favor. This way, he wouldn't have the arrogant and volatile young man to deal with, and best of all, he wouldn't have him to share the take with. Everyone's cut of the pie from the bank robbery just got bigger.

When Matt returned to the boardinghouse, he was met by Mrs. Foley.

"Are you all right?" she asked.

"You heard?"

"Everyone has heard," Mrs. Foley said.

Matt shook his head. "I'm sorry about all this. I know it's not the kind of notoriety you would want from one of your boarders."

"Don't be silly," Mrs. Foley said gently. "I know it couldn't be helped."

"Thank you for understanding."

"Oh," Mrs. Foley said, handing an envelope to Matt. "I don't know how this got here or where it came from, but I found it in front of the door this evening. But it has your name on the envelope."

"Thank you," Matt said, taking the envelope. He didn't open it until he reached his room. When he did open it, he removed a single .50-caliber bullet, with the piece of paper held in place by a strip of rawhide. He knew what he would see, even before he unwrapped the paper.

MATT JENSEN

But this time, there was also a short letter.

"I'm glad you were not killed tonight," it said. "I am reserving that privilege for myself."

Matt sighed in frustration. For a while, he had entertained the hope that Clay was the mysterious man who was after him.

Chapter Four

Clouds, heavy with the promise of snow, clung to the tops of the Sangre de Cristo Mountains and drifted west toward Cuchara, Colorado. Despite that, or perhaps because people wanted to beat the impending storm, business was brisk. Wagons and buckboards moved up and down High Street, and bundled-up pedestrians, their breath forming vapor clouds, moved quickly along the boardwalks. Mrs. Emma Foley nodded in response to greetings from a couple of strollers as she stepped into the bank.

The bank was empty except for one employee, and he was standing by the little potbellied stove taking in the warmth. He looked up and smiled as Mrs. Foley stepped through the door.

"Good morning, Mrs. Foley," the teller said. "What brings you out on a cold, dreary day like this?"

"Good morning, Mr. Meade. I got a letter from my son yesterday, and he sent me a draft drawn on a bank in San Francisco," Mrs. Foley said, taking the document from her handbag. "I'm just wondering if there will be any difficulty in depositing it."

"I'm sure there will be no problem at all," Meade replied. "I'll be glad to take care of that for you," Meade walked over to the teller's cage. "How are you getting along?"

"Just fine, thank you," Mrs. Foley replied. "I have a wonderful group of people staying with me now. They keep me from being lonely, now that Mr. Foley is gone."

"I don't believe you'll ever have to worry about being lonely, Mrs. Foley. Not in this town anyway. Why, you've got dozens of friends all over," Meade said as he accepted the draft from her and started filling out a deposit slip. "I suppose you heard about the little fracas in the saloon last night involving one of your guests."

"Yes, you are talking about Mr. Jensen," Mrs. Foley said. "He came to tell me about it himself last night. He said he wanted me to hear it from him before I heard it from anyone else. It was self-defense."

"Oh, yes, it was that, all right," Meade said. "There's nobody questioning that. Matt Jensen had no choice, the other fella drew on him."

"Poor Mr. Jensen feels terrible about it," Mrs. Foley said.

"No need for him to feel bad about it," Meade said. "He was in the right. Will you be wanting any cash back?"

"No, just deposit it all to my account," Mrs. Foley said.

"Very good," Meade replied.

Suddenly, the front door of the bank was thrown open and three men, all wearing masks and carrying pistols, rushed into the room.

"Get your hands up!" one of the men shouted. "This is a holdup."

"Oh! Oh, my!" Meade said in a frightened tone of voice.

"You!" the robber ordered, pointing to Meade and throwing him a cloth bag. "Fill this bag with money."

As a nervous Meade began complying with the bank robber's request, Mrs. Foley stared at the three robbers.

"What are you lookin' at, old woman?" one of the obbers asked gruffly.

"I know you," Mrs. Foley said.

"No, you don't."

"Yes, I do. And I know you too," she said, pointing to one of the others. "The two of you worked for my husband one summer. You are Boone Parker and you are Al Hennessey."

"Damn you!" Boone said. He shot her, the sound of the gunshot sudden and unexpected. Mrs. Foley's eyes grew large as she realized she had just been shot. She fell back against the front of the counter, then slid down into a sitting position on the floor.

"What did you do? Are you crazy? You shot that old woman!" one of the other robbers said.

"She recognized us. We couldn't let her live, she would tell everyone."

"What about him? He heard her," the robber said, pointing to Meade.

"No, I've never seen you before!" Meade said, his voice rising to a high pitch in fright. He handed a full bag of money to Boone. "Here, take your money! I filled it up! I won't say a word, I promise."

Boone took the money bag, then raised his pistol. "I'm sure you won't," he said as he pulled the trigger.

"Let's get out of here," Hennessey said.

The three men ran out of the bank, then leaped up onto horses that were being held by a fourth man. They galloped out of town.

* * *

Matt Jensen, totally unaware of the tragic events that had just taken place in town, was in the nearby hills setting up for his deer hunt. Matt knew how sensitive a deer was to a strange scent, and that a male deer would always go downwind to check for danger, so he was positioned crosswind of the buck's line of travel in order to avoid detection.

Matt knew also that the buck would try to stay in cover as much as possible, so he found an area that he felt sure the buck would use. Then, leaving that area for the deer, he got out of sight and waited.

Matt was confident enough of the game that he allowed the first two deer to pass undisturbed. Then he heard a soft, nearly inaudible tapping sound. Most men would not have heard it at all, and most of those who might hear it would have no idea what it was.

Matt knew exactly what it was, and he gripped his rifle and stared at the place where he knew the deer would make its appearance. The leaves and branches of the low-limbed trees at edge of the forest across from where Matt had set up were waving gently in the wind. But buried within that sea-wave of vegetation was a movement in the opposite direction—a movement against the wind.

Even though Matt could not see the deer, he knew where it was, tracking him by the gentle movement of the branches as surely as if the deer were in plain view.

Then the deer appeared, at first only his nose sticking out from the bushes, nearly invisible as it sniffed for any sign of danger. Then the head stuck out and the deer looked all around it. Finally, the entire deer stepped out into the open, sniffing the wind, assessing the danger by smell and sight. It was a magnificent eight-point buck and Matt lifted the rifle to his shoulder, aimed, and fired.

* * *

It was several hours after the robbery when Matt Jensen rode into town with the deer slung across his horse in front of him. He headed straight for the Mountain View Café, where he had an agreement with the owner to store and cook for him any game he brought in. There seemed to be a lot of activity in the town, and Matt wondered what had everyone so agitated, but he didn't ask. Instead, he rode around to the back of the café, dismounted, and was pulling the deer off when Jason Cumbee stepped outside.

"That's a nice one," Jason said.

"He is a pretty good one," Matt replied as he hung the deer's back two feet up on a hook so that it could be dressed.

"Did you hear?" Jason asked.

"Hear what?" Matt replied as he pulled his knife to start to work on the deer.

"The bank was robbed. The robbers killed Frank Meade and Mrs. Foley."

Matt looked up sharply.

"Did you say they killed Mrs. Foley?"

"Yes. She was in the bank at the time of the robbery. Apparently there were only two there, Mrs. Foley and poor Frank Meade."

"Why would they shoot a helpless old woman?"

"Seems she recognized two of them, so they shot her to keep her quiet. Only, she didn't die right away. She lived long enough to tell the sheriff who did it."

"Who was it?"

"There were four of them, but she only named two. Boone Parker and Al Hennessey."

Matt shook his head. "I don't know either one of them."

"You wouldn't. They cleared out of here a couple of years ago. They did odd jobs, worked for Mr. Foley for a while, but they was always in trouble, what with fightin', gettin' drunk, destroying public property, and the like. Sheriff had them in jail about as much as out."

"Is he going after them?"

"Yes."

"I want to go too."

Cumbee smiled. "He figured you would. He asked me to send you down to see him soon as you got back in town."

Matt made a gesture toward the deer.

"Leave the deer, I'll take care of it for you," Jason said. "I want those sons of bitches caught too."

"Thanks," Matt said, sheathing his knife.

"There were four of them," Sheriff Craig said to Matt. "There would've been five, but you killed one of them."

"I beg your pardon?"

"More than half-a-dozen men have told me that Boone Parker come into the saloon with Rufus Clay yesterday. I figure Clay pushed you into that fight to get you out of the way so they could rob the bank today."

Matt nodded. "Could be," he said. "Since I had never met the man, I couldn't figure out what put the burr under his saddle."

"I'm hoping that you will take a hand in finding them," Craig said.

"Absolutely," Matt said. "They killed Mrs. Foley. I definitely want to find them."

"Good, I was hoping you would feel like that. I've got

more than a dozen men volunteering to be in the posse," Sheriff Craig said. "But I want you to lead it, if you will."

"No posse," Matt said, shaking his head.

"What?"

"I'll go after the men for you, but I don't want anything to do with a posse," Matt repeated. "If I'm going, I want to go alone."

"There are four of them, Matt," Sheriff Craig said. "Why on earth would you want to go alone?"

"Because if I go alone, I can find them," Matt said. "Stick a big posse behind me and I might as well be followed by a brass band. I can track, and I can move quietly if I'm by myself. But if there is a posse involved, we might never find them."

Sheriff Craig let out a long sigh and ran his hand through his hair. "I've heard you can track a fish through water," he said. "Is that true?"

Matt smiled. "Sometimes," he said. "It depends on the fish and it depends on the water."

"Yeah, well, you may have to track these guys through water if this storm moves in."

"I'll find them."

"All right, let's say you do find them. How will you get them back if you are by yourself?"

"I'll get them back," Matt promised.

"I do want them back, Matt. Alive. I want them to stand trial and hang legally."

"I'll get them back," Matt repeated.

Craig shook his head. "Damn if I don't think you can," he said. "I may be crazy for doing this, but I hereby deputize you, and I'll let you go out on your own."

"Thanks," Matt said. "I'll have them back by tomorrow afternoon."

Craig chuckled. "Whoa, now, that's biting off quite a load, isn't it? Tomorrow afternoon?"

"You're right, that might be a little early. I'll have them back by tomorrow night," Matt corrected.

Craig chuckled. "I'll keep the office open late," he said.

Fifteen minutes later, Matt rode out of town on the trail of the robbers. He had a week's supply of jerky, an extra box of .44 cartridges, and a rain slicker worn over his coat. In the mountains, there was a distant rumble of thunder, suggesting that the storm to come would more likely be rain than snow. Matt was grateful for that. It would be hard enough to track them in the rain, but practically impossible to track them under a mantle of new-fallen snow.

Just after dark, the rain started. It was a cold, driving rain, laced with little pellets of ice. Matt found a rock overhang that was large enough to give both him and Spirit a degree of shelter, and he prepared to wait through the night.

The one-room cabin that clung to the side of a mountain was built from logs and chinked with mud. Carved into a log just over the door was a message left by the original owner:

THIS HEER HOUS WAS BILT BY
JED. MORTON IN 1839.

Boone Parker had found the cabin, long deserted, about three months earlier. He laid in a supply of food, candles, and wood, specifically making this a place to go after the bank robbery. He even built a lean-to behind the cabin so the horses would have a place to stay.

It was morning of the next day and the four men had spent the night in the relative comfort of the cabin. The room was permeated by the smell of brewing coffee and frying bacon.

"Damn, Taylor, that smells pretty good," Hennessey teased. "You'd make someone a pretty good wife."

The others laughed.

Coleman, did you check the horses?" Boone asked.

"Yeah, I checked 'em while ago," Coleman answered. He was lying on one of the bunks with his hands laced behind his head. "Boone, how long we goin' to have to stay in this place?" he asked.

"Prob'ly till about spring," Boone answered.

"Till spring? Son of a bitch! Are you tellin' me we have to stay in this cabin till spring?"

"We've got food, coffee, wood, a place to stay out of the weather. What's wrong with staying here?"

"I just hate the thought of being stuck here when we have all that money to spend," Coleman said. "I mean, what good does that money do us if we are goin' to stay here?"

"Tell you what, Coleman. Why don't you just go back into Cuchara and spend it?" Taylor asked.

"Hell, Taylor, I ain't askin' to start spendin' it today," Coleman said. "I was just wonderin' how long we're goin' to have to stay here, that's all. Besides which, what if someone tracked us here?"

"That's not very likely," Boone said. "It's for sure that the rain last night wiped out our tracks so's no one could trail us. We'll just winter here, and by springtime, things will have died down a bit and we can go on our separate ways."

"If we hadn't killed that woman and the banker, the whole damn state wouldn't be lookin' for us," Taylor suggested.

"If you think robbin' a bank wouldn't have the whole state lookin' for us, you are crazy," Boone said. "Anyhow, she recognized us, I didn't have no choice."

"She didn't recognize all of us. She just recognized you and Hennessey."

"Recognizing one of us is like recognizing all of us," Boone said. He walked over and picked up a piece of bacon. "You want to go on, do it," he said as he took a bite of the bacon. "Only, the money stays here till we can all divide it."

"No, no, I ain't wantin' to go on by myself," Coleman answered. "I was just curious, that's all."

The rain had washed out much of the trail, but there were still little puddles of water that indicated hoof indentations, here and there a broken twig, and a few horse droppings. Much of it would have gone completely unnoticed by the average person, but Matt Jensen wasn't the average person, and to him the trail was as clearly defined as if there were a series of road signs directing him to his destination.

He smelled the cabin before he saw it, the aroma of wood smoke drifting from at least a mile away. As he got closer, he could also smell the bacon and coffee. He dismounted, tied off his horse, took four sets of handcuffs from his saddlebag, then moved, unobserved, to the front door. He stood just outside the door for a moment, listening to the conversation from within.

"If you hadn't killed that woman and the banker, the whole damn state wouldn't be lookin' for us."

"If you think robbin' a bank wouldn't have the whole state lookin' for us, you are crazy. Anyhow, she recognized us, I didn't have no choice."

"She didn't recognize all of us. She just recognized you and Hennessey."

"Recognizing one of us is like recognizing all of us. You want to go on, do it. Only, the money stays here till we can all divide it."

"No, no, I ain't wantin' to go on by myself. I was just curious, that's all."

Matt smiled. What he heard was as good as a confession. There was no question but that these were the men he had been trailing. Pulling his pistol, he kicked open the door and rushed inside.

Boone let out a shout of fear and alarm and jumped back from the stove. Hennessey started toward his pistol belt, which was hanging from the head of the bed. Matt fired at the belt, the bullet hitting just in front of Hennessey's reaching hand.

"I could've killed you just as easily," Matt said.

"What the hell? Who are you, mister?" Hennessey asked.

"It's Matt Jensen," Boone said. "The one who killed Clay. What the hell are you doin' after us? Is there a reward already?"

"I'm Sheriff Craig's deputy."

"Deputy, huh? I don't see no badge," Boone said.

"I didn't take the time to pick one up," Matt said. "Get down on your belly, all four of you."

"What? What do you want us to do that for?" Coleman asked.

Matt shot at the floor between Coleman's legs, the bullet poking a hole in the wide, unpainted planks and sending up a puff of dust.

"Do it," Matt repeated. "Or my next shot will take off one of your balls."

Coleman did as ordered, immediately followed by the others. Matt reached back outside the door, then picked up the four sets of handcuffs. He tossed all four to Boone.

"Cuff their hands behind their back," he ordered.

Boone did so, then Matt cuffed him. After that, he marched them out to his horse, where he took his rope and made four nooses. He put the nooses around the necks of each of his prisoners, then led them back to their own horses and ordered them to get mounted. As Taylor started to get on his horse he slipped, causing a pull against the neck of the other three men.

"Careful there, you dumb bastard!" Boone growled. "You want to break all our necks?"

Once all four prisoners were mounted, Matt tied the end of the rope to his saddle, then swung up onto his horse.

"Okay, gents," he said easily. "Let's head for Cuchara."

"It's a two-day ride to Cuchara," Hennessey protested.

"Then we better get going, hadn't we?"

"Hey, mister, when are you going to give us a chance to rest up a bit?" Boone asked late that afternoon. "We've been ridin' all day long without a break."

"You can rest when we get there," Matt replied.

"It'll be night soon. You plannin' on pushin' us through the night?"

"If need be."

"We ain't had nothin' to eat since breakfast."

"You can rest and eat when we get there."

"I'm so tired now, I'm about to fall out of the saddle," Boone said.

"I wouldn't recommend that," Matt said. "You could wind up breaking your neck. Fact is, you could break everyone's neck."

"Don't you be fallin' out of no saddle, Boone," Hennessey said. "We wouldn't be in this fix if you hadn't shot that old woman and the bank teller."

"Shut up, Hennessey," Boone said. "You was plenty ready to spend the money."

"All of you shut up," Matt said. "I'm not in any mood to listen to you talk."

"You can go on if you want to, but I ain't goin' no farther," Boone said. "Whoa, horse."

When Boone stopped his horse, Matt jerked hard on the rope. As the rope was looped around Boone's neck, it had the effect of choking him.

"Watch it!" Boone said. "You could jerk me off here an' break my neck!"

"That's right, I could," Matt said. "So my advice to you is to shut up and keep moving."

Chapter Five

Matt pushed his prisoners throughout the rest of the day, arriving in Cuchara around eight o'clock that night, well after dark. The five horses plodded down the dirt street, the hollow-clopping echoing back from the darkened false-fronted stores and houses. The jail, like many other buildings in town, was dimly lit by a single lantern.

Matt tied his horse off at the hitch rail, then stepped up onto the wooden porch in front of the jail, then pushed the door open. "You in here, Sheriff?" he called.

"Yeah, I'm here. That you, Matt?"

"Yes, it's me. I've got some prisoners for you."

Sheriff Craig stepped up to the door, then looked outside at the four men who were bound together by ropes around their necks. He chuckled. "Damn if you didn't say you'd have 'em back by tonight and here you've gone and done it," he said.

"You men climb down," Matt ordered.

Craig reached up beside the door. When he pulled his hand back, it was clutched around a Greener ten-gauge shotgun. He pointed the double-barrel weapon at the four men.

"Okay, you boys, just come on in real easy now," he said. "I've got a nice room all ready for you."

Sullenly, the four men, still connected by the rope around their necks, filed in through the jailhouse door. Sheriff Craig jabbed Boone in the ribs with the barrel of his shotgun.

"Hey, watch it. That hurts," Boone complained.

"Does it, now?" Craig replied, jabbing him again. "Well, now, that's too bad."

Matt returned to his horse and took the bag that had been tied to the saddle horn. "Here's the money they took," he said.

Craig held up his hand. "Don't give it to me," he said. "Give it to Mr. Matthews. That goes back to the bank."

"All right," Matt said, keeping the bag. "Tell Mr. Matthews if he wants his money to come see me in the Dog Bar Saloon. I'm going to get supper and a beer."

"I'll have a beer, Paul," Matt said when the bartender moved down to stand in front of him.

The bartender, who was sucking on a toothpick, nodded without speaking, then turned to draw a glass, then slid it in front of Matt.

"I heard you brought them four in a while ago," Paul said. "Is that right?"

Matt nodded, then took a drink of the beer. After the long, hard ride, it tasted very good.

"After what they done to Mrs. Foley and Frank Meade, I hope all four of the sons of bitches hang," Paul said.

"I expect they will, but that's not for me to decide," Matt said. "That'll be up to a jury."

"Ain't much question about it, far as I'm concerned,"

Paul said. "The jury will find 'em guilty for sure, and that's one hangin' I don't aim to miss."

A tall, gray-haired man came into the saloon then, accompanied by Sheriff Craig.

"I'll be damn," Paul said. "That's the banker. In all the time I've worked here, I don't believe Mr. Matthews has ever come in before. I wonder what brings him in now."

"He probably wants the money," Matt said calmly.

"What money?"

Matt picked up the bag that was on the floor by his feet. "This money," he said.

"Damn! You've had a bag full of money with you all the time you've been in here?"

"Yeah," Matt said. He handed the bag to Matthews.

"Thanks," Matthews said. "I'm glad to get the money back. I just wish it hadn't of cost Frank and poor Mrs. Foley their lives."

"Yeah," Matt said. He nodded toward an empty table. "Paul, bring me something to eat. I haven't had anything but jerky this whole day."

"Bring him anything he wants, Paul," Matthews said. "The bank will pay for it."

"Yes, sir," Paul said. "And Matt, the beer is on the house too."

Matt nodded, but said nothing as he took his beer over to the empty table.

Santa Clara, Colorado

Seeing a newspaper blowing down the street, Strayhorn picked it up and took it into the City Pig Café with him. Teech was already at the café, sitting at a table near the stove.

"I ordered you bacon and eggs and coffee," Teech said as Strayhorn sat down.

"You goin' to pay for it?" Strayhorn asked.

"What? Hell, no, I ain't goin' to pay for it."

"Then don't be orderin' nothin' for me."

"I was just tryin' to save some time is all."

"Save time for what?" Strayhorn asked. "What have we got to do?"

"Well, nothin', I don't reckon."

"Then don't worry 'bout savin' time."

"I'll tell 'em to cancel the order."

"Never mind, I'll eat it," Strayhorn said.

"And pay for it?"

"And pay for it," Strayhorn agreed.

"Did you buy a paper?" Teech asked.

Strayhorn looked up and frowned. "You ever know me to pay for a paper?" he asked.

"No, I just seen you with that one and I was wonderin', that's all."

"I picked it up when it was a'blowin' down the street," Strayhorn said. Looking at the paper, he suddenly chuckled. "I'll be damn," he said.

"What is it?"

"They should'a listened to me."

"Who should'a listened to you?"

"Boone and the others," Strayhorn said. "The dumb sons of bitches have done been caught."

Strayhorn read the article in silence.

BANK ROBBERS CAUGHT !

Trial to Be Held Quickly.

Rarely in the annals of human history has there been a crime so foul, a deed so dastardly, as that perpetrated in this fair community last Wednesday. On that day four dregs of humanity visited their evil upon this place by robbing the local bank, and murdering Mrs. Emma Foley and Mr. Frank Meade, two much beloved Christian citizens.

It is, however, with great pleasure that this newspaper can report that the cowardly desperadoes who perpetrated this foul deed are now in custody. Despite a summer storm which threatened to eliminate any sign, Mr. Matt Jensen, a well-known man of the mountains, tracked the villains to a cabin where, singlehandedly, he made the arrest.

Now, these scurrilous vermin, Boone Parker, Al Hennessey, Billy Taylor, and Ed Coleman, wait in the local jail for the appearance of Judge Amon Heckemeyer to conduct the trial which will send them to the gallows, and to an even harsher judgment when He, who created us all, will consign their miserable souls to eternal damnation.

In the same newspaper, Strayhorn also found an article about the gunfight between Matt Jensen and Rufus Clay. As he read this article, he began laughing out loud.

"What are you readin' that's so funny?" Hennessey asked. "Do they have jokes in that paper?"

"Jokes?" Strayhorn asked, still laughing. He shook

his head. "This ain't no joke," he said. "But it's funny. Fact is, it's funnier than any joke. What was it Clay liked to call himself?"

"You mean Ruthless?" Teech asked.

"Yeah, Ruthless," Strayhorn said. "Well now, he can call hisself dead." He passed the paper across the table to Teech. "Here. Read all about it."

Shootist Hurled into Eternity.

FIGHT OVER IN BLINK OF AN EYE.

A young man with misplaced confidence in his proficiency with a six-gun met his fate when he engaged Matt Jensen, a man whose skill has been proven many times over. The young pistoleer was named Rufus Clay, and it was reported by all witnesses to the event that it was he who demanded that their relative proficiencies be put to the test.

With the challenged issued, both men went for their guns, and while young Clay was very fast, he wasn't fast enough and came in second. In such a deadly contest as dueling, coming in second is not the desired outcome. Caps and powder exploded and pistol balls were sent on their flight. The ball from Matt Jensen's pistol found its mark while Clay's missile did no damage, save to a beer mug.

Though Clay had no family nor friends to mourn him, his funeral and burial in Boot Hill on the day subsequent was well attended by the citizens of the town, who collected money to erect a tombstone for him which reads:

> To all who pass this way
> My name is Rufus Clay
> In a gunfight quicker than the blink
> of an eye
> The other man lived—and I did die.

Cuchara

It was two more weeks before the trial was held, which was the time it took for Circuit Judge Amon Heckemeyer to come to Cuchara to hold court.

The first order of business was to empanel a jury of twelve men, good and true. Felix Gilmore, a young and eager lawyer from Wallenburg, was appointed as the defense attorney. He began his defense, by conducting a very aggressive voir dire.

"You are Mr. Anthony Tate?" he asked a prospective juror.

"I am."

"Did you know Emma Foley or Frank Meade?"

"I knew both of them."

"How well did you know them?"

"Cuchara is a small town," Tate replied. "Everybody knows everybody very well."

"Uh-huh," Gilmore said. "And is it true, Mr. Tate, that you did business with Mrs. Foley?"

"I own a butcher shop," Tate replied. "I have done business with everyone in town."

"What was your opinion of Mrs. Foley?"

"She was a fine, upstanding woman."

"And did you do business with Mr. Meade?"

"Yes, of course, every time I went into the bank."

"What was your opinion of Mr. Meade?"

"He was a fine, upstanding gentleman."

"Your Honor," Gilmore said, turning to the judge. "I would like to strike this juror for cause. I believe he was too close to the victims to be able to render a fair verdict."

"Counselor, I doubt you can find anyone in this town who did not know Mrs. Foley and Mr. Meade, who did not do business with them, and who did not have a high opinion of them," Judge Heckemeyer said. "That is not cause for striking."

"Then, Your Honor, I request a change of venue on the grounds that we cannot have a fair trial here."

"Request denied. Continue with your voir dire, Mr. Gilmore."

With the jury empaneled, the trial began. After his opening statement, Doug Jeter, the prosecutor, called his first witness. Dan Dunnigan testified that he had heard gunfire, then saw three masked men run from the bank, mount horses that were being held by a fourth man, unmasked, then gallop out of town.

He further testified that he then ran into the bank, where he saw Mrs. Foley sitting against the front of the teller's cage, bleeding from a wound to her chest.

"Did she say anything?" Jeter asked.

"Yes, sir. She said it was Boone Parker and Al Hennessey what done it."

"Thank you. Your witness, Counselor."

"You said the three men who ran from the bank were wearing masks, did you not?" Gilmore asked.

"Yes, sir, they was."

"Did you recognize any of them?" Gilmore asked.

"No, sir."

"So then you can't be certain that any of my clients are the ones you saw."

"Oh, yes, sir, they was the ones," he said, pointing to the men sitting at the defense table.

"How can you be certain of that?"

"They's more ways to recognize a person than just their faces."

"Oh?" Gilmore said. "And pray tell us, Mr. Dunnigan, what those ways are."

"Well, sir, one of 'em was tall, with big floppy ears and a nose that you could tell was big, even behind the kerchief he was wearin'. Like that first feller there."

"Let the record show that Mr. Dunnigan has pointed out Boone Parker," Jeter said from his table.

"Another'n had a scar come down over his left eye, like that second feller there."

"Let the record show that Mr. Dunnigan has identified Al Hennessey," Jeter said, again without getting up from his chair.

"Then they was the short bandy-legged feller there." Dunnigan pointed to the third man.

"That would be Edward Coleman," Jeter said.

"And that there one there was just sittin' on his horse holdin' the other three. He didn't even have no mask on, first time I seen him."

"Let the record show that Mr. Dunnigan has identified Billy Taylor."

"But it could be anyone with big ears, bandy legs, or

tall and thin—not necessarily these men," Gilmore said. "Because the truth is, you didn't see their faces."

"It was these—" Dunnigan began, but he was interrupted by Gilmore.

"You did not see their faces, did you?"

"No, sir, I didn't see them three men's faces," Dunnigan admitted. "But I seen his."

"No further questions, Your Honor."

The prosecutor brought three more witnesses who testified that they heard Mrs. Foley identify her killers before she died. Then Matt Jensen was brought to the stand. He testified as to the conversation he heard through the door of the cabin when he found the men.

"Objection, Your Honor, that's hearsay evidence," Gilmore said.

"Your Honor, Mr. Jensen is reporting what he heard directly from the mouths of the defendants, not what someone told him they heard. That makes his testimony directly relevant, not hearsay," Jeter said.

"Objection overruled," the judge said.

When Jeter was finished with his examination, Gilmore stood for the cross-examination.

"Mr. Jensen, were you involved in a shooting incident last week?"

Matt nodded.

"Please, for the record, you must give a verbal answer."

"Yes, I was involved in a shooting last week."

"Tuesday night, I believe?" Gilmore asked.

"It was Tuesday."

"Who did you kill?"

"The man's name was Rufus Clay."

"Did you know Mr. Clay?"

"Your Honor, I object," Jeter said. "Where is Counselor going with this?"

"I will show relevancy, Your Honor," Gilmore said quickly.

"Please do," Judge Heckemeyer said.

"Did you know Mr. Clay?" Gilmore repeated.

"No, I'd never seen him before that night."

"Did you know that when Mr. Clay came to town that day, he was with Boone Parker?"

"I've been told that."

"Is it not possible, Mr. Jensen, that your testimony against Mr. Parker might be self-serving?"

"Self-serving? In what way?"

"You did kill Rufus Clay, did you not? And he was with Boone Parker. I suggest, Mr. Jensen, that you have some personal animus against Boone Parker because he was with Rufus Clay on the night Clay tried to kill you. Is it not possible that you fear some possible future retaliation from Parker as a result of you having killed his friend? So, you have taken it upon yourself to blame him for the bank robbery and murder, just to get him out of the way?"

"Your Honor, I object," Jeter shouted. "There is not one bit of evidence to support this ridiculous suggestion, and my esteemed colleague knows it."

"I withdraw the comment and I have no further questions," Gilmore said. He was smiling as he returned to the defendants' table.

"What are you smilin' about?" Boone asked. "You withdrew the statement."

"I withdrew my statement, but you can't un-ring a bell. I made my point before the jury," Gilmore said.

Following Matt's testimony, the banker Matthews

testified that the amount of money in the sack Matt brought back with him was exactly equal to the amount of money that had been taken on the morning of the robbery. After that, the state rested its case.

"The state's entire case is built upon hearsay evidence," Gilmore pleaded in his summation. "Prosecution could not produce one eyewitness. Oh, they had witnesses who said they heard Mrs. Foley identify Boone Parker and Al Hennessey. But how much weight can we actually give their testimony?

"There is a reason for not accepting hearsay evidence, and that is because you cannot cross-examine them to check on their story. Think about it. The robbers were masked. She was an old, frightened woman. She may have just thought she recognized them and, without her here to question, we'll never know, will we?

"Mr. Jensen testified as to what he heard when he was standing outside the door of the cabin. But at best, that is self-serving testimony. After all, he may have his own reasons for wanting Boone Parker out of the way."

"Counselor," Judge Heckemeyer interrupted. "You withdrew that statement. I'll not allow it to be revisited."

"I beg your pardon, Your Honor, you are quite right," Gilmore said. Smiling at the jury, he said, "Forget that comment. But, gentlemen of the jury, even forgetting the suggestion that Jensen might have his own reasons for wanting Boone Parker to go away, and considering that there were no eyewitnesses to the bank robbery and murder, we have only hearsay as to the guilt of my clients. That, my friends, constitutes doubt, and if there is any doubt, you cannot, and must not, find these men guilty."

Jeter got up for his closing comments, and he applauded Gilmore quietly.

"I want to compliment my esteemed colleague on mounting a brilliant defense under extremely difficult conditions," he said. "It is our constitutional duty to see to it that everyone gets the best defense possible, and I do not believe the accused can say they did not.

"However, despite Mr. Gilmore's best effort, the evidence is overwhelming and compelling. You heard Mr. Dunnigan give very accurate descriptions of each of the men, doing so in a way that would identify them whether or not you saw their faces. You heard Mr. Jensen tell what he heard through the door before he captured the defendants. You heard Mr. Matthews testify that the money Matt Jensen recovered from the robbers matched exactly the amount of money that was stolen in the robbery. And lastly, there is such a thing as dying testimony. Whether or not Emma Foley is present to be cross-examined, she did make the accusation in front of three witnesses, and the fact that it was dying testimony gives it a great deal of weight. Gentlemen of the jury, there is no doubt here. Boone Parker, Al Hennessey, Ed Coleman, and Billy Taylor are all guilty as charged."

Chapter Six

After hearing arguments from both sides, the jury found all four accused guilty and, despite the protestations of the other defendants that it was Boone Parker who killed both Mrs. Foley and Frank Meade, the judge sentenced all four to die, the execution to be carried out that very day.

With their legs hobbled by chains, Deputy Goodson was given the responsibility of taking the four prisoners from the court to the holding cell. The prisoners shuffled by the crowd of people who had gathered around the courthouse in order to get a ticket that would allow them to watch the hanging. Although all four had been sentenced to hang, the gallows could only accommodate three at a time. Because it was generally agreed that Boone Parker was the one who actually did the shooting, he was selected to hang alone, after the others.

Once outside, Deputy Goodson took them across the courtyard toward a small holding cell. It was quiet in the yard since, as yet, no spectators had been allowed around the gallows. As they passed through the shadow of the gallows, someone was up on the deck, oiling the hinges to one of the three trapdoors. He pulled the lever and the door swung open with a bang. When it did so, Coleman let out a little cry of alarm and Boone laughed.

"You think it's funny, do you?" Coleman growled at Boone.

"I was just wonderin' if you were goin' to pee in your pants when they drop you through the trapdoor," Boone said. "Come to think of it, that might not be such a bad idea. If you pee in your pants, maybe you'll put out the fires in hell and it'll be cool by the time I get there."

Goodson laughed.

"What are you laughin' at?" Coleman asked.

"You," the deputy answered.

"Well, I'm glad we can be so entertainin' to you."

"Quit your cryin', Coleman," Hennessey said. "We're all in the same boat here."

"It ain't fair," Coleman said. "We wouldn't none of us be here if Boone hadn't been so trigger-happy. He's the only one should be hanged."

The four men were put in the holding cell, where they waited for no more than fifteen minutes. Then Goodson came back to get Hennessey, Coleman, and Taylor.

"Wait, what are you takin' us out now for?" Coleman asked. "There ain't even nobody out there yet."

"The judge wants you boys already up on the gallows before we let anyone in to watch," Deputy Goodson said.

"Boys, if you get there in time for supper, save a place at the Devil's table for me, will you?" Boone called out to them as they were taken from the cell.

As they started across the courtyard, the man who had been working on the gallows came down and started walking toward them. As soon as he was even with them, he pulled a gun and pointed it at the deputy's head.

"Cut 'em loose," he said.

Goodson looked up in surprise, then his face reflected his shock.

"Why, you ain't Jules," he gasped. "Where's Jules? Who are you?"

"I'm the man that's already killed Jules, and I'm gonna blow your brains out too if you don't do what I tell you to," the man with the gun answered. "Now, unlock those hobbles like I said."

"Howdy, Strayhorn," Hennessy said. "It's good to see you."

"Strayhorn! Strayhorn, don't forget me!" Boone called from the cell.

"Sorry, Boone," Strayhorn called back to Boone. "But I got me some ideas of my own, and there ain't room for two leaders."

"You son of a bitch! You can't leave me here!" Boone shouted angrily.

"Yeah, I can," Strayhorn replied easily.

From behind the courthouse a rider appeared, leading four horses. Strayhorn looked up at him. "Have any trouble, Teech?"

"Yeah, I had to knife the guard at the back gate," Teech said. "You boys hurry up and get mounted. We gotta get out of here."

Suddenly, two guards came into the courtyard from the front of the building.

"Stop!" one of them shouted. He fired a shot, which missed. Strayhorn returned fire and he didn't miss. The guard who had fired collapsed with a hole in his chest. The other guard, suddenly aware that he was alone, and not realizing that only two of the outlaws were armed, retreated back around the corner.

"Let's go!" Strayhorn shouted.

For just a moment, the prisoners took their eyes off the deputy. Goodson used that moment to draw his own pistol.

"Hold it!" he shouted. "You ain't goin' nowhere!"

Strayhorn turned toward the deputy and fired. Goodson fired back, hitting Coleman. Coleman went down. Strayhorn fired again, and this time the deputy went down.

"Come on, boys, let's go!" Strayhorn shouted, swinging into his saddle.

"What about Coleman?" Taylor asked.

"What about 'im?" Strayhorn replied as he dug his spurs into the side of his horse. His horse bolted toward the back of the plaza, followed by Teech, Hennessey, and Taylor. Coleman lay in a spreading pool of blood on the ground behind them.

"Don't leave me, you bastards! Don't leave me here like this!" Boone shouted angrily.

By now the shouts and gunfire had alerted the others, and several armed men appeared in the courtyard, just in time to see the four riders gallop through the back gate. They fired at the outlaws, but not one bullet found its mark. The entire band had gotten away.

Later that same day, Boone Parker was led to the gallows. His legs weren't hobbled, but his hands were handcuffed behind his back. He hesitated at the foot of the thirteen steps.

"Get on up there, Parker," Sheriff Craig said. "These good folks have already missed one hangin'. I don't intend to disappoint them again."

"Well, maybe you could come on up here and hang

alongside me," Boone suggested. "The folks ought to really like that."

"You know, there might be some who would be pleased at that," the sheriff replied with a chuckle. Then, more gently, and using his first name, Craig said, "Come on, Boone, the sooner we get this over with, the better it is for all of us."

Boone moved onto the scaffold, and was positioned under the noose. From there he had a very good look into the faces of the spectators, and he glared at them defiantly.

A clergyman stepped up to Boone, then began to pray.

"Oh, Holy Jesus, who of thine infinite goodness didst accept the conversion of a sinner on the cross; open thine eyes of mercy upon Boone, thy servant, who desireth pardon and forgiveness, though in his last hour he turneth unto thee. Renew in him whatsoever hath been decayed by the fraud and malice of the devil, or by his own carnal will and frailness. Consider—"

"That's enough of that," Boone said. "Get this Holy Roller off here and let's be done with it."

"But my son, will you not now repent?" the minister asked.

"I ain't repentin' for a goddamned thing."

"Mr. Parker! You are going to meet God with heresy in your heart and blasphemy on your lips! You'll spend an eternity in hell for that!"

"Thank's for the words, Padre," Parker said sarcastically. "They was just real comfortin'."

The clergyman, shaking his head in sadness, stepped down from the gallows.

"Any last words, Boone" Sheriff Craig asked.

"Just get it done," Boone said.

The sheriff nodded, and the hangman stepped up to

slip a hood over Boone's head. Once the hood was in place, he fit the noose.

"When the trap opens, don't hunch up your shoulders," the hangman suggested. "Just relax and it'll be better."

"Really? How the hell do you know?" Boone mumbled from under his hood.

"You aren't my first hanging," the hangman replied. He stepped over to the handle, then looked at Sheriff Craig. The sheriff nodded, and the hangman pulled the handle.

The trapdoor swung down on its hinges and Boone's body dropped through the opening. Either Boone didn't follow the hangman's instructions, or the hangman's instructions were wrong, because Boone didn't die right away. He was still alive, and for almost four minutes he kept drawing his body up as if in that way he could relieve the weight on his neck. His stomach heaved, and those nearest the scaffold could hear rasping sounds from his throat.

Chapter Seven

There were more than two dozen men gathered at the sheriff's office after the hanging. These were the men who had answered the call to join the posse in pursuit of the escapees and the ones who had helped them escape.

"Sheriff, how long are we going to be out?" one of the men asked.

"As long as it takes," Craig replied.

"The reason I ask is, I can't be away from the store too long. I mean, my wife can run it for a while, but we got kids to raise and she's goin' to have to be with them."

"Potter, there's nobody goin' to hold it against you if you don't go," Craig said. "This here posse is strictly voluntary."

"Maybe I better stay home too," another suggested, and after a little more discussion, the posse was cut down to ten plus the sheriff.

"Is Matt Jensen goin' with us?" someone asked.

Sheriff Craig shook his head. "I think he would go by himself if I asked him to, but Jensen don't believe in posses," he said.

"What do you mean, he don't believe in posses?"

"I don't know," Craig said. "It's just a thing with him."

"Well, by damn, I aim to be on this here hunt whether he wants me to or not. Deputy Goodson was my wife's brother, and I aim to get some revenge."

Craig shook his head. "We aren't going out for revenge, Staley," he said to his deputy's brother-in-law. "We're goin' out to bring them back—to hang for those who have already been convicted. And for trial for the others."

"Yeah, well, don't worry, I ain't plannin' on doin' nothin'. Watchin' 'em hang is revenge enough for me," Staley said.

"Good, I'm glad you feel that way. All right, those of you who are goin' out, go home and get yourself an extra box of ammunition and a warm coat to wear. Better pack an extra blanket in your bedroll. Take some oats for your horse, some bacon, beans, coffee, and jerky for yourselves. I figure on us ridin' out of here in no more'n half an hour."

Matt was playing cards in the saloon when the sheriff came in a few minutes later.

"Matt, can I talk to you for a few minutes?" the sheriff asked.

Matt looked at his hand and smiled, then laid it down. "Sure," he said. "As bad as this hand is, you're probably saving me a couple of dollars by pulling me out of the game. I'm out, boys."

Matt scooped up the money that was in front of him, then followed the sheriff back to the corner of the saloon. They stood alongside the silent piano to hold their conversation.

"I've got a posse together," he said.

"How many men do you have?"

"Ten. I started out with over twenty, but about half of them backed out."

"You would be better off if about half of what you have left quit as well."

"I know you feel that way," the sheriff said. "But there are at least four out there that we know about, and there may be a few more. One of them was Marcus Strayhorn, and he's known to have a few men riding with him."

"My offer still stands, Sheriff. If you would like, I'll go after them myself."

Craig shook his head. "I appreciate your offer, but there's no way I can send my posse home. These men want to go, Matt."

"I know, I know. I'm not saying give up your posse. I'm just saying I'll go after them myself independent of your posse, if you would like."

"No, I'd rather you not," the sheriff replied. "What I really want you to do is to stay on here and act as my deputy while I'm gone. What with Goodson dead, I don't even have a deputy to look after the peace right now."

"All right," Matt said. "I'll do that for you if you like."

"Yes, I would very much like," Craig said. "And I thank you for agreeing to take on the job."

"Sheriff Craig!" someone called loudly. Looking toward the front door, they saw Staley standing there. Staley was wearing a wool-lined, sheepskin coat and carrying a Winchester rifle.

"I'm back here, Staley," Sheriff Craig called back.

Staley looked around the room until he spotted Craig. Then, when he saw Matt, he scowled.

"I thought you said he wasn't goin' with us," Staley said.

"He's not going with us. I've just asked him to be my deputy while we're gone," Craig said.

"Good. I don't want to be ridin' with anyone who don't want to be ridin' with us."

"What is it, Staley? What do you want?"

"Oh," Staley said, as if just remembering why he had come in. "All the rest of the boys is down to the sheriff's office waitin' on you," he said.

"Good," Craig said. "We'll get on our way then."

"Good luck, Sheriff!" one of the saloon patrons called.

"Yeah, good luck," another called, and by the time Craig and Staley left the saloon, there were good wishes from everyone in the place.

Five minutes later, much of the town had turned out to watch the mounted posse ride off in pursuit of the escaped prisoners. There were a few more good wishes called, and some of the men said aloud they regretted the pressing reasons that prevented them from going along as well. But a cold wind and low-hanging clouds in the west made them secretly glad that they would be spending this night in the warmth and comfort of their own homes.

Cairo, Illinois

Layne McKenzie was a strikingly pretty woman with raven-black hair, brown eyes, high cheekbones, and lips that were a little fuller than average. After graduation from Southern Illinois University in Carbondale, she returned home to Cairo to apply for a job as a teacher in the Cairo school system. The examination process had been much more difficult than she anticipated, perhaps because there were four teachers applying for one position. All four had had to take a test, then be interviewed by the members of the Cairo School Board. After more than a week of waiting, Layne had finally received a letter from the school board asking her to appear before them at two P.M. today.

Because Cairo sat at the confluence of the Ohio and Mississippi Rivers, it was a major hub of river traffic, not only from the North, but from the East. Also, because it was the railroad gateway that connected the South to the North and the West to the East, it was a major rail hub.

Layne could see ample evidence of that now, because from the anteroom she had a view of the many boats that were tied up at the bank of the Ohio River. And from the window on the opposite side of the room, she could see the depot where, even now, two of the sixty-five passenger trains that passed through Cairo daily were standing in the station, taking on or discharging passengers.

She waited nervously in the anteroom, wondering what she had forgotten, or what questions she had failed to answer properly. When the door to the meeting room opened and Mr. Stallings stepped out into the anteroom, Layne took a deep breath. Stallings was the secretary of the school board and, or so she had perceived, had been the most difficult questioner during the interview proceedings. She hoped that his summoning her was not a bad sign.

"Miss McKenzie, would you please step into the meeting room?" Stallings asked.

Nodding, Layne picked up her handbag and followed his invitation.

Layne knew two of the school board members, and had known them for most of her life. One was a banker, the other was the minister at her church. They smiled at her as she entered the room, and that eased her nervousness.

"Congratulations, Miss McKenzie," Mr. Travelsted, the Superintendent of Schools, said. "The school board is pleased to offer you employment as a teacher in our system, with a starting salary of forty dollars per month. You will start next fall."

Layne was thrilled by the offer, though the excitement was somewhat tempered by the fact it was still seven months until fall.

"This offer is contingent upon two things," Travelsted continued. "You must take no other employment in the interim, and you must remain single for the duration of your employment by the Cairo school system. Do you agree to our terms?"

"I agree," Layne said.

"Here is a ruler," Mr. Stalling said, now smiling for the first time. "The ruler is symbolic of your position as a schoolteacher."

"Thank you," Layne said, returning the smile.

"The question now," Layne said to her mother and father that evening, "is what do I do from now until school starts next fall? I shall go crazy hanging around, doing nothing." She was holding the ruler in one hand and slapping it quietly into the palm of her other hand.

"I have an idea. My brother has been wanting you to come West for a visit. Suppose I write to him and see if this is a good time," Layne's mother suggested.

"I don't know," Layne's father said. "Denver, Colorado, is a long way to go."

"Nonsense, by train she can be there in less than a week," Layne's mother said.

"Oh, yes, I would love to go," Layne said enthusiastically. "Father, please say that it is all right."

Layne's father frowned for a moment, then he smiled and nodded.

"Of course it is all right," he said. "But you will be on your own for a long time so please, be very careful."

"I shall be, Father, I promise," Layne said.

Sangre de Cristo Mountains

"Boys, we've got 'em!" Staley said, looking around the area to which they had tracked the men they were chasing. "I've been here before. This here is a dead-end canyon. There ain't no way out of here 'ceptin' to come back this way. We got 'em trapped!"

Sheriff Craig stopped at the mouth of the canyon and took a drink from his canteen while he studied the canyon.

"Staley is right, this is a dead-end canyon, all right," Craig said. "The question is, do Strayhorn and his men know that it is a dead end? If they know, why would they go into it?"

"Why would they go into it?" Staley replied. "Easy, they don't know it's a dead end."

"But what if they do know?" Craig asked.

"All right, maybe they do know. But maybe they figure we wouldn't count on them going into a dead-end canyon like this."

"Or maybe they figure to draw us in so they can set up an ambush for us," Craig suggested.

"So what if that is their plan?" Staley asked. "What are we going to do, just let them stay in there? I mean, come on, there are only four of them, there are ten of us. I figure that, no matter what they have planned, we can handle it."

Craig hooked his canteen back onto the pommel and pulled his rifle from the saddle holster, then jacked a round into the chamber.

"All right," he said. "Let's play this hand out." He started walking into the canyon, leading his horse.

The others followed, the horses' hooves falling sharply on the stone floor, then echoing back loudly from the canyon walls.

"If they are in here, we damn sure ain't sneakin' up on 'em, are we?" one of the others said nervously.

"If you're afraid, you can always go back, Mitchell," Staley said.

"I didn't say nothin' 'bout bein' afraid," Mitchell replied sharply.

"Brass band," Craig said quietly.

"What? What's that you say?" Staley asked.

Craig sighed. "I was thinking about something Matt Jensen told me about posses. He said you may as well have a brass band with you."

"I don't understand," Staley said.

"You wouldn't," Craig replied.

The canyon made a forty-five-degree turn to the left just in front of him, so Craig held up his hand as a signal for all to stop.

"What are we stopping for?" Staley asked.

"If they're waiting for us, this is where they'll be," Craig replied.

"Hell, there's one good way to find out," Staley said. He slapped his horse on the rump and sent it on ahead. The horse broke into a gallop, the staccato beat of the hooves echoing back to them.

When the sound of the hooves stopped, the canyon was very quiet once more, the only sound being the whisper of the wind through the canyon.

"There's nobody there," Staley said. "If there was, they would'a shot at my horse."

"They have to be here," one of the other riders said.

"We found their tracks goin' in, but not comin' out. And you said yourself, there's only one way in and out."

"If you want to know what I think, I think they are up at the far end, trying to climb out. Like I said, we've got 'em trapped. Come on, let's go."

Without waiting for Sheriff Craig, Staley moved around the bend in the canyon. Suddenly, the canyon exploded with the sound of gunfire, the sound of the shooting greatly amplified by the confines of the canyon. The missiles raised sparks as they hit the rocky ground, then careened off into empty space, echoing and re-echoing in a cacophony of whines and shrieks.

Staley went down.

"Staley's hit!" Mitchell said.

"Keep me covered, I'm going after him," Sheriff Craig said.

"Keep you covered? Keep you covered how?" Mitchell asked.

"Move up to the edge here and start shooting," Craig said.

The rest of the posse moved up to the edge of the canyon and started shooting up toward the canyon walls. For the next minute, it sounded like a full scale battle, the canyon not only amplifying the sounds of shooting, but multiplying it many times over by the echoes that bounced from wall to wall.

Sheriff Craig moved toward Staley. He saw Staley moving.

"How bad are you hit?" he called.

"In my leg," Staley called back, his voice strained with pain.

"Turn over on your belly and try to crawl toward me," Craig called.

Staley did so, then started wriggling forward on his belly. Bullets hit all around him and Craig, but neither of them were hit. Finally, he got close enough to Craig that Craig was able to reach out and pull him behind the relative safety of a large outcropping of rocks.

As the shooting continued, Craig and Staley, able to stand now because of the rocks, moved back to join the others, Staley supported on his wounded leg by Craig.

"Bartlett's been hit," Mitchell reported when Craig got back.

"How bad?" Craig asked.

"He's dead," one of the others said.

"Anyone else hit?"

"No, but we're all goin' to be killed if we stay here any longer," Mitchell said. "I say we get out of here."

"No need to do that," Craig said. "Like Staley said, we have them trapped in there. All we have to do is wait them out."

"Wait them out? How are we going to do that? We got, what, two more days of food and water?" Mitchell asked.

"What do you think they have?" Craig replied.

"Who knows what they have? They could have a month's supply of food and water hidden up there for all we know. I mean, why else would they come into a canyon that they know is dead end? I think they was just settin' a trap for us."

"I think Mitchell is right," one of the others said. "I mean, you're a sheriff, you get paid for this. But I drive a wagon. It ain't my job to risk my life, and I ain't a'goin' to do it. I'm goin' back home."

"Yeah, me too. I work at the livery," another said. "I don't get paid for this. I think we should all go home and let the law handle this."

"Funny," Craig said. "I thought we were the law."

"You might be the law, but we ain't," Mitchell said. "We're just a bunch of clerks and workers, that's all. It would'a been good if we could'a got 'em, but there's no way we're goin' to do that now. And Staley has to get back to a doctor."

Craig sighed. "Yeah," he finally said. "All right, get mounted. We'll go back."

"I ain't got nothin' to ride," Staley said. "My horse didn't come back."

Ride Bartlett's horse, he won't need it," Craig suggested.

"What about Bartlettt? We goin' to just leave him here?" Mitchell asked.

"We'll tie him on behind Staley," Craig said.

Cuchara, Colorado

When the posse rode out of Cuchara a week earlier, they had been confident and determined, cheered on by the people of the town. But when the posse returned, they were defeated and dispirited, showing the effects of exhaustion, cold weather, and even hunger. Several of the citizens of the town saw the blood on Staley's leg. Others, knowing the makeup of the posse as it left, now put together the fact that the man thrown over the horse behind Staley was Barlett, and that he was probably dead.

The posse broke up the moment they came into town and most went individually to their homes. Staley went straight to the doctor's office, while Craig took Bartlett's body to the undertaker. After making arrangements for him, Craig rode on down to the sheriff's office.

Matt was holding a cup of hot coffee, and he handed it to Craig the moment the sheriff came into the office.

"Thanks," Craig said. He took a big swallow of the coffee, then set the cup on his desk as he removed his coat. He had a week's growth of beard, and he ran his hand across the stubble. "They got Bartlett," he said. "I'm going to have to ride out to his ranch and tell his widow."

"I don't envy you that," Matt said.

"I should have listened to you," Craig said. Picking up the coffee again, he sat down behind his desk. "It was just like you said. We couldn't have announced our presence any more if we had hired criers to go in front of us. They were waiting for us when we got to Wahite Canyon. They killed Bartlett and they shot Staley."

"And the outlaws? What happened to them?"

Craig shook his head. "Who knows? They could be in Mexico by now, for all I know," he said. "My . . . posse . . . lost its enthusiasm." He set the word *posse* apart sarcastically.

"When you are tracking someone like that, the element of surprise is always your strongest ally," Matt said. "But surprise is damn near impossible with a posse."

"Any trouble while we were gone?"

Matt shook his head. "Nothing," he said.

"Well, thank God for that at least. After a week like I've just been through, I would hate to come home to something new. I appreciate your sitting in for me while I was gone."

"I didn't mind it," Matt said. He took the badge from his shirt and laid it on the desk in front of Sheriff Craig.

Craig looked at the badge, but he didn't pick it up. "You know, Matt, that badge is yours for as long as you want it."

"I appreciate that," Matt said. He stretched. "I really do. But I think I'll be moving on."

"Moving on to where?"

"I don't know," Matt said. Then he smiled. "Maybe Denver."

"Denver? What's in Denver?"

"Apple pie," Matt said.

"I beg your pardon?"

"There is a place in Denver called Vi's Pies. The lady who owns it, Vivian McCain, makes the best apple pie in the world. I'm going to go have a piece."

For a long moment, Sheriff Craig looked at Matt as if he didn't understand. Then, he laughed out loud.

"By damn," he said. "What a life you lead, Matt, that you can just pull up stakes and go a hundred miles away for no reason other than to have a piece of pie." He laughed again. "Damn, if I weren't married and didn't have this job, I'd go with you."

Wahite Canyon

Hennessey was laughing as he watched the posse ride away. "Son of a bitch!" he said. "Son of a bitch!" He slapped his leg with his hand. "You was right."

"So, you've changed your mind, have you?" Strayhorn said. "Coming into a dead-end canyon wasn't the dumbest thing you ever heard of?"

Hennessey shook his head. "I never would'a thought it," he said. "I mean, I figured for sure we'd be trapped in here, but they come in like sittin' ducks, just like you said they would."

"Strayhorn is a smart man," Teech said. "You're better off with him than you were with Boone Parker."

"Yeah," Hennessey said. "I got to admit, I don't think ole Boone would'a thought of anything like this. Course, it don't matter none now nohow, seein' as ole Boone is pushin' up daisies."

"Let's go," Strayhorn said. "I want to be outta here before they decide to come back."

"Where are we goin'?" Taylor asked.

"Dorena," Strayhorn answered.

"Who is Dorena?" Hennessey asked.

"Dorena ain't a who," Teech said. "Dorena is a town. A very special town."

"What's so special about it?"

"You'll see."

Chapter Eight

Dorena, New Mexico Territory

Dorena was a very small town. The small adobe buildings that housed the mostly Mexican residents were either in total darkness, or barely illuminated by burning embers of mesquite wood or fat-soaked rags, because few could afford candles, and fewer still kerosene lanterns.

The outlaws passed a sign that announced the town.

YOU ARE ENTERING
DORENA

We've got our own Law.
We don't need none of yours.

The town had only one street, with a few leaning shacks constructed from rough-hewn lumber, the unpainted wood turning gray and splitting. There was no railroad serving the town, and no signs of the outside world greeted them. It was a self-contained little community, inbred and festering.

Strayhorn had been here many times before, and so

had Teech, but this was the first time for Hennessey and Taylor.

"And you say this town has got no law?" Hennessey asked as they rode into town.

"Oh, it's got law, alright," Strayhorn said.

"It's got law? Then, what the hell are we doin' here? What if they've got word on our jail break?"

Teech laughed. "It ain't that kind of law," he said.

Hennessey shook his head. "Then I don't understand. What kind of law are you talkin' about?"

"It's a law we make among ourselves," Strayhorn said. He headed his horse toward a building that sported a big red sign that said simply:

SALOON

"Hah," Taylor said. "I don't think I ever seen a saloon that didn't have no name."

"This one has a name," Strayhorn said as they swung down from their horses. "It's called Saloon. What more do you need?"

"How long are we goin' to be here?" Hennessey asked.

"As long as I say we are," Strayhorn answered. "Unless you have a hankerin' to ride out on your own."

"No. You're the one came to save my ass," Hennessey said. "I reckon I'll see what you have in mind."

"What I have in mind is twenty-five thousand dollars," Strayhorn said.

"What?" Hennessey replied, practically shouting the word.

Strayhorn laughed. "I thought that might get your attention," he said. "I didn't rescue you just 'cause I'm a good guy. I rescued you because I need you and the others to help me pull this off."

"What is it? A bank?"

"No," Strayhorn said. "It's better than a bank. It's like two banks in one. Next week the Midnight Flyer of the Denver and Rio Grande is going to be carrying twenty-five thousand dollars to be deposited in two different banks." Strayhorn smiled, then held his hand out and rubbed his fingers together. "But the only transfer is to be into our pockets," he said.

The others laughed.

"So, to answer your question, Hennessey, as to how long we are going to stay here—we are going to stay here until that transfer is made."

"And you say that will be sometime next week?" Hennessey asked.

Strayhorn nodded. "Unless you have some other idea."

"No, no, your idea is fine with me," Hennessey replied.

Strayhorn nodded. "Good. I thought you might see it my way."

"My only question is, what are we supposed to do until next week?" Hennessey asked. "Neither me nor Taylor has got a penny to our name."

"That's your problem, it ain't mine," Strayhorn replied. "I didn't take you to raise. I got you out of jail—the rest is up to you." He smiled. "All I'm askin' is for you to meet me here in the saloon next Tuesday."

"Where will we stay till then? What will we eat?" Taylor asked.

"See Boomer," Teech suggested.

"Who's Boomer?"

"Boomer owns the saloon. He's nearly always got some

job to do. And if he likes you, he'll lend you some money until you do the job. At least enough to eat on."

There were no hotels in Dorena, and no restaurants except for the food served in the American saloon or the Mexican cantina. The influx of lawless Americans, however, did create a market for whores, and this market was served by American soiled doves who worked out of the single American saloon in the town. Most of the women had aged beyond their prime so that they could no longer make a decent living in the whorehouses and bars of the more Anglo cities. But because there were so few American prostitutes here, they could still command a good price.

There were also Mexican women who were engaged in the trade, and most of them operated out of their own houses. In many cases, the Mexican whores had children who were comfortable with the knowledge that their mother was a *puta*, because they knew of no other existence. Most of the customers of the *putas* were American, some attracted to the women because of their dusky beauty, others because the Mexican women cost only one half of what the Americans were charging.

Strayhorn was one who frequented the Mexican *putas*, and after he left the others, he went straight to the house of Frederica Arino, a *puta* he had visited many times before. Strayhorn was also a brutal man who enjoyed hurting, and often left the women whimpering in pain when he finished. The Anglo whores would not put up with that, but the Mexican *putas* just gritted their teeth and bore it in silence.

Maria Arino, fourteen years old, was used to having

men visitors in the tiny house she occupied with her mother, two younger brothers, and baby sister. She felt no shame for her mother. She realized that it was a means of making a living for all of them. But when a man like Strayhorn called, Maria was sometimes frightened. She didn't like the way he treated her mother, and she didn't like the way he looked at *her*.

A gaily decorated blanket hung from a rope that divided the house into two rooms. On the other side of the blanket, Maria could hear the squeaking of the rope and wood-frame bed, the gurgling grunts of the Anglo, and the barely controlled whimpers of pain of her mother.

She heard her mother cry out.

"Shut up, bitch," Strayhorn's voice growled.

"You are hurting me, Señor," Maria's mother replied.

"Hurting you gives me pleasure," Strayhorn said. "And you are in the business of giving me pleasure."

There was a loud smack, and Maria's mother cried out again.

"Shut up, bitch! I know you like it! All you Mexican whores like it."

"Maria," Esteban asked. "Why is Mama crying?"

"Shh," Maria answered very quietly. She held her finger across her lips. "Remember, when Mama is on the other side of the blanket with a visitor, there is to be no talking."

"But I am frightened," Esteban said.

"Do not be frightened, *poqueño*," Maria said. She had a piece of string, tied in a circle, and she put her fingers into the string, then began showing her brothers all the tricks she could perform. It kept them so entertained over the next few minutes that they were unaware of the building crescendo of sound behind the blanket that

Maria knew signaled the beginning of the end of the Anglo's visit.

When she knew it was over, she handed the string to Esteban, suggesting that he try to manipulate it as she had. Esteban's efforts kept him and Juan occupied, which was what she wanted, because she needed some time to carry out her plan.

Moving quietly to the part of the room where the cooking utensils were kept, Maria found a butcher knife. Then, before her mother's visitor appeared from the other side of the blanket, she went outside to wait beside the outhouse. The smell was strong and she shivered in the cold.

In the cantina, someone was playing a guitar.

From the American saloon she heard loud laughter.

A cat screeched in the dark.

Finally, Strayhorn stepped outside the small house.

"Señor?" Maria called.

"What? Who is it? Who is there?" Strayhorn asked.

Maria stepped out from the shadow of the outhouse into the silver splash of moonlight.

"Who are you?" Strayhorn asked. Then, when he examined her more closely, he recognized her. "Wait a minute, you are the whore's daughter, ain't you?" He pointed toward the house behind him with a jerk of his thumb. "I seen you in there."

"Si, Señor. I am Maria."

"Well, what do you want, Maria?"

"I want one dollar."

"A dollar? Haw!" Strayhorn said. "Now, why would I want to give you a dollar?"

"Because I will give myself to you for one dollar," Maria said. Quickly, she pulled her dress up over her head, then off, holding the bunched-up cloth in her right hand. She stood before him, totally nude, her young body barely mature, with small breasts and a silky fuzz of emerging pubic hair. Her skin quickly filled with gooseflesh, brought on by the chill of the night air.

"Damn!" Strayhorn said.

"You do want this, don't you?" Maria asked. With her left hand, she touched herself. "I have seen how you look at me when you visit Mama."

"Well, now, you're gettin' started a little early, ain't you, girlie?" Strayhorn asked. "All right, if you want to learn what it's all about, I'll show you."

"One dollar?" Maria asked.

"A dollar? Girlie, I didn't give your mama but a quarter. But I ain't never had me a whore as young you, so you might just be worth it."

Maria waited until Strayhorn stuck his hand into his pocket, then, dropping the bunched-up dress, she lunged at him with the butcher knife.

"What the hell?" Strayhorn gasped when he saw what she intended. Moving quickly, he stepped to one side managing to avoid her rush. Then he reached out to grab her knife hand, causing Maria to lose her only advantage, the element of surprise. Strayhorn easily took the knife from her hand; then he pushed her up against the outhouse, clamping his left hand over Maria's mouth so she couldn't cry out.

"See what you did?" Strayhorn said. "I was goin' to give you that dollar. Now I'm goin' to get it for nothin'."

From their vantage point at the top of the hill, Hennessey, Taylor, and Hodge Decker, a somewhat shorter-than-average man they had recently met, could hear the driver whistling and calling to the six-horse team as they strained and struggled to pull the stagecoach up the long hill.

"I hear 'im comin'," Hennessey said. "It won't be long now."

"Shouldn't we have told Strayhorn what we're doing?" Taylor asked.

"Why?" Hennessey replied. "You heard him the same as I did. He said he didn't care what we did until next Tuesday. Boomer set this job up for us, and Teech is the one who told us to go see Boomer."

"Yeah, but—" Taylor began, but Hennessey interrupted him.

"Yeah, but what?" Hennessey said. "Without any money, what were we supposed to do? Starve? We need to get a little money from somewhere, and robbing a stagecoach is about as good a way as any."

The whistles and shouts of the driver grew louder as the stage came closer.

"All right, get ready," Hennessey said. "It'll be here any minute now."

When the coach reached to top of the long hill, it stopped.

"All right, folks, we're goin' to let the team take a breather here," the driver called down to his passengers. "You can stretch your legs here. Ladies, there is a necessary on the left side of the road. Gents, there is one on the right."

The doors opened on either side of the coach and the passengers, four men and one woman, got out. The passengers started toward the little outhouses that had been put here for that purpose, while the driver climbed down and began examining his team. He checked the harness on each horse, spoke gently to them, then turned to go back to the coach. That was when he saw Hennessey, Taylor, and Decker standing there with their guns drawn.

"Who the hell are you?" the driver asked.

"Who we are don't matter none," Hennessey answered. "We'll take whatever you're carryin'."

"Mister, I ain't carryin' nothin'," the driver said. "Maybe you noticed that I don't even have a shotgun guard ridin' with me."

"Check it out, Decker," Hennessey said.

Decker climbed up onto the driver's seat and looked under the seat.

"Here's a mail bag," he said.

"Throw it down."

"Mister, don't you know it's a federal law to steal the mail?"

Hennessey laughed. "There ain't no law wrote that I ain't done broke," he said. "Do you think I care whether it's a federal law or not?"

Decker tossed down the bag, which was closed by a draw rope.

"Go through it, Taylor," Hennessey said. "See if there's anything there."

Taylor opened the bag, then began rifling through the letters, opening several of the envelopes. After a minute or two, he threw the bag down in frustration.

"Nothin' here," he said.

"That's what I told you," the driver said.

There was the sound of laughter and conversation as some of the passengers returned from the necessary. They stopped in shock when they reached the edge of the road.

"What is this? What's going on here?" one of them asked. The man who asked the question was wearing a three-piece suit. He was overweight and, though he didn't have a beard, he did have sideburns than ran down either side of his face like saddlebags. Several chins worked their way from his rubber lips down to what would have been his neck, if his neck could be seen.

"We're collecting a toll," Hennessey said. "Give us all your money."

"What? See here, you have no right to—" His protest was interrupted when Hennessey fired a bullet at the ground near his feet. The bullet ricocheted into the woods behind, the shot and whine echoing back from the nearby mountains. The expression in the man's eyes turned from anger to fear.

"Whatever you are carryin' isn't worth your life, is it?" Hennessey asked.

The overweight man shook his head.

"Then do what I tell you. Give us your money," Hennessey ordered. He looked at the others, all of whom had returned to the coach by now. "All of you," he said. "Give us whatever money you are carrying."

Frightened and with shaking hands, the others pulled out their wallets and emptied them. Only the woman, who, seeing what was going on, had remained hidden off the road, escaped.

"Hey," Taylor said with a broad smile. "This fat old fart was carrying over one hundred dollars!"

"And here's fifty," Decker said.

"Damn, this one don't have but three dollars here," Taylor said after examining one of the others.

"Take it," Hennessey called back to Taylor. "Three dollars will buy a lot of beer."

Taylor chuckled. "Yeah, it will at that, wont it?" he said, putting the money in his pocket.

Hennessey walked up to the team and put his pistol to the head of one of the horses and pulled the trigger. The horse fell and the others reacted in fright.

"Why did you do that?" the driver asked.

"Just to keep you folks busy for a while," Hennessey said. He looked at Taylor and Decker. "All right, we've got what we came for. Let's go."

When Hennessey, Taylor, and Decker showed up at the Saloon the next Thursday to meet with Strayhorn and Teech, they saw four more men with them. The four were Loomis, Kale, Malone, and Mills. Hennessey had met them since coming to Dorena, but he didn't know any of them from before.

"Well, I see you boys managed to survive," Strayhorn said mockingly.

"Yeah, we picked up a few dollars," Hennessey replied.

Strayhorn nodded. "I heard about your great stage-coach robbery," he said. "How much did you get?"

"Enough," Hennessey replied without being specific.

Strayhorn chuckled. "You got one hundred fifty-three dollars," he said. "And you had to give half of that to Boomer."

"What difference does it make to you what we got?" Hennessey replied. "It was enough to keep us going until today. So now, where is this twenty-five thousand dollars you say we are going to get?"

"Like I told you, it's on the Midnight Flyer," Strayhorn replied. "Get your horses saddled and meet out front in fifteen minutes. We've got a long way to ride."

Chapter Nine

Cuchara, Colorado

It was growing dark as Matt Jensen stepped out onto the platform of the Cuchara depot. He had bought his ticket and made arrangements for Spirit to be loaded onto the stock car that was part of the train. He was now waiting for the train that would take him to Denver. Matt could hear the echoing puffs of the engine and see the almost luminescent white steam billowing from the drive cylinders.

"The train for Denver and all parts north!" the station manager shouted through his megaphone, though no such announcement was necessary. Cuchara was a one-track town and everyone knew where every train that passed through was bound.

Layne McKenzie had been on trains for three days and two nights now, having boarded in Cairo, Illinois. She had but one more night on this train before reaching Denver. It had been an exciting adventure, but as her only sleep had been what she could grab by trying to get comfortable in uncomfortable seats, she was very tired.

As the train began slowing for another stop, she shifted

positions and looked through the window at the little town. A sign attached to the end of the station house read CUCHARA, and she rolled the name over on her tongue. The further west she got, the more melodic and exotic-sounding were the names of the towns.

One of the men standing on the platform caught her attention. He was tall and blond, and even from the train she could tell that his flashing blue eyes were deep and unexpectedly expressive. He carried some packages onto the train for a woman and two children, and Layne felt a twinge of envy for the woman, who was apparently his wife.

"Thank you, sir," the woman said as the man put the packages in the overhead rack for her. "You have been most kind."

"Glad I could help, ma'am," the man said, touching the brim of his hat.

So, they aren't married, Layne thought. Again, the thought was followed by, *Not that it matters.* The terms of her employment were very specific about that. She could not get married while she was teaching school.

I must really be tired, she thought. *Why am I even thinking about such a thing?*

There were two short whistles from the engine, then a series of jerks as all the slack was worked out of the couplings when the train got under way.

The Denver and Rio Grande Train Number Eighty-three, known as the Midnight Flyer and consisting of an engine, tender, two express cars, and six passengers cars, was on the midnight run, working its way up toward Thunder Pass. Scheduled to arrive in Denver at just after sunrise, it was a marvel of nineteenth-century progress in which a person could be whisked some 150 miles in one night.

One of the 131 passengers making the trip was Matt Jensen. Matt was sitting alone, halfway down the left-hand side of the second of four passenger cars. There was a wood-burning stove at the rear of the car, but the small bubble of heat it put out did very little to push back the numbing cold that permeated the car.

As night fell, a porter came through handing out blankets to all the passengers, but Matt gave his to the woman who was traveling with two children, a boy about nine and a girl of six. He then turned the collar up on his wool-lined, sheepskin coat, and looked through the window at the dark mass of coniferous trees that climbed the sides of the mountains nearby.

Although night had fallen, the illuminated cars were projecting little squares of golden light that slid alongside the track with the train, creating a sparkling effect with the falling precipitation of sleet mixed with snow. Matt saw a wolf dart from some shrub covering, keep pace with the train for about one hundred yards, then dart back into the woods.

"Mama, how long before we get to Denver?" the nine-year-old asked.

"We'll be there by morning," the woman answered.

"Will Daddy be there?" the little girl asked.

"Oh, yes. He'll be there in a buckboard to pick us up."

"I hope he has a lot of buffalo robes to wrap up in," the boy said. "It's really cold."

"I'm sure he will. You know that Daddy is always prepared," the woman answered. "Now, why don't the two of you try to sleep?"

Listening to the dialogue between mother, son, and daughter caused Matt to think back to his own sister and mother. It had been a long time since he thought about them, not because they were unimportant to him, but because the memories were too unpleasant.

The gentle rocking of the train, the rhythmic sound of the wheels passing over the track joints, and the warmth of his sheepskin coat enabled Matt to fall asleep.

It was a fitful sleep, one in which Matt dreamed that he was back in the orphanage under the tutelage of an evil man who called himself Captain Mumford.

Matt had committed some breach of Mumford's regulations and for it, he was to be punished.

"Gag him, Simon," Mumford said. "We wouldn't want to wake the others with his screams."

Simon stuck a rolled-up sock down Matt's throat, then tied a cloth around around his mouth to secure the gag.

"Connor, you may begin," Mumford said.

"Yes, Cap'n Mumford," Connor said, his own voice reflecting his excitement over the task before him.

At first, Matt wasn't sure what was going to happen, but it took little more than a second for him to find out. He heard the swish of the whip as Connor swung it toward him.

The pain of the lash across his back was immediate, but he was surprised that the pain seemed to go deeper than the flesh. He felt it in the pit of his stomach and his groin. He tried to scream, but the gag silenced him.

Within three more lashes, Matt lost control of his bladder and began urinating.

"Hee, hee, hee, he's a'peein' in his pants," Simon said. "Hell, he ain't no more'n a baby."

Matt could no longer count the number of lashes. They

seemed to fall one on top of the other until, eventually, he was no longer able to distinguish individual lashes. The impact of one lash blended into the next so that he was experiencing a constant and excruciating pain. He felt his head beginning to spin; then everything faded away and his head dropped.

"Hold it, Connor," Mumford called out.

Connor let the whip drop by his side and he stood there, breathing hard from the exertion. He, Mumford, and Simon looked at the boy, who now hung in the manacles, his head forward and his eyes closed.

"Is he dead?" Simon asked. There was a sense of morbid excitement to Simon's question, as if he hoped Matt was dead.

Mumford stepped up closer to Matt. The back of Matt's long underwear was striped and pooled with blood from his shoulders, all the way down to his knees. Mumford put his hand on Matt's neck, feeling for a pulse.

"He's alive," he said. "Take him back to his bed."

Connor nodded, then undid the manacles. Without them to hold him up, Matt collapsed on the floor.

The train ran over a rough section of track, and the clacking and jerking of the car caused Matt to wake up. It took him a second to gather his thoughts, to realize that he was not back in the orphanage, but was on a train bound for Denver.

Although he had told Sheriff Craig that he was going to Denver for a piece of apple pie, the truth is, he had no particular reason for going to Denver. But then, he had no particular reason for being anywhere. He had no plans beyond spending a few weeks in the city enjoying the restaurants, hotels, and gaming houses. And why not? He was young, and he had no familial encumbrances or obligations.

The train started up the long incline that would take it to the pass at the top of Thunder Pass, and as it did so, it slowed noticeably. Matt had taken this same train trip before, and he knew that it would get much slower before finally cresting the peak.

Getting up from his seat and stretching, Matt walked to the rear of the car, where he stood for a moment in the warmth of the little coal stove. After that, he stepped over to the wooden water scuttle, pulled a flat paper cup from a dispenser, opened it up, and drew himself a cup of water, wishing that it was whiskey, or at least a beer.

Two miles ahead of the train, Strayhorn and the others waited alongside the track. Strayhorn blew on his hands, then stamped his feet in the snow.

"Damn, it's cold," Hennessey said, wrapping his arms around himself.

"I'll bet ole' Boone ain't cold right now," Teech said with a giggle. "Yes, sir, I'll bet ole' Satan has the fires turned up just real hot for him."

"That ain't none funny a'tall," Hennessey said. "Me'n Taylor was almost hung too, you know. Could be us down there burnin', 'stead of up here freezin'.'"

"Yeah, well, right now I don't know which is the worst," Decker said as he stamped his feet on the ground. "Freezin' up here, or burnin' down in hell."

"What are you doing here, Decker? I thought I told you to stay with the horses," Strayhorn said, his voice showing his irritation.

"Them horses ain't goin' nowhere," Decker answered. "I've got 'em tied up real good."

"They damn sure better not go anywhere."

At that moment, inexplicably, one of the other men laughed. "Lookit that," he said.

"What is it? Look at what?" Strayhorn asked.

"I just took me a piss on the railroad track and now it's smokin'. I bet there ain't none of you ever pissed smoke before."

"I swear, Loomis, you may be about the dumbest son of a bitch I've ever met," Malone said. "Your pee ain't smokin'. It's steamin'. See, when you take a pee on a day as cold as this, why, your pee starts to boilin' soon as it comes out."

"So, you mean if I peed on my hand when it's this cold, it would burn?" Loomis asked.

"Yeah," Malone said.

Strayhorn shook his head in disgust. "You're both dumb as dirt," he said.

They heard the distant sound of a train whistle.

"Here comes the train, so hush up, the lot of you," Strayhorn said, holding up his hand. "Mills, you're sure you know what to do?"

"Yeah, I know what to do," Mills said. "When the train reaches the top of the grade, it'll be comin' slow enough for me to climb up into the engine cab. I'll make 'em stop so you folks can get into the express car." He smiled. "Then we all ride away rich."

"You're sure they're carryin' twenty-five thousand dollars?" Hennessey asked.

"That's what it said in the newspaper story I read," Strayhorn replied.

"I sure hope so. We been out here in the cold this

whole night," Hennessey said. "I just want to be sure it's worth it, that's all."

"You can ride away now and get warm if you want to," Strayhorn offered.

"No, no, I was just wonderin', that's all."

"Hey, Strayhorn, how 'bout if Taylor'n me goes through the cars and takes whatever money the passengers is carryin' on 'em?" Hennessey suggested.

"We're here to get twenty-five thousand dollars and you're worrin' about a few measly dollars the passengers might have?"

"We got over a hundred and fifty dollars for that stage coach we robbed," Hennessey said. "There's a lot more people on a train than there is on a coach."

"Yeah, you may be right," Strayhorn said. "But I want you and Taylor out here with me. Kale, you go with Loomis. Go though ever' car. Don't bother none with watches or jewelry and sech. Just take whatever money they got."

"All right," Kale agreed with a nod. He looked at Loomis. "You start at the back of the train, I'll start up front."

"Right," Loomis replied.

By now the train was close enough that they could hear the puffing of the steam engine as it worked its laborious way up the long incline.

"Mills, you ready?" Strayhorn called.

"I'm ready."

"Get down there then," Strayhorn said, pointing to a spot by the track. "It'll be slow enough when it reaches that point that you can climb on real easy. By the time it gets here, you'll have the engine stopped. You know how to do it, right?"

"Yeah, I just point my gun at the sons of bitches who

are drivin' the train and tell 'em to stop," Mills said with a chuckle.

"What if one of the passengers comes out to see why they've stopped and starts up puttin' up a fight?" Hennessey asked.

"It's Kale and Loomis's job to see that they don't," Strayhorn said. "Kale, Loomis, you hear that? If you see any passenger who looks like he's going to get off the train, shoot him."

Kale and Loomis nodded.

Seeing that Mills hadn't left yet, Strayhorn waved his hand. "Go on, get goin'," he said.

Mills nodded, then hurried down to the spot by the track that Strayhorn had pointed out to him. The train approached, puffing loudly as the throttle was full open, working hard to make the long climb. At this point, the train was moving no faster than a slow walk.

Mills trotted alongside it, overtaking it until he drew even with the engine. Then, reaching up to grab the boarding ladder, he stepped easily onto the bottom rung.

Chapter Ten

Back in the second passenger car of the train, Matt returned to his seat. His walk to the back of the car had been less to get warm and to get water than it had been to stretch and get the kinks and soreness out. Looking around at the others, and noticing their pained attempts to get comfortable, he couldn't help but wonder about them. Then, with a quick intake of surprise, he noticed that one of the other people in the train was staring back at him. She was a young, and very pretty, woman.

"I've been watching you," the woman said. The voice was soft and melodic.

"Beg your pardon?" Matt replied.

"I've been watching you," the woman repeated. "You were obviously having a dream, but the dream wasn't a pleasant one."

"How do you know it wasn't a pleasant dream?"

"Because your face is remarkably reflective," the woman said. In addition to being pretty, she had a subtle hint of perfume about her. Perfume that carried with it a note of lavender.

"I suppose I was dreaming," Matt replied. He made no effort to tell her what he had been dreaming.

"Well, dreams, like thoughts, are quite private, so I shall make no inquiries as to what it was," the woman said. Smiling, she extended her hand. "My name is Layne. Layne McKenzie."

"I'm Matt Jensen. I'm pleased to meet you, uh, Miss or Mrs. McKenzie?"

Layne laughed. "Definitely Miss," she said. "Will you be getting off in Denver, Mr. Jensen?"

"Yes. And you?"

She nodded. "I will as well. I've come to spend some time with my uncle," Layne replied. "It's my first time out West. Have you been to Denver before?"

"Yes."

"How is it? The city, I mean."

"Hasn't your uncle told you about it?"

"He says Denver is wonderful, but then he is so sold on the West in general, and Colorado and Denver in particular, that I don't know how much credence to give his reports."

"I would listen to your uncle. Denver is very nice," Matt said. "I've no doubt that your stay will be most pleasant."

"I certainly hope so," Layne replied. "I don't mind telling you that I am a little apprehensive about it."

"Don't be. I'm sure you will have a fine time," Matt promised.

"Listen to me, prattling on so to a perfect stranger," Layne said. "Why, my mother would be just mortified if she could see me now."

"No reason she should be," Matt replied, smiling warmly. "We have introduced ourselves. That means we are no longer strangers."

Layne laughed. "Yes, that's right, isn't it? I mean, since we know each other's names, we aren't strangers at all."

"Not at all," Matt agreed.

"Mr. Jensen, I know this is very forward of me, and I wouldn't want you to get the wrong impression, but I certainly hope we find the opportunity to meet again while we are both visiting Denver. Do you think we will?"

"I don't know," Matt replied. "Denver is a very big town."

"But if the opportunity arose for us to meet again, would you welcome it?"

"Well, now, who wouldn't welcome the opportunity to meet such a pretty young woman?"

Layne smiled and blushed appropriately. Then, she pulled a card from her handbag and handed it to Matt. "This is my *carte de visite*," she said. "I have written my uncle's address on the back. I do hope you will call on me while you are in town."

"Thank you," Matt said, taking the card. He put the card in his shirt pocket without looking at it.

Up in the engine the fireman, his face covered with soot, threw in another shovel of coal, then stood up and looked over at the engineer. The engineer, like the fireman, was illuminated by the soft, golden glow of the storm lantern they used for light.

"George, what's the pressure now?" the fireman shouted.

"Two hundred PSI. She's at the maximum, Hank. You can take a break now."

"I don't know. We're going to have to keep the pressure up," Hank said. "Leastwise, until we reach the top of the grade. Then we can back off a bit."

"No!" a third voice suddenly called out. "I'll thank you boys to back off right now!"

"What the hell?" the engineer shouted, startled by the man's sudden and unexpected appearance. "Who the hell are you and where did you did you come from?"

"The name's Mills and you just guessed it, I came from hell," Mills said, laughing at his own joke. The pupils of his eyes were reflecting the orange light from the boiler furnace and with a little imagination, they could have been reflecting the flames of hell. "Now, shut this thing down like I told you," Mills said. He made a motion with his gun.

"Better do what he says, George," the fireman said. "Looks like he means business."

Mills smiled. "Well, now, mayhaps you ain't as dumb as you look," he taunted.

The engineer closed the throttle and applied the brakes, bringing the train to a squeaking, rattling halt. Steam escaped from the relief valve and the engine sat motionless on the track, emitting rhythmic puffs of steam.

"All right, she's stopped," George said. "What now?"

"Get down from the train, both of you," Mills said, waving his pistol to emphasize his order.

"Mama, why are we stopping?" the boy across the aisle from Matt asked. "We aren't there yet."

"I don't know why we have stopped, dear," the boy's mother replied. "Maybe they have to let the engine rest a bit. You know they always stop the stagecoach at the top of a long hill to let the team rest."

The boy laughed. "Mama, you don't know nothin'

about steam engines. They ain't like horses. They don't get tired."

"It's know anything, Timmy. And don't say ain't."

Suddenly, a man appeared at the front of the car. He was holding a gun and he pointed it down the car toward the passengers.

"All right, folks, this here is a holdup!" he shouted at the top of his voice. "And if any of you men is carryin' a gun, I'd advise you to take it out and put it on the floor right now."

Besides Matt, there were four other men in the car, and all four complied with the robber's request, laying their pistols on the floor. Matt stood up, the gun on his belt in plain sight.

"Mister, did you hear what I said?" the robber asked, waving his pistol toward Matt.

"Yeah, I heard what you said," Matt said. "Now I'm tellin' you to drop your gun."

"The hell you say. I'm just goin' to kill you and be done with—" That was as far as the robber got because even as he was thumbing back the hammer, Matt drew and fired. The noise of the gunshot and the brilliant flash of the muzzle pattern was like lightning and thunder in the confines of the car. Layne and the young mother screamed and the men called out in shock and fear, but even before the smoke from the discharge rolled away, Matt was bailing out of the back end of the car. Hitting the ground, he dropped to his stomach, then rolled down the berm that elevated the track. At the bottom of the berm he got up and, moving in a crouch, started toward the front of the train, where he saw several men gathered around the express car. The fireman and the engineer were both outside, standing alongside the engine with their hands in the air.

One of the train robbers stepped up to the express car and banged on the side of it with the butt of his pistol. "Open the door!" the train robber shouted.

"I ain't a'goin' to do it!" a muffled voice replied from inside the express car.

"I ain't goin' to fool around with you, mister," the leader of the robbers said. "Open the door right now, or I'm going to start killin' people."

The door still did not open, so Strayhorn turned to Malone. "Malone, kill the engineer," he said.

Malone shot the engineer in the head and he went down.

"We just killed the engineer," Strayhorn shouted to the closed door of the express car. "If you don't open that door in five seconds, I'll kill the fireman too."

"Hold it!" Matt shouted, bringing his pistol up and pointing it at Malone.

Seeing the unexpected appearance of a passenger, Malone turned his gun away from the fireman and shot at Matt. He missed.

Matt fired back and the outlaw went down. Realizing that they were under fire, the other robbers scattered, looking for cover.

Suddenly, a bullet fried the air by his ear and, turning, Matt saw what had to be one of the robbers coming toward him from the rear of the train. Matt returned fire, but just as he pulled the trigger, the robber leaped behind a rock, causing Matt to miss. Matt dropped to his stomach and fired again, watching his bullet take a chip out of the rock right where he had last seen the robber.

Behind Matt, the fireman had taken advantage of the

situation to climb back up into the engine cab. As soon as he got there, he moved the throttle into the full position and the train lurched forward.

"Strayhorn! The train is getting away!" one of the robbers shouted.

"Mills, stop it!" Strayhorn yelled.

Mills jumped up onto the mounting ladder and climbed up to the cab. Just as he got there, though, the fireman smashed Mills in the head with the shovel. At the same time the fireman hit Mills, Mills pulled the trigger. Mills fell from the mounting ladder, his shout of horror cut off in mid-yell as he was ground up by the wheels of the tender car when the train passed over him.

"Strayhorn, the train is still going!" Hennessey yelled.

"Hennessey? Hennessey, is that you?" Matt called, recognizing the voice of the man he had brought in for hanging a few weeks earlier.

"Son of a bitch!" Hennessey shouted. "Strayhorn, it's Jensen! Jensen is on this train!"

"Get to the horses, let's get out of here!" Strayhorn ordered.

Upon hearing Strayhorn order the others to get mounted, the robber who had been engaging Matt stood up.

"No you don't, Strayhorn! You fellas ain't leavin' me behind!" he shouted.

"We ain't comin' back for you, Kale! You gotta run for it like the rest of us!" Strayhorn shouted.

"Drop your gun, Kale," Matt ordered, using the name he had heard Strayhorn use. Matt was standing now, and he pointed his pistol at the would-be train robber.

"The hell you say!" Kale called back, and with a challenging scream, he started toward Matt, firing his pistol as he did so. Matt took careful aim and dropped Kale with one shot.

Behind him, Matt heard the muffled sound of hoofbeats in the snow, and he knew that the remaining outlaws were getting away. He looked in the direction of the sound, hoping to be able to get a shot, but the riders had already disappeared into the darkness of the night, leaving behind four bodies, two killed by Matt, one killed when he fell under the train, and the engineer, who was killed by the outlaws. In addition, there was one more dead outlaw on the train, killed in Matt's very first confrontation with them. The attempted train robbery was a bloody failure, due primarily to the fact that Matt had been a passenger on the train.

The train!

Matt suddenly realized that the train was under way and already picking up a good deal of momentum.

"Whoa, hold it!" Matt shouted, his call sounding small and tinny against the noise of the passing train. Facing the possibility of being left out here alone, Matt broke into a run to catch up to it. He barely grabbed the boarding ladder at the very end of the train, then pulled himself up onto the rear vestibule. When he opened the door to go into the last car, he was met with three armed passengers, all of whom were pointing their pistols at him.

"It's one of the robbers!" one of the armed men shouted.

"No!" a woman called out. "I saw this man through the window! He was shooting at the robbers!"

"The lady's right," Matt said. "I'm a passenger, just like you."

The three men lowered their pistols. "Sorry," they said.

"No, don't apologize," Matt said. "I admire you for being willing to fight them off."

"We didn't fight them off. I reckon you're the one who did that," one of the men said.

"Whoever did it, we're safe now," another said. "At the rate we're going, we aren't likely to run into that bunch again."

The train was going fast, much faster now than it had been when Matt managed to catch the last car.

"I've taken this trip before," the first passenger said. "We've never gone this fast through here. They must really be scared up there to be going this fast."

As the speed of the train increased even more, the cars began jerking back and forth, throwing the passengers from side to side.

The conductor came into the car then, and he was barely able to stand, negotiating the center aisle only by holding onto the backs of the seats. The expression on the conductor's face was one of fear.

"Conductor, what's going on?" Matt asked. "The danger is over now, why are we going so fast?"

The conductor shook his head. "God help me, I don't know!" he said. "After we clear Thunder Pass, we're supposed to go down the hill not much faster than we went up it. But we are going over sixty miles per hour! If we don't slow down before we get to Miller's Curve, we'll go off the track."

"Well, that will certainly slow us down," Matt said.

"No, you don't understand! There's a fifty-foot-high trestle at Miller's Curve. If we go off the track we'll tumble down into a gulch."

"Oh, my God!" someone shouted.

"We'll all be killed!"

"Why doesn't the engineer do something?"

"The engineer isn't driving this train," Matt said.

The conductor looked at Matt in surprise. "How do you know the engineer isn't driving this train?" he asked.

"Because I saw the robbers kill the engineer," Matt replied.

"Oh, my God," the conductor said, pinching the bridge of his nose. "George's wife just had a new baby." He shook his head.

"Well, if the engineer isn't driving the train, who is?" one of the passengers asked.

"It has to be the fireman," the conductor said. "He can operate the engine as well as the engineer."

"If he can drive the train as well as the engineer, he should know better than to go this fast, shouldn't he?" Matt asked.

"Yes," the conductor replied. "He certainly should know. I have no idea why he is running the train this fast."

"It could be that he isn't," Matt suggested.

"I thought you just said that he was."

"No. What I said was that the robbers killed the engineer. I know that to be true because I saw it. But it could also be true that they killed the fireman as well. I did see someone fire into the engine cab just before he fell from the train."

"That doesn't make sense. If both of them are dead, the train wouldn't even be moving," the conductor said.

"Unless the fireman got the train started before they killed him," Matt suggested.

"Oh, Good Lord in Heaven, do you mean to tell me there's nobody driving this train?" one of the women passengers asked, her voice choked with fear. This was the woman who had pointed out to the other passengers that Matt was not one of the robbers.

"I'm beginning to think that is very possible," the conductor said. "Otherwise, we wouldn't be running downhill with the throttle full open!"

"So, what do we do now?" the woman asked fearfully.

"About the only thing we can do is pray," the conductor said.

"Praying is always good," Matt agreed. "But I've always heard that the Lord helps those who help themselves. I think I'd like to have another option available."

"At this point, there is no other option," the conductor said.

"No, I can't accept that. There is always another option," Matt insisted. "All we have to do is get to the engine and stop it."

The engineer shook his head. "The problem is, there is no way to get the engine."

"Why not? Seems to me like all you'd have to do is go through all the cars until you get to the tender," Matt said. "Climb over it, and you're in the engine."

"Not possible," the conductor said.

At that moment, the train whipped around another curve, going so fast that it threw the conductor down. A couple of the women passengers screamed, and one of the men passengers began praying out loud.

Matt helped the conductor back to his feet.

"Why can't we get to the engine?" Matt asked again.

"Because there are two express cars between the passenger cars and the engine, and you can't get through them," the conductor said, holding onto the seat to keep his balance. "The only way you are going to get to the engine is if you climb over the top of those two cars."

"Is there a brakeman on board?" Matt asked. "Someone who is used to doing that sort of thing?"

The conductor shook his head. "No need for brakemen on this train, mister. This is a passenger train. We're equipped with Westinghouse air brakes."

The train seemed to increase speed, and the back-and-forth whipping motion of the car became even more extreme.

"Damn," Matt said. He started toward the front of the car.

"Where are you going? What are you doing?" the conductor asked.

"I'm going to go through this train and get to the engine," Matt said.

"You're crazy, you'll never make it."

"Doesn't look like I have much of a choice, does it?" Matt replied. "I either die trying to stop this train, or I die when it goes off the trestle and crashes into the gorge. So I'm going to try. Now the question is, once I get there, how do I stop it?"

"It's impossible," the conductor said again.

"Stop telling me what is impossible and tell something that can help me!" Matt shouted. "Now, once I get to the engine, how do I stop this damn train?"

"There will be a big lever running horizontally across the cab from the left to the right," the conductor explained. "That's the throttle. Pull it all the way back. Also, there's a Johnson bar, which is a sturdy-looking ratcheted lever with a hand release; this is a vertical bar on the right. And right next to it you'll see a chunky-looking brass handle sticking out to the left. That's the air brakes."

"What do I do with the Johnson bar?"

"You don't have to do anything with it. I was just pointing it out to you to help you find the air brakes, is all. The Johnson bar controls the direction the steam takes in going into the cylinders. That's what makes the train run forward, or in reverse. But when you close the throttle, no steam will be going into the cylinders anyway."

The train bucked again and the car rattled as it ran over a rough section of track.

"Hurry, man, hurry!" one of the men in the car shouted. "Don't stand here talking about it!"

"God go with you," the woman said.

"Thank you, ma'am," Matt said. He started to open the door, then paused long enough to take off his coat.

"You better keep that coat on, mister," the conductor said. "It's not more'n ten degrees outside, and with the wind blowin' on you at sixty miles per hour, you're likely to freeze to death before you get there."

"I think I'll feel more secure up there if I'm not bound up by the coat," Matt explained.

Matt stepped out onto the vestibule, then into the car ahead. Here, the people were as frightened as they were in the car he had just left.

When Matt reached the second car, Layne gasped when she saw him.

"Thank God you are alive!" she said. "We thought you had been killed!"

"What's happening, mister?" the mother of the children asked, her voice tinged with fright. "Why are we going so fast?"

"I'm not sure," Matt said. "But I intend to find out." He looked toward the body of the robber, who was lying facedown in the aisle near the front door.

"A couple of you men, drag this body out onto the vestibule," he said, pointing to the dead robber. "There's no need for the good folks to have to look at it any longer."

"I ain't settin' foot on that vestibule, goin' as fast as we are," one of the men said.

"I'll do it," another said.

"I'll help," his seat companion added.

"Thanks," Matt replied.

Matt passed through four more cars before reaching the first of the two express cars he was going to have to negotiate.

When he reached the vestibule platform here, he saw why he would not be able to go through the express cars. Unlike the passenger cars, the express car had no end doors. He was going to have to climb up to the top.

Matt grabbed a ladder rung, then jerked his hand back. The metal rung was so cold that it had almost the same effect as if he had grabbed a piece of hot iron from a blacksmith's forge.

Matt steeled himself, then grabbed it again, this time forcing himself to hold on. He put his foot on the bottom rung, then climbed to the top of the car. Just as he reached the top, though, his foot slipped off the icy rung, causing him to fall. He managed to grab the top rung, though his face hit the corner of the car, cutting a deep gash in his cheek. Disregarding the bleeding wound, he held on until he was able to gain purchase with his foot. Then he propelled himself up over the edge, and onto the top of the car.

Chapter Eleven

The sleet had taken effect on top of the car so that it was covered with a sheet of ice. Also, the train was traveling so fast that he was in a sixty-mile-per-hour slipstream. In addition, the top of the car was like the end of a pendulum, so that the lateral movement was more extreme up here than it had been down inside the cars.

Matt tried to stand up, hoping he could sustain himself by bending forward against the wind. But his foot slipped on the ice and he fell, painfully barking his shin, managing to keep from falling off only by grabbing hold of a small pipe that acted as a smokestack coming through the roof. After that, he quit trying to stand and instead, moved forward on his hands and knees, crawling as quickly as he could.

When he reached the front end of the car, he realized that, under these conditions, he would not be able to bridge the gap between them without climbing down this car, and then up on the next.

Taking pains to be more careful this time, Matt climbed down, stepped across the connecting plates, then climbed up the other side. As he raised his head above the top of the car, though, he saw that they were approaching a tunnel. He ducked back down as the train entered the tunnel, then hung on for dear life as the noise of the train roared back at him from the tunnel walls.

Finally, the train emerged from the tunnel, and he crawled across the roof of this car as he had the previous one.

The tender was a little easier to navigate because he was down inside, rather than on top. That way, he didn't feel as if he were about to be thrown off. Then, climbing down the front of the tender, he stepped across the foot-plate until he was inside the engine.

The cab was lit by a storm lantern, which put out just enough light to be able to see the valves, levers, handles, protuberances, coils, chains, and gauges that made up the mysterious workings and mechanical contrivances of the engine. The light also showed what had happened to the fireman. He was lying on the floor with a black hole in his forehead.

The engine was loud and vibrating, and Matt could feel the heat emanating from the boiler. That, at least, gave him some relief from the bitter cold.

As he wiped some of the blood away from his cheek, he studied the back of the huge, round boiler. There was a large gauge on top, with a needle that was quivering just inside a red wedge on the face of it. Attachments, hoses, coils, faucet handles, cylinders, canisters that looked like coffeepots and deep-fry cookers protruded, extended, sat upon, and hung from every part of the boiler. Then he saw the long, horizontal bar that the conductor told him would be the throttle. It was in a full forward position. He pulled it all the way back while, at the same time, he pulled the brass handle back that the conductor had identified as the brake handle.

Matt's action had an immediate consequence as he felt the driver wheels lock into place, allowing the train to slide along the rails. But the rails were coated with ice and, even though the heavy train and the friction of sliding steel wheels on steel rails generated enough heat to cut through the ice, Matt realized that it wasn't braking effectively enough.

Matt looked down at the Johnson bar, remembering that the conductor told him that its only purpose was to make the train go in reverse.

Getting an idea, Matt pulled the Johnson bar all the way back; then he pushed the throttle all the way forward. Once more, the cylinders and actuating rods began operating, but this time in the opposite direction. The huge driver wheels started a backward rotation, and Matt was rewarded by seeing a tremendous shower of sparks flying out from either side of the engine, generated by the wheels spinning in reverse.

Gradually, the train began to slow, but as he looked ahead in the beam of light thrown out by the gas headlamp, he saw that the track ahead was making a sharp curve to the left and onto a trestle. The light also picked up a sign along the edge of the track.

ENGINEERS:

PROCEED <u>SLOWLY</u>

"I'm trying to, I'm trying to!" Matt shouted at the sign as the train slid by, still at considerable speed.

The braking became more and more pronounced until,

finally, just as it was entering the curve, the train came to a stop.

Matt breathed a sigh of relief, but it was short-lived as the train suddenly started backing up.

For a moment Matt was surprised, then he remembered the Johnson bar. He closed the throttle and put the Johnson bar in the middle, and the train stopped. He stood there in the engine cab for a long moment, listening to the hiss and gurgle of the boiling water.

"You did it! By damn, you did it!"

Turning, Matt saw that the conductor had climbed the boarding ladder and was stepping into the engine cab with him.

"Yeah, I did it," Matt said. "But now what?"

"What do you mean, now what?"

"How are we going to get this train into the station?"

"Not to worry," the conductor said. "There is an engineer and fireman deadheading back to Denver. They'll take us in."

"Yeah? Where were they a few minutes ago when I needed them?" Matt quipped.

For a moment or two, the conductor didn't realize that Matt was joking. Then, when he did realize it, he laughed, his laughter greater than the joke deserved, but brought on more by relief than by humor.

"Strayhorn, hold up!" Hennessey called.

Strayhorn stopped, then looked around. "What do you want?"

"I thought you had this all planned."

"Things don't always go like they are planned."

"This didn't even come close. We were supposed

to come away from this little adventure with twenty-five thousand dollars. How much did we get?" Hennessey asked.

"What are you trying to say, Hennessey?"

Hennessey pointed back in the direction from which they came. "I'm not trying to say it, I'm saying it," Hennessey said. "We left four men dead back there because of you. You let Boone hang because you wanted to be the leader? You couldn't lead a starvin' horse to oats."

"Do you think you can do better?"

"Yeah, I think I can do better. Taylor, Decker, and me robbed a stagecoach. We got money, and nobody got killed."

Strayhorn laughed. "You got what? A hundred fifty dollars?"

"That's one hundred fifty dollars more than we got from the train," Hennessey said.

"Look," Strayhorn said. "The greater the reward, the greater the risk. If you are afraid of risk, then I suggest you go into another line of work. Try being a store clerk."

Some of the others laughed at Strayhorn's derisive comment.

"I'm not afraid of a little risk, if I think there is really some chance of a reward," Hennessey said. "With you, I doubt there is a chance."

"If you don't want to ride with me, don't," Strayhorn said.

"I don't intend to," Hennessey said. He turned his horse away from the others.

"Hennessey, wait," Taylor called. "I'm coming with you."

Hennessey stopped, then looked back at the others. "Anyone else want to come with us?" he asked.

Although a few of the others looked nervous, none of them joined Hennessey.

"Decker?" Hennessey called.

Decker shook his head. "I'll stay with Strayhorn," he said.

"All right," Hennessey said. "Have it your own way. But you might want to ask yourself who is going to be the next person to get ground up like Mills."

The arrival in Denver of the Midnight Flyer caused quite a stir. The city police came to interview Matt, the conductor, and many of the passengers. Upon learning that in addition to the two bodies on the train, there were at least four bodies back at the site where the robbery attempt was made, a telegram was sent to order the next train to stop and retrieve the bodies.

The passengers were full of praise for Matt, not only for confronting the robbers, but also for saving the train. However, Matt tried to downplay it, explaining that he really had nothing to lose because if he had not attempted to stop the train, he probably would have died anyway.

"There's nothing heroic about saving your own life," he insisted.

"Maybe," the police captain replied. "But you have about one hundred and thirty people who don't agree with you."

When all the interviews and reports were over, Matt excused himself and got a room in a hotel, certain that he had heard the last of it.

* * *

When Hennessey and Taylor rode into Denver a couple of days later, they saw a crowd gathered around the front of a hardware store. Approaching to see what was drawing the crowd, they saw the flash of a pan of phosphorous powder.

"What was that?" Taylor asked.

"Somebody's takin' a picture," Hennesey said. "Ain't you ever seen nobody take a picture before?"

"What are they takin' a picture of?"

"How the hell do I know?" Hennessey replied. "I just got into town, same as you."

The two men headed over toward the hardware store. Dismounting, they tied off their horses, then moved in to see what was going on.

"Damn, Hennessey, lookit that! That's ole Loomis there!" Taylor said.

"Yeah, and Malone and Kale," Hennessey added grimly.

Loomis, Malone, and Kale, their skin now a pale blue-white, had been tied into their coffins and propped up against the front of the hardware store. On an easel alongside them was a sign:

EMIL CARTER, *photographer.*

Take your picture with dead outlaws,

25 cents.

The photographer was doing a booming business by charging citizens twenty-five cents apiece to be photographed standing alongside the bodies. When he saw Hennessey and Taylor looking at the bodies, he smiled broadly and waved at the two men.

"Would you like your picture took with the outlaws?"

he asked. "Just cost you a quarter. And for an extra ten cents, why, you can hold a gun while I take the picture."

"Why would I want to do that?" Hennessey asked.

"Could be, some years from now, folks will look at that picture and think you're the one that brought 'em to justice, never mind that it was Matt Jensen."

"Matt Jensen, huh?"

"Yes, sir, quite the hero he was too, what with killin' the outlaws and savin' the train and all. So, what'll it be, gents? Do you want your picture took with the outlaws?"

"No, I ain't interested in that," Hennessey said. He took in the three bodies with a wave of his hand. "Where's the other one?"

"The other one?"

"There was four of them," Hennessey said. "Where's the other one?"

"Oh, it could be that you are talking about the engineer and the fireman," the photographer said. "Their bodies have been took down to the Railroad Hall, where they'll stay till the funeral."

The photographer looked back at the three dead outlaws and chuckled. "Don't reckon these boys will be havin' much of what you would call a funeral."

"I'm not talkin' about the fireman and the engineer. There was another man with these three," Hennessey said.

The photographer shook his head. "No, I don't think so."

"Sure there was another one, Emil, don't you mind what the undertaker said? There was one that got runned over by the train."

"Oh, yes. Well, I think the undertaker has him somewhere in the back. What's left of him, that is. Wasn't nothin' he could do with that fella 'cept put a few bloody pieces in a box. Surely you don't want to see him, do you?"

"No, I reckon not," Hennessey said.

"Come on, Al, let's go get us a drink," Taylor suggested.

"Yeah," Hennessey agreed.

Five minutes later, the two men were sitting at a table drinking a whiskey. Several others in the saloon were talking about the incident with the train and how heroically Matt Jensen had been in fighting off the would-be robbers and stopping the train.

"That Jensen fella is one son of a bitch we need to avoid," Taylor said.

"Or kill," Hennessey said as he took another swallow of his whiskey.

Chapter Twelve

Matt was passing through the lobby of the hotel when someone called out to him.

"Mr. Jensen?"

Looking toward the person who called his name, Matt saw a very short, bald man holding a pencil and a narrow tablet.

"You are Matt Jensen, are you not?"

"Yes."

"Mr. Jensen, my name is Brandon. Alan Brandon. I'm a reporter for the *Rocky Mountain News*. I would like to do a story about you."

Matt was silent for a moment. He didn't particularly enjoy notoriety, but he didn't know how to send Brandon away without being rude. He motioned toward the chairs and sofas that were in the lobby. "Would it be all right to talk here?"

"Yes, sir, this would be fine."

"I don't know understand why anyone would want to do a story about me."

"You're much too modest, Mr. Jensen. You are a hero. The public has a right to know all about you."

Matt shook his head. "No, I'm no hero," he said. "And the public has no right to know anything about me," Matt replied.

"Please, Mr. Jensen. I'm just a man trying to make a living," Brandon replied. "Won't you let me interview you?"

Matt let out a sigh. The reporter had taken just the right tack by not saying he would make Matt famous. Matt was not interested in any self-aggrandizement, but he could understand how a man might need to make a living.

The reporter was someone who belonged to something that Matt referred to as "the other life." The other life consisted of hardworking, honest men who ranched or farmed, who drove wagons or stagecoaches, who clerked in stores and worked in banks and offices, or who, like this man, worked for a newspaper. It also consisted of the women and children who were there in support of those same hardworking, honest men. And though Matt referred to them as "the other life," it wasn't meant as a derisive sobriquet. On the contrary, they were people he admired, respected, and envied.

"All right," Matt finally agreed. "Ask your questions, I'll answer as best I can."

"Thank you for agreeing to talk to me, Mr. Jensen," the reporter said. He raised his pencil to the tablet. "What brings you to Denver?"

"As it turns out, I wasn't doing anything in particular, and you can do nothing in particular anywhere. So, I decided to do nothing in particular here in Denver," Matt said.

The reporter laughed.

"Wonder what all the passengers on the Midnight

Flyer would say if they knew that their hero was coming to Denver for no reason in particular."

"I told you, I'm not a hero," Matt said.

"That's what you told me, all right, but that's not what the governor's niece says."

"The governor's niece? What does the governor's niece have to do with anything?"

"She says she met you on the train, and she credits you with saving her life."

"The governor's niece?" Matt shook his head. "No, I don't recall meeting anyone like that."

"You didn't meet the governor's niece on the train?" Brandon asked, his eyebrows raised in question.

Matt shook his head. "No."

"Hmm. I wonder why Miss McKenzie told me that she met you."

"Wait a minute," Matt said quickly. "Did you just say McKenzie? Would that be Layne McKenzie?"

"Yes. Layne McKenzie is the governor's niece," Brandon explained.

Matt chuckled, surprised by the announcement. "In that case, I guess I did meet her," Matt said. "Only, she never told me that she was the governor's niece."

"She is, and if she sings your praises to the governor the way she did to me, why, I wouldn't be surprised if the governor didn't invite you to the mansion for a dinner."

Matt chuckled. "I don't think that is very likely."

"You would go, wouldn't you?"

"I don't know. I suppose it would depend on what he is serving," Matt answered easily.

Brandon chuckled, then continued with the interview. Two days later, the story ran in the newspaper.

HEROIC ACTION SAVES TRAIN.

Hero to be Honored.

On April 5 of this year, passengers on board the Midnight Flyer en route to this city had their journey interrupted by a band of brigands who lay in wait at the crest of Thunder Pass. The outlaws knew that at this point the train would be traveling at no faster than a slow walk, the decreased velocity necessitated by the long, steep climb.

It was here that the would-robbers managed to board the train, whereupon they immediately began to implement their nefarious plan. They forced the engine to stop; then they sent two men onto the cars to relieve the hapless passengers of any coin of the realm they might be carrying on their person.

While the robbers made careful plans as to where, how, and when to board the train, they failed to take into account the presence on board of a man who proved not only to be their nemesis, but more than their equal.

When one of the robbers entered the car in which Matt Jensen was traveling, the bold young man confronted the bandit, ultimately besting him in a shootout. Jensen then left the train to engage the others, and his spirited attack, though one man against many, interrupted the robbery, setting to flight the remaining outlaws.

In the meantime, the road agents killed both the engineer and the fireman. Although exact details are unknown, it is believed that the fireman managed to put the engine in motion immediately prior to receiving his fatal wound. That resulted in a drastic increase in the train's velocity on a section of track that railroad experts deem as quite hazardous due to the many sharp turns that are necessitated by requirements of geography. The train, which should have been traveling at no greater speed than ten miles per hour, was going downhill with the throttle at full open. As a result, it accelerated to an excess of sixty miles per hour.

Reboarding the train, Jensen realized rather immediately that something was terribly amiss, and he decided upon a course of action that would slow the speeding cars. That course of action, however, required that he reach the engine, and as he was separated from the engine by two express cars that would not allow interior passage, he could accomplish that mission only by climbing over the top.

It should be noted here that, in addition to the train's great speed, a raging ice storm added to the danger. Despite these perils, the intrepid Mr. Jensen, with total disregard of and great risk to his own life, braved both elements and the law of physics by climbing to the top of the speeding, oscillating, and ice-covered cars. The realization that the 131 hapless passengers were being hurtled to a sure death, and the concern for their safety being paramount in his mind, Matt Jensen undertook the task before him.

Our intrepid hero succeeded in reaching the engine cab, where he found Fireman Hank Mabry dead as a result of a gunshot wound. Acting quickly, Passenger Jensen, who knew naught of the operation of a modern locomotive, save that which had been provided him by Conductor Cooper prior to his undertaking the adventure, managed to bring the speeding train to a halt just before it reached Miller's Curve where, no doubt, it would have plunged over the trestle, resulting in the untimely death of all on board.

At a special ceremony to be held on the 21st instant, in the ballroom of the Palace Hotel, Governor John Long Routt will present Mr. Jensen with a proclamation expressing the thanks of the State of Colorado. In addition, a representative of the Denver and Rio Grande will give an award of five hundred dollars, and a one year's free pass upon any Denver and Rio Grande train.

Matt was sitting at a table in the Parker House Café as he read the article. Although he considered the entire article to have inflated his exploits, it wasn't until he reached the last paragraph that he reacted. "Wait a minute!" Matt said out loud, even though he was sitting alone at the table. "Nobody said anything to me about some special ceremony."

He heard someone clearing his throat and, looking up, saw a tall, thin, bald-headed man sporting a goatee, standing at his table. A pair of pince-nez glasses perched on the end of his nose, and he was carrying a bowler hat.

"Mr. Jensen?" the man said. "Are you Mr. Matt Jensen?"

"Yes, I'm Matt Jensen."

"My name is George Highgate, Mr. Jensen. I am a private secretary to His Honor John Long Routt, Governor of the State of Colorado." Highgate handed Matt a small, white envelope. "The governor asked me to give this to you," he said.

"What is it?" Matt asked, taking the envelope.

"It's not my place to say, sir," Highgate replied.

"Fair enough," Matt said. He opened the envelope, then removed the card.

The card was beautifully written:

John Long Routt, Governor of the State of Colorado,

Requests the presence of Matthew Jensen,

At a reception in his honor to be held in

The Ballroom of the Palace Hotel

On the 29th of April

"Do you have a response for the governor, Mr. Jensen?" Highgate asked.

"Yeah, I have a response."

"And your response would be?"

"My response is I'm not going."

"But, surely you are not serious sir," Highgate said, chagrined at the response. "One simply does not refuse an invitation from the governor."

"This . . . one . . . is refusing," Matt said, setting the word *one* apart as a sarcastic response to Highgate. "Just tell the Denver and Rio Grande to send me a draft for the money."

"I'm sorry, sir, I can't do that," Highgate replied. He smiled. "The governor anticipated something like this, so he has made getting the money from the railroad company contingent upon you being present for the ceremony."

For a brief instant, Matt was angry with the governor for doing that, then realizing that the governor's method was one sure way of making certain that he attend, Matt smiled.

"I'll give the governor this," he said. "He's a smart old coot. Because there is absolutely no way I would attend such a thing without this incentive."

"Your word for the governor, sir?" Highgate asked.

"Tell the governor I will be honored to attend," Matt said.

Highgate smiled and nodded. "I'm sure that the governor, and his niece, Miss Layne McKenzie, will be quite pleased you have accepted the invitation," he said.

Chapter Thirteen

At that very moment, Layne McKenzie was in the same café as Matt Jensen, though she was standing behind a post and a potted plant, keeping herself out of sight. She watched as Highgate approached Matt and presented him with the invitation from her uncle. With Layne was a new friend she had met since arriving in Denver.

"There he is," Layne said. "Do you see him?"

"The man Mr. Highgate is talking to?" Millie replied. "Yes."

"So that is the dashing and heroic Matt Jensen, is it?" Millie asked. "Oh, my, I can see why you are so taken with him. He is a very handsome man."

"Yes, he is," Layne agreed. She looked at her friend. "Oh, Millie, please don't stare. I would simply die if he caught us staring at him."

"I thought you and he were old friends."

"We met on the train," Layne said. "That doesn't make us old friends."

"Why don't you introduce me?"

"No, I couldn't do that."

"I see. You want to keep him for yourself, do you? Well, I can't say as I blame you."

"No, it isn't that," Layne said. "It's just that, well, I rather foolishly threw myself at him on the train. I invited him to call on me when we reached Denver and he hasn't done so."

"He may yet," Millie suggested.

Layne shook her head. "I doubt it. It has been nearly two weeks now, and he has made no effort to contact me."

"Maybe he doesn't know where to find you."

"He knows. When Mr. Highgate delivered my uncle's invitation to him, I made certain that Mr. Highgate would remind him that I was the governor's niece."

"Well, there you go," Millie said. "It could be that he is intimidated by you."

"What do you mean, intimidated?"

"You are the governor's niece, after all," Millie explained. "I can see how that might give most men pause before they called on you."

Layne laughed. "Millie, you are talking about a man who faced a gang of outlaws all alone, then climbed on the top of a train doing sixty miles an hour in an ice storm. I cannot see such a man being intimidated by the mere fact that I am the governor's niece."

"No, I suppose not," Millie admitted. "I was just trying to give you an excuse for why he hasn't contacted you—other than the fact that he might find you ugly."

"What?" Layne gasped, then, as she saw the smile on her friend's face, they both laughed.

"I know what you can do," Millie said.

"What?"

"You can invite him to the Firemen's Charity Ball tomorrow."

"Oh, no, I don't think I could do that," Layne said. "Ask him to escort me to a dance? That would be very unseemly."

Millie laughed. "You aren't asking him to escort you. You are merely asking him to come to the ball. After all, it is a charitable function. The volunteer fire company will be taking up a collection there, to be used for the widows and orphans fund."

"Yes," Layne said. "Yes, I suppose I could do something like that. That wouldn't be forward, would it?"

"Not at all," Millie said. "Would you like me to come with you? We can ask him now."

"Oh, yes. Would you?"

"Of course I will," Millie said. "I fear you will never introduce me if I don't."

Layne laughed. "All right, come with me."

Layne and Millie walked over to Matt's table. Seeing them approach, Matt stood.

"Good afternoon, ladies," he said with a slight nod of his head.

"Good afternoon, Mr. Jensen," Layne said. "I wonder if you . . ."

"Uh-humm," Millie said, clearing her throat.

Layne looked at her friend for a second, then smiled as she realized that Millie was hinting at an introduction.

"Oh, uh, Mr. Jensen, this is my friend Millie St. Cyr."

"I'm so pleased to meet you, Mr. Jensen," Millie said, extending her hand palm down.

Matt took her hand and shook it. The expression on Millie's face indicated that she had intended him to kiss her hand, but she recovered quickly.

"It is nice to meet you, Miss St. Cyr. Would you ladies like to join me for lunch?" he invited.

"Oh, no, thank you, but we have already eaten," Layne said.

"Perhaps another time," Matt suggested.

"Another time, yes," Layne said.

"Layne, aren't you going to invite the gentleman?" Millie asked.

"Yes," Layne said. "Mr. Jensen, there is to be a dance tomorrow, the Firemen's Charity Ball, being held at the Court House Hall. It is a benefit for widows and orphans, and the fire company has asked that we invite as many as we can to attend. Do you think you might find the time to attend?"

"Both Layne and I will be there," Millie said. "And we promise to leave a spot open on our dance cards for you."

"Well, then, how can I refuse an invitation like that?" Matt asked. "Of course I will come."

"Oh, good," Layne said. "Then, we shall look forward to seeing you there."

"Mr. Jensen," Millie said with a slight curtsy.

"Ladies," Matt replied as the two young women turned and walked away.

"That wasn't so hard now, was it?" Millie asked.

"No, it wasn't hard at all," Layne replied. "And, oh, Millie, I have had the grandest time out here. I'm so glad Uncle John invited me. Why, I would have never met a friend like you if I hadn't come out here. And you must come back to Cairo to visit me sometime."

"I will," Millie promised. "I will. I just wish you didn't have to return."

"I do too. But I can't stay with my uncle forever. He

has his own family, and I need to get back to mine. Plus, I will need to make preparations for my teaching job this fall."

"When are you going back?"

"Not until late summer. I have several weeks remaining."

"Good," Millie said. "That will give us a lot more time together."

"Oh, and I've asked Uncle John," Layne said. "You can sit at the table with me at the reception and ceremony honoring Mr. Jensen."

"That will be fun," Millie said. "I wonder if Matt Jensen is married."

Layne gasped. "Oh, heavens, I don't know," she answered. "Surely he is not married, or he would have told us so when we invited him to the dance, don't you think?"

"Why? We didn't ask him to escort either one of us; we just invited him to a charitable event," Millie said.

"One in which you volunteered that we would save a place on our dance cards for him," Layne replied, laughing. "You said that as if our dance cards were nearly filled."

"As far as Mr. Jensen is concerned, our dance cards *are* nearly filled," Millie said. "It will increase his interest if he believes we are so popular that we can barely find time for him."

Layne laughed. "If you say so," she said.

"So, are we going to go shopping, or are we just going to stand here and prattle on all morning?" Millie asked.

Layne laughed. "We're going shopping," she said.

When they stepped out of the hotel they saw some men, standing on ladders on opposite sides of the street, erecting a sign. The sign, a huge banner that stretched all the way across the street was attached on the north side of the street, to the front of the hotel, and on the south side of the street to Drew's Hardware Store.

COLORADO HONORS MATT JENSEN

"Oh, my, look at that," Layne said, pointing to the sign. "They have Mr. Jensen's name spread all the way across the street."

"I bet he will be very proud to see that," Millie suggested.

Layne shook her head. "I'm not so sure," she said.

"What do you mean, you aren't sure? Who wouldn't appreciate such an honor?"

"Just from what I have observed by being around him, I get the feeling that Mr. Jensen is a very reserved man, not given to self-aggrandizement. I think, all things considered, he would rather not have the sign so prominently displayed."

"I hadn't thought about that," Millie said. "You may be right."

"Come, let's go shopping," Layne said. "I would not want him to come out of the restaurant now and see us standing here, looking up at the sign."

"All right. There are some new hats at Graber's Emporium," Millie said. "Let's go see them before they are all sold."

Later that afternoon, Layne stepped off the omnibus when it stopped in front of the Governor's Mansion and, gathering her two purchases, one a straw hat, the other some ribbon, started up the walk to the house.

"Good afternoon, Miss McKenzie," Highgate said as he let her into the house. "I trust you had a pleasant day."

"Oh yes, very pleasant," Layne replied. "Is my uncle home?"

"Yes, miss, you will find him sitting out on the back porch."

Layne put her packages on a table, then walked through the house and stopped out onto the back porch. The governor was reading a newspaper.

"Hello, Uncle."

Governor Routt looked up and smiled at his beautiful young niece.

"Ah, Layne, my dear. How nice to see you."

"Are you reading about Matt Jensen?" he asked, pointing to the paper.

"Yes, it is quite a story," the governor replied. The smile left his face. "It makes me realize all the more the danger you were in. Had anything happened to you, my dear, I would never be able to face my sister again."

"Of course you would, Uncle," Layne replied. "You had nothing to do with putting me in danger. I am the one who wanted to come."

"I hope that ordeal hasn't soured you on Colorado," the governor said.

"On the contrary," Layne said, smiling brightly. "I have found the entire adventure to be quite exciting. To say nothing of having met Matt Jensen again. Millie and I invited him to the Firemen's Charity Ball tomorrow. I hope that wasn't too forward of us."

"Too forward? Of course not," the governor replied. "Well, I'm sure you will have a fine time at the dance tomorrow night. And I must confess, I am looking forward to presenting him with a proclamation at the reception."

"Yes, I am looking forward to being there as well," Layne said.

The governor chuckled. "I'm glad that you will be there. I'm sure your presence will brighten the occasion for everyone."

Highgate appeared on the porch and discreetly cleared his throat.

"Yes, George, what is it?"

"I wonder if I might have a word with you, sir?" he asked.

"Yes, yes, of course. Pour yourself a cup of coffee and join us."

Highgate looked pointedly at Layne, but he said nothing. However, Layne took the hint and standing quickly, she excused herself.

"Uncle, if you will excuse me, I'm going to my room to look at some of the purchases I made today."

"Of course I'll excuse you," Governor Routt said. "I'm glad you had a good day," he added with a broad smile.

After Layne was gone, the governor looked up at Highgate.

"Yes, George, what is it?"

Highgate took off his pince-nez glasses and began polishing them, paying particular attention to them so he wouldn't have to look the governor in the eyes. "I—uh—was wondering, sir, if I might not have an advance on my salary," Highgate said.

The governor sighed. "How much is it this time?"

"A hundred and fifty dollars," Highgate said.

"One hundred and fifty dollars?" the governor gasped. "George, that's three months!"

"I know, I know," Highgate said contritely. He placed the glasses carefully upon his nose. "I apologize, Governor, I do. But it's for my sister. I got a letter from her today saying that she and her husband may lose their farm if they can't pay off the mortgage."

Governor Routt stroked his mustache for a moment before he answered.

"All right, I tell you what. I don't know that I can authorize an advance in your salary without going through a lot of explanation. After all, the state pays you, not I. But I will personally lend you the money and you can pay me back whenever you can."

"Thank you, Governor," Highgate said. "From the bottom of my heart, I thank you."

"That's all right," the governor said with a dismissive wave of his hand. "Things like this can happen to anyone. I'm just glad that I can help."

"I will write my sister today and tell her not to worry," Highgate said.

Although drinks were served in the establishment, there was no bar. And although pretty women wandered around the floor between the tables, they were not soiled doves, nor were they bar girls. The name of the establishment was Pair-O-Dice, and it existed for the sole purpose of gambling.

There were many games of chance taking place in Pair-O-Dice, from the roulette wheel to craps to various card games. Highgate's particular passion was for "bucking the tiger," or faro, and when he stepped up to the window to buy some chips, he was met by the manager.

"I'm sorry, Mr. Highgate," he said. "But I have given my tellers instructions, no further credit. From now on you must play on a cash-only basis."

"I have the money to pay what I owe," Highgate said. "And enough money to buy more chips for tonight."

The manager smiled and nodded. "Then in that case, Mr. Highgate, you are welcome. You are welcome indeed. Callie," he called out to one of the young women who happened to be passing by.

"Yes sir, Mr. Toomey?"

"Get the governor's secretary a drink. On the house."

Sue smiled prettily at Highgate. "I'll bring it to your table," she said.

"Thanks," Highgate replied as he started toward an empty seat at one of the faro tables.

As Highgate played at the table, his fortunes seemed to turn for the better early in the game. He started winning, and the pile of chips grew higher in front of him. He was an animated player, exclaiming with joy each time he won, and expressing his frustration each time he lost. Then, even as his losses began to exceed his winnings, he continued to play. He played until every last chip was gone.

Highgate hurried to the cashier's window for a new supply.

"I need more chips," he said.

"Certainly. How many do you want?"

"One hundred dollars worth," Highgate said. "Put it on my account."

The cashier, who had been counting the chips, stopped and shook his head.

"I'm sorry, sir, but I have my orders. We can't extend you any more credit."

"But I paid my debt. You were here when I came in and paid it."

"Yes, sir, and we are grateful for that. But no more chips unless you have cash to pay for them."

"Do you know who I am?" Highgate asked.

"Yes, sir. You are the governor's private secretary."

"I could have the governor close this place down," Highgate said.

"No, Mr. Highgate, I don't think you can," another voice said.

Turning, Highgate saw Toomey, the manager.

"You don't think so?" Highgate asked.

"No, I don't," Toomey said. "And I don't think you would close us if you could. You have the disease, Mr. Highgate. You can't stop gambling. If we were closed, where would you go?"

Angry and frustrated, Highgate formed his hands into fists and left the establishment. He knew that Toomey was right. He was addicted to gambling. But with this last loan, he had exhausted every avenue he had of getting more money.

What would he do now?

Chapter Fourteen

Although the Firemen's Charity Ball wasn't due to start until seven o'clock of the evening, the Court House Hall was busy for most of the afternoon. Millie belonged to a young woman's group called Denver Maidens of Mercy, an organization dedicating to helping others.

The Maidens of Mercy were in the Court House Hall helping with the decorations, and helping to get set up for the evening's entertainment.

At the rear of the hall, a hydrant was placed upon a pedestal. Attached to the hydrant and running down each wall were fire hoses. At the moment, Millie was standing on a ladder, weaving a long strand of greenery and garland around one of the hoses. Others from the club were polishing the brass nozzles so that they flashed and glistened in the light.

"All right, I'm ready for another strand," Millie said.

"Coming right up," Layne offered. She turned toward the table where the strands had been laid out and Norma Jean Proud, a short, dark-haired girl and friend of Millies, handed it to her.

"What is he like?" Norma Jean asked.

"What is who like?"

"You know. Matt Jensen," Norma Jean said. "Is he handsome?"

"I suppose you could . . ." Layne started to reply, but Millie's laughter interrupted her.

"Yes, he is very handsome," Millie said. "Don't listen to Layne. She's just trying to keep him for herself."

"I am not!" Layne said, blushing at the remark.

"Pay no attention to Millie," Anne Jones said. Like Layne, Millie, and Norma Jean, Anne was helping to decorate for the dance. And like Millie and Norma Jean, Annie was a member of the Maidens of Mercy. "Millie is just trying to embarrass you so she can have him all to herself."

"This is all so funny," Layne said. "Don't you think Mr. Jensen ought to have some say-so in all this?"

"Oh, don't be silly," Millie said. "Men just think they have a say so. Everyone knows they do only what their women allow them to do."

The girls laughed at Millie's observation, but the laugh was interrupted with the arrival of the band.

"Oh, look!" Norma Jean said excitedly. "The band is here!"

For the next hour, as the girls and the firemen continued to prepare the Court House Hall, the band practiced, the high skirling sound of the fiddles, interspersed with the ringing of the banjos and the strum of the guitar.

"Oh, my, look at the time!" Millie said. "We barely have time to go home and get ready for the dance."

In a nearby saloon, a man sat alone in a table at the back of the room. From time to time, one of the bar girls would drop by his table and with a practiced grin would inquire as to his needs.

"The only thing I need is for you to leave me the hell alone," he said gruffly and, as the girls shared his reaction to them with the others, they stopped trying to be nice to him.

The man was drinking whiskey and reading the paper. He had already read the article about Matt Jensen being feted by the governor of Colorado. That was what brought him to Denver. Now, he was reading an article about the Firemen's Charity Ball and noticed that Matt Jensen would be in attendance.

It was the last line that caught his attention:

As the purpose of the Firemen's Charity Ball is to raise funds to be dispersed to widows and orphans of the city, anyone who is disposed toward financial participation in the eleemosynary endeavor is welcome to attend.

When Matt Jensen arrived at the Court House Hall, there was a table set up just inside the door. The table was manned by firemen in uniform. There was a big bowl on the table and a hand-lettered sign in front of the bowl.

> *Friend, our plea is not for much,*
> *Give only what you are able.*
> *Your donation will help widows and orphans and such*
> *Put food upon their table.*

Matt dropped five dollars into the bowl, then he stepped out onto the floor. The hall was very crowded as the men in clean jeans and pressed shirts intermingled with the women in their butterfly-bright gingham dresses.

"Ah, Mr. Jensen, there you are!" Layne said, coming toward him with a big smile. "I'm so glad you could come."

"Well, I thank you for inviting me," Matt replied.

"Gents, choose your ladies and form up your squares!" someone shouted loudly, and looking toward the sound of the voice, Matt saw the caller standing in front of the band, holding a megaphone to his mouth.

"I hope your dance card isn't taken for this dance," Matt said.

"I've left this one open," Layne replied, giving Matt her arm.

Several couples, including Matt and Layne, hurried to their positions within one of the squares.

The music started then, with the fiddles loud and clear, the guitars carrying the rhythm, the banjos providing the counterpoint, and the dobro singing over everything. The caller began to shout, and he clapped his hands and stomped his feet and danced around on the platform in compliance with his own calls, bowing and whirling as if he had a girl and was in one of the squares himself. The dancers moved and swirled to the caller's commands.

> Swing your partner round and round,
> Turn your corner upside down.
> Hang on tight like swingin' on a gate,
> Meet your partner for a grand chain eight.
> Chew some 'backy and dip some snuff,
> Grab your honey and strut your stuff.

"Friend, aren't you going to make a donation?" one of the fireman called to a short, swarthy, dark-haired man who had just walked past the table without stopping.

"What?" the man replied, turning toward the table.

"A donation," the fireman repeated. "It doesn't matter how much you donate—just give what you can. But the purpose of this dance is to raise money for charity."

"Oh," the man said. Reaching his hand into his pocket, he pulled out ten cents, then dropped it into the bowl.

The fireman looked pointedly at the donation.

"You said it don't matter how much," the man said.

"Yes, I did," the fireman replied. "Thank you, sir."

The man nodded, then moved out onto the dance floor. Wandering over to the punch bowl, he accepted a cup from a smiling young woman, then moved up to stand with his back against the wall and look out onto the floor at the swirling dancers.

That was when he saw him. Matt Jensen was dancing with a very pretty woman. He watched for a while, then seeing someone who was bussing empty cups and plates, he went over to talk to him.

"Do you see that man in the blue shirt dancing with the black-haired girl in the green dress?"

"Yes, sir."

"I'll give you a dollar if you will give him this envelope," he said, holding up a dollar bill and an envelope.

"All I got to do is give him the envelope?"

"That's all."

The busboy smiled broadly. "Yes, sir, I'll do that for you."

"Thanks."

The short, swarthy man watched as the busboy moved through the crowd of dancers to find Matt Jensen.

When the dance ended and the square broke up, Matt thanked Layne for the dance. With a curtsy she told him that he was welcome, and that she had enjoyed the dance. That was when the busboy approached him.

"Excuse me, sir," the busboy said. "But a gentleman asked me to give you this envelope."

"What gentleman?" Matt replied.

"The one standing over . . ." the busboy said, pointing toward the punch bowl. He stopped in mid-sentence. "He's a short fella, dark hair, kind'a swarthy skin. That's funny. He ain't there no more."

"Let me see the envelope," Matt said, taking the small package from the busboy.

Looking inside the envelope, Matt saw a .50-caliber bullet. A little piece of paper was wrapped around the bullet, secured by a strip of rawhide. On the paper was his name and the same symbol he had seen before.

"Look around, man," Matt said. "Do you see him anywhere?"

The busboy surveyed the entire room, then shook his head.

"No, sir," he said. "He ain't nowhere in the buildin'. That seems strange, him givin' me somthin' to give you, then not even stayin' around so's you could see who done it."

"Under the circumstances, maybe not so strange," Matt said.

"Beg your pardon, sir?"

"Nothing," Matt said. "Thank you."

"You're welcome," the busboy said as he hurried off to attend to his duties.

"Matt, what is it?" Layne asked. "What's in the envelope?"

"Nothing, particular," Matt replied.

"I don't believe that. I told you once before when we were on the train, remember? I told you then that you have a remarkably expressive face. I don't know what was in the envelope, but it did disturb you."

"I think curious would be a better word than disturb," Matt said. "I'm curious as to why anyone would send me something like this."

Matt opened the envelope to allow Layne to look inside.

"What is it?" she asked. Then, seeing the bullet, she gasped. "My word!" she said. "What a strange thing to send to someone."

"Ahh, it's probably just someone's idea of a joke," Matt said, purposely making light of it.

When Matt went into his hotel room that night, he turned up the gas lights, then walked over to sit on the bed to remove his boots. Just as he was sitting on the bed, a bullet smashed through the window and smacked into the wall on the opposite side.

Rolling off the bed and onto the floor, Matt snaked his revolver from the holster that hung on the headboard, then crawled over toward the window. Another bullet came through the glass, and he could hear it whizzing by just over his head. It too slammed into the wall on the opposite side.

Raising himself just high enough to peak through the window, he saw a muzzle flash in the hayloft of a barn across the street. The bar housed the mules for a wagon freight company. The bullet from that shot whizzed by him so close that he could feel the wind of its passing. He fired toward the black maw that opened into the hayloft, but because he had no specific target, he didn't expect to hit anything.

He crawled across the floor to the door, opened it,

then went out into the hall and ran toward the window at the end of the hall. Just as he reached the window, the door to the end room opened.

Whirling quickly, Matt brought his pistol to bear on the man who had stuck his head out the door.

"What's going on?" he said. Then, seeing the pistol in his face, he gasped. "Oh, my Lord!" he said, throwing his hands up.

"Sorry," Matt said, lowering the pistol. "Get back in your room and stay away from the window."

"Yes, sir," the man answered, even as Matt was opening the window at the end of the hall. Stepping up onto the windowsill, Matt jumped down into the area between the hotel and the neighboring building. Then, with pistol in hand, he darted across the street, and began working his way toward the barn.

Reaching the side of the barn, he backed against it, then started working his way toward the main door. Just as he reached the door, though, he heard the sound of galloping hoofbeats.

Matt ran to the front of the barn, then dashed into it through the smell of mule and manure, hay and oats. When he reached the back of the barn, he saw a mounted rider dart behind a row of buildings. With a sigh of frustration, Matt lowered his pistol, then returned to the hotel.

The night clerk met Matt as he came into the lobby.

"Oh, my, what are you doing out here?" he asked. "I thought you were in your room."

"I went for a walk," Matt said simply.

The expression on the face of the night clerk was one of confused bewilderment as he watched Matt, gun in hand, climb back up the steps to go to his room.

Chapter Fifteen

Denver

As Smoke Jensen rode down Wynkoop Street the next day, he had to maneuver his horse from side to side in order to negotiate his way through the heavy traffic of coaches, carriages, and wagons.

There was a large banner stretched across the street, and looking up, Smoke smiled when he saw the name.

COLORADO HONORS MATT JENSEN

This was a proud moment for Smoke, having Matt honored by the state of Colorado. Smoke and Matt had shared their time together long before Smoke married Sally, and long before his two most loyal hands, Pearlie and Cal, had come to work at Sugarloaf. But Sally understood the bond between the Smoke and Matt, and it was she who, having read the article in the *Rocky Mountain News,* suggested to Smoke that he go to Denver for the ceremony.

After getting a room in the hotel, Smoke took a bath and put on a suit. Then he went downstairs and walked through the lobby to a large ballroom that was being used as a reception hall. Through the open door of the room, he could see several well-dressed men and women standing around, laughing and talking.

A large man was standing near the open door, looking out into the lobby. By the man's demeanor and by the expression on his face, Smoke could see that he was not a guest of the reception, but was a guard. The guard came toward Smoke, shaking his head and with his hand extended.

"Sir, this is a closed reception," the guard said.

"That's good," Smoke said. "It shouldn't be open for just anyone. Why, there's no telling what kind of disreputable figure might try to come in."

"You don't understand, sir," the guard said. "I'm talking about you. You can't come in here."

"Wait a minute. Are you calling me a disreputable figure?"

"No, sir, I'm just telling you that this is a closed reception and unless you have a personal invitation from the governor, you cannot come in."

"Well, the gentleman being honored and I are old friends," Smoke said.

"Do you have an invitation?"

"No."

The guard smiled triumphantly. "Well, if you were old friends, you would have an invitation now, wouldn't you? I'm sorry, sir, but you can't come in. I'm going to have to ask you to leave."

"Why don't we just ask the man being honored?" Smoke suggested. He started into the room.

"Sir, if you don't leave now, I am going to personally throw you out of here!"

Smoke looked at the guard. The guard was a big man and it was obvious that he could handle himself. But at the same time Smoke was looking over the guard, the guard was taking stock of Smoke, and Smoke could see by the expression in his face that he wasn't looking forward to any encounter with someone Smoke's size.

Smoke sighed. The guard was just doing his job.

"All right," Smoke said. "I don't want to cause any trouble." He pointed to the lobby. "I'll wait out here. I would appreciate it, though, if you would tell Matt Jensen that Smoke is here."

With Matt Jensen

If it weren't for the fact that the Denver and Rio Grande was giving Matt a five-hundred-dollar reward and a year's free pass on their railroad, he would just as soon have missed the governor's reception. But it was all tied together. The railroad wanted some consideration from the governor, Governor John Long Routt wanted the political recognition he would receive from such an event, and Matt wanted the money.

Matt stood in his room of the Palace Hotel, examining his reflection in the mirror. He was wearing a suit, vest, and tie. This was a rare affectation, but he thought it necessary for the occasion.

There was a light knock on his door and, with a final adjustment of his tie, he walked over to open it. It was a hotel valet.

"Mr. Jensen, I was sent to inform you that the governor has arrived, sir."

"Thank you," Matt said. "You may tell the governor that I will be along shortly."

"Very good, sir."

* * *

Layne was enjoying the reception. Many of the new friends she had made were there as well, and Millie commented on it.

"They are all here so they can get a glimpse of Matt Jensen," Millie said. "Why, there is not a one of them who would be here if your uncle were honoring some sixty-five-year-old man for developing a new way of curing cowhides or something," she added with a laugh.

"Why are you here, Millie?" one of the others asked.

"Oh, I admit it, my dears. I am here just to get a closer look at the handsome and heroic Mr. Jensen." She looked over at Layne. "Although it is clear that Layne has a claim on him."

"I do not," Layne said, laughing and blushing as she responded.

"Oh, but my dear, you were with him on the train when he performed his heroics. Indeed, you were one of the people he saved. Why, what better claim can one have than to be that very damsel in distress?"

Unaware that he was the center of such conversation, Matt went downstairs, through the lobby, and into the large ballroom. Here, several dozen tables were scattered about, already filled with elegantly dressed representatives of Denver's citizenry. Despite its brief history, Denver, with a population of well over one hundred thousand people, was already the largest city between St. Louis and San Francisco. It was also one of the wealthiest cities, so that the net worth of those gathered here tonight could compete with any similar gathering in any city in America.

He was met just inside the door by George Highgate, who escorted him to the long table on the dias.

"Where is the governor?" Matt asked.

"He will be here in a moment, sir," Highgate answered.

"Good evening, Mr. Jensen," Layne said.

Smiling, Matt nodded at her. "Good evening, Miss McKenzie," he replied.

"Speaking on behalf of the widows and orphans of the city, may I tell you how much I—that is, we," Layne corrected, "appreciated your presence at the Firemen's Charity Ball last night?"

"Believe me, the appreciation and the pleasure were all mine," Matt said.

"You remember all my friends, I believe," Layne said, taking the other girls in with a wave of her hand.

"Let me see if I can remember," Matt said. He looked at each of the girls he had met last night, and called them each by name, in turn. "This is Miss Millie St. Cyr, Miss Norma Jean Proud, Miss Sue Kendal, and Miss Annie Jones."

"Oh, my," Millie said. She clapped her hands, and the others clapped as well. "I am very impressed."

"Yes, especially as you are so famous now," Norma Jean said.

"And a true American hero," Sue added.

"Hardly famous, Miss Proud," Matt said. "And definitely not a hero, Miss Kendal."

"I think Mrs. Jensen would argue that fact," Millie said. "Surely, your wife believes you to be a hero."

"Oh, there is no Mrs. Jensen," Matt said. "That is, I have no wife."

"Millie, what a shameless way to ask if the gentleman is married," Layne scolded, though her scolding was alleviated both by the expression in her voice and the smile on her face.

At that moment, the governor was just passing through the lobby when he saw Smoke Jensen. Breaking into a wide smile, the governor hurried over to extend a personal greeting.

"Smoke Jensen," Governor John Long Routt said, extending his hand. "How good to see you."

"Hello, John," Smoke replied, returning the smile.

"Governor, this man doesn't have an invitation," the guard said.

"Really? Well, don't worry about it, Mitchell," the governor said. "Mr. Jensen and I are old friends," the governor said. "I would have certainly extended the invitation if I had known he would come. And I do so now."

"Oh. Mr. Jensen, I'm sorry I didn't know. I hope you don't take offense."

"Don't be sorry, my friend," Smoke said. "You were just doing your job. And if I may say so, you were doing it quite well."

"Uh, yes, sir. Thank you, sir. But you should'a said you were a friend of the governor. You said you were a friend of the man being honored."

"Indeed he is, Mitchell," Governor Routt said. "In fact, he is much more than a friend. Perhaps you didn't catch his last name. It is Jensen."

"Jensen? Oh, you mean like Matt Jensen, the man getting the award tonight?"

"Yes," Governor Routt said. "Come with me, Smoke, I'm sure Matt is looking for you."

Smoke shook his head. "I doubt it," he said. "I didn't tell him I was coming. I wanted to surprise him."

"Oh. Well, that is even better. Come along."

* * *

Inside, Matt was still surrounded by Layne and her friends. They were all pretty, and the company was pleasant, but they were almost fawning over the story that had appeared in the paper, and that was making him a little uncomfortable. The only way he could handle it was with self-deprecating humor.

"Is it true that you had to walk on top of a train doing sixty miles an hour in order to reach the engine?" Sue Kendall asked.

"I didn't walk."

"I beg your pardon?"

"I didn't walk," Matt repeated. Unconsciously, he stroked the small, crescent-shaped scar on his cheek, the result of the slip on the ice that almost caused him to fall off. "I fell, then I had to crawl like a baby, hanging on for dear life, cursing myself for the fool I was to try such a thing."

The ladies laughed out loud.

Smoke followed the governor through a cloud of aromatic tobacco and pipe smoke. He saw Matt before Matt saw him. It was easy to pick Matt out from the crowd. His young protégé stood over six feet tall with broad shoulders and narrow hips. His blond hair seemed even more yellow than Smoke remembered.

Matt didn't see Smoke right away, because he had his back turned and he was surrounded by about half-a-dozen very beautiful women, each woman vying for his attention. As Smoke approached, the women broke out into laughter over some story Matt was telling.

"You always were able to spin a good yarn," Smoke said.

A huge smile spread across Matt's face, and he turned to greet the man who had just spoken.

"Smoke! What are you doing here?"

"You are getting an award from the governor, aren't you?" Smoke replied. "I had to be here."

Matt took Smoke's hand in his, and the two shook hands and clasped each other on the shoulder.

"Ladies, I would like to introduce Smoke Jensen," Matt said.

"Did you say Jensen?" Millie asked.

"I sure did."

"Is he your brother?"

Matt nodded. "Yes, indeed," Matt said. "Smoke is my brother."

There was a dinner after the reception, and though Smoke offered to leave, he was persuaded to stay when he learned that the governor had made special arrangements for him at the head table. When all were seated, Governor Routt tapped his spoon on the crystal goblet. The clear ringing sound could be heard above all the laughter and conversation, and it had the desired effect of silencing the guests.

"Ladies and gentlemen, it is my distinct honor and privilege tonight to host this banquet in honor of Matthew Jensen, one of Colorado's leading citizens."

Although everyone in attendance had read the newspaper article and heard the story of Matt's exploits, the governor repeated it all in his speech, pausing occasionally to allow the crowd to react with exclamations of awe and wonder at Matt's skill and bravery.

"And now, as governor of the state of Colorado, I

hereby issue this proclamation declaring this day to be officially entered into the state historical records as Matthew Jensen Day."

After the presentation, the crowd responded with applause and calls for Matt to make a speech.

Clearing his throat, Matt got up from his seat and walked to the podium. Looking out over the room, he saw over one hundred people, all of whom were looking at him in admiration. He cleared his throat before he began to speak.

"I'm not a hero," he said. "A hero is someone who takes a great risk to do something very dangerous for the good of others. I had no choice. If I had not tried to stop the engine, the train would have gone off the track and I would have been killed along with the others. When you do such a thing as a matter of necessity rather than as a matter of choice, it is not heroic, it is basic animal survival.

"Nevertheless, I am grateful to Governor Routt for this honor, and grateful to the Denver and Rio Grande Railroad for their generosity. Thank you very much."

Matt resumed his seat to the applause of all.

After the reception and dinner, Matt was pleased to see that the people seemed as genuinely pleased to meet Smoke, and shake his hand, as they were to meet Matt and shake his. This was as it should be, Matt knew, because long before anyone had ever heard of Matt, Smoke Jensen was performing heroic deeds. As Matt watched the others react to Smoke Jensen, he recalled his connection with the famous mountain man.

After his parents were murdered by Payson and his gang, young Matt Cavanaugh wound up in an orphanage.

Conditions in the orphanage were as brutal as any delinquent detention home, and unwilling to take it anymore, Matt ran away. He would have died had Smoke not found him shivering in a snowbank in the mountains. Smoke took him to his cabin and nursed him back to health.

It had been Smoke's intention to keep the boy around only until he had recovered, but Matt wound up staying with Smoke until he reached manhood. During the time Matt lived with Smoke, he became Smoke's student, learning everything from Smoke that Smoke had learned from Preacher many years earlier. He learned how to use a knife or a gun to defend himself; he learned how to survive in the wilderness, and how to track man or beast. But the most important lesson of all was how to be a man of honor.

By the time Matt reached the age of eighteen, he felt that the time was right to go out on his own. Smoke did not have the slightest hesitancy over sending him out, because Matt had become one of the most capable young men Smoke had ever seen.

But just before Matt left, he surprised Smoke by asking permission to take Smoke's last name as his own. Smoke was not only honored by the request, he was touched, and to this day there was a bond between them that was as close as any familial bond could be.

Therefore, when Millie asked if they were family, Matt was able to say—truthfully—that Smoke was his brother.

At breakfast the next morning, Smoke commented on his surprise over the number of people who had made a special effort to greet him.

"You shouldn't be surprised," Matt replied. "Surely, you know that you are one of the best-known men in the entire state of Colorado. Why, if you ran for governor today, I've no doubt but that you would be elected."

Smoke chuckled. "Don't tell John that," he said. "Though he has no need for worry, I have no intention of ever entering politics," he said. "But maybe you should. You are getting quite an enviable reputation yourself, and you are still young enough—why, you could have a very successful political career."

"Thanks, but no, thanks," Matt replied, clearly uncomfortable with any such suggestion. Clearing his throat, he changed the subject. "How is Sally?"

"Sally sends her love."

"You tell her that I send mine as well," Matt said.

"I'll do that," Smoke said.

"Smoke, I need your advice on something," Matt said.

Smoke smiled. "Well, now, that warms my soul," he said. "It's good to know that the student still thinks he can learn something from his teacher."

"Are you kidding?" Matt replied. "There will never be a time when I can't learn from you."

"What is it?" he asked.

Matt reached into his shirt pocket and pulled out three .50-caliber shells, three strips of rawhide, and three pieces of paper, each of them bearing the same thing.

MATT JENSEN

"Where did you get these?" Smoke asked as he examined the symbols.

"They were given to me," Matt replied.

Smoke looked up in surprise.

"In a manner of speaking," Matt said. He explained how there had been three attempts on his life, and how, after each attempt, he had found one of these little symbols, wrapped around a bullet and held in place with a strip of rawhide.

"Have you made any Indian enemies?" Smoke asked.

Matt shook his head. "None that I know of."

"Then you've made one that you don't know of," Smoke said. He pointed to the symbol.

"This is called the Maasaw. It is the Hopi Indians' God of Death. Whoever is leaving this for you is Hopi. Or at least, part Hopi."

"Hopi?" Matt replied. "But the Hopi have always been peaceful. Even their name means peace."

"That's true," Smoke said. "But you can have a bad apple in any barrel. Just because the Hopi as a people are peaceful, doesn't mean you can't have one of them who is a mean son of a bitch. Do you know anyone who is Hopi?"

"No," Matt answered.

"Well, some Hopi knows you. And he doesn't like you very much. So keep your eyes open."

"I will," Matt promised.

"I need to get started back," Smoke said, putting some money on the table as he stood.

"No," Matt said resolutely. He picked the money up and gave it back. "I'm buying breakfast."

Smoke took the offered money and laughed. "All right. But don't you think for one moment that a measly breakfast is going to pay me back for all the meals I furnished you when you were a snot-nosed kid."

Matt laughed as well and walked to the door with his friend. It was always like this when the two encountered each other. Matt had never made an effort to dissuade him from leaving, nor had he ever put forth any notion to join him. Each man was supremely confident in his own life, and in the absolute certainty that their friendship would remain strong, despite lengthy and distant separations.

Shortly after Smoke left, Matt returned to the hotel to move out of his room. When he asked the clerk what the charge was, the clerk shook his head.

"No charge to you, Mr. Jensen," he said. "The owner of the hotel instructed me to tell you that your stay with us is free. He was at the ceremony last night when you were honored by the governor."

"That's very nice of him, but it isn't really necessary," Matt said.

The hotel clerk chuckled. "Don't worry, Mr. Jensen. We've doubled the price on the room where you stayed. There will be people who will be more than willing to pay the price, just so they can tell their friends where they stayed. The hotel will make the money back within one week."

Matt shook his head and chuckled. "I don't know why anyone would want to do such a thing, but I thank you for the room," he said.

The train fare was also free, thanks to the offer made by the Denver and Rio Grande.

"Where would you like to go, sir?" the ticket agent asked.

"You suggest a place," Matt said.

"I beg your pardon, sir?" the clerk replied, surprised by Matt's response.

"I don't have any particular place to go," Matt said. "What would you suggest?"

"Oh, well, Colorado Springs is certainly nice this time of year."

Matt smiled. "Then Colorado Springs it will be," he said. "For me and my horse."

Chapter Sixteen

The Butrum ranch

On the very night Matt was leaving for Colorado Springs, at the Butrum Ranch near Greenborn Creek, Silas Butrum laid his pocket watch on the night table and blew out the lantern.

"So, you are finally coming to bed, are you?" his wife asked from the bed.

"I'm sorry, Karla, I didn't mean to wake you," he said. "I was just going over the books. It looks like we have finally turned the corner, old girl. Paying off the mortgage was a good thing."

"I thought it would be," Karla said.

"Wait a minute," Silas said.

"What is it?"

"I don't know, I thought I just saw a light outside."

"A light? Why would there be a light way out here?"

"That's just what I was thinking," Silas said.

Walking over to the window, he pulled the curtain aside to stare out into the darkness. On the bed alongside him, the mattress creaked, and his wife raised herself on her elbows.

"What is it, Silas?" she asked. "Do you see anything?"

"No, I guess not," he said.

Silas looked through the window for a moment longer. He saw only the moon-silvered Purgatory Peak.

"Ah, don't worry about it, Karla," Silas replied, still looking through the window. "It's prob'ly just the moon reflectin' is all."

"Come on to bed. You've been up too late and you have to get up too early in the morning," Karla said.

"Is it my sleep you're worryin' about, woman?" Silas teased. "Or is it that you're just wantin' me to lay beside you?"

"A woman takes comfort in lyin' alongside her man," Karla replied in a welcoming voice.

Three hundred yards away from the house, Marcus Strayhorn twisted around in his saddle and looked back at the others. "Put that cigar out!" he hissed.

"Sorry, Marcus, I guess I wasn't thinkin'," Decker said.

Strayhorn, Teech, and Decker were all wearing hats pulled low over their faces and long dusters that were hanging open to provide access to the pistols that stuck from their belts.

"You sure there's money here?" Teech asked.

"You heard what them fellas said same as I did," Strayhorn said. "Butrum got hisself almost fifteen hundred dollars for the cows he sold last fall, and he keeps ever' cent of it in the house."

"That's what they said all right," Teech agreed.

"Besides, we ain't only goin' to get the money, we'll get

some vittles as well. Decker, you hit the smokehouse, take ever' bit of meat they got a'curin'."

"Hope they got a couple slabs of bacon," Decker said.

"Teech, you go in with me," Strayhorn said.

Inside the house, Silas had just gone to bed when he heard men talking.

"Damn, Karla, there *is* somebody outside," he said, suddenly sitting up in bed.

"What? Are you sure?"

"You damn right I'm sure. I can hear 'em talkin'," Silas said. He relit the lantern, then got out of bed and started to pull on his trousers. Suddenly, there was a crashing sound from the front of the house as the door was smashed open.

"Silas!" Karla screamed.

Holding up his trousers, Silas started toward the living room and the shotgun he kept over the fireplace.

"You lookin' for this?" Teech asked. He was holding Silas's shotgun.

"Who the hell are—" That was as far as Silas got. His question was cut off by the roar of the shotgun, and a charge of double-aught buckshot slammed him back against the wall. Silas slid down to the floor, painting the wall behind him with blood and viscera from the gaping exit wounds in his back.

"Silas! No!" Karla shouted, hurrying into the living room. She knelt on the floor beside him, holding his head in her lap.

"What about the woman?" Teech asked.

"If she tells us where the money is, we'll let her live," Strayhorn said. "If she don't, we'll kill her."

"It's in the bedroom, under the mattress," Karla said.

Strayhorn smiled. "Well, now, that's more like it." Rushing into the bedroom, Strayhorn flipped the mattress over and, seeing a small cloth bag tied to the springs under the mattress, he opened it.

"Here it is!" he said excitedly, but as he counted the money, the expression on his face changed from one of excitement to one of anger and frustration.

"Where's the rest of it?" he asked.

"Rest of it? What rest of it?" Karla asked. "That's all we have. Take it."

Moving quickly to Karla, Strayhorn reached down and pulled her to her feet. Then he slapped her viciously in the face.

"Where is the rest of it?" he demanded.

"Please!" Karla screamed. "There is no rest of it! This is everything we have!"

Strayhorn slapped her again. "You're lying!" he shouted angrily. "There's not more than a hundred dollars here. I know damn well you got almost fifteen hundred dollars for them cows you sold last fall."

"We paid off the mortgage on our place," Karla said. "There is no more money."

"Ahhh!!" Strayhorn yelled in anger. Then, seeing the lantern Silas had lit, he picked it up and threw it against the wall. The lantern broke, and flames began leaping up onto the kerosene-soaked wall paper.

"Let's get out of here," Strayhorn said.

"What about her?" Teech asked, pointing to Karla.

"Drag her out to the barn," Strayhorn said. "No more money than we got, we may as well have a little fun with her."

Teech looked at Karla and smiled. His face, bathed

orange now in glow of the fire, gave him the appearance of a demon from hell.

"Yeah," Teech said. "That's what I figure as well."

"No!" Karla said. She began fighting when Teech reached for her.

Teech slapped her so hard that it knocked out one of her teeth. She began bleeding from the mouth.

"Woman, whether you're dead or alive, we're goin' to have our way with you," Teech said.

"I won't fight you anymore," Karla said. She pointed to her dead husband. "But please don't leave him in here to burn up."

"You don't understand, do you?" Strayhorn said. "You ain't in no position to bargain."

The flames were growing higher and hotter, and a strip of burning wallpaper fell onto the floor.

"Damn!" Teech said. "We're all goin' to cook if we don't get out of here."

"Grab her, and let's go," Strayhorn said.

As Teech reached for the woman's shoulders, she suddenly, and unexpectedly, pulled his gun from his holster.

"What the hell!" Teech shouted, jumping back away from her.

Karla pointed the gun at Teech, then at Strayhorn. Then, to the shock of both men, she put the gun to her temple and pulled the trigger. Blood and brain tissue sprayed from the opposite side of her head, and she fell across her husband's body.

"Son of a bitch! What did she do that for?" Teech asked.

By now, the smoke was so thick that both men were beginning to cough.

"Let's go!" Strayhorn said. "If we don't get out of here now we'll choke."

Coughing, the two men ran from the room, then out of the house. Decker was already standing out front, holding a slab of bacon and a sack of coffee beans.

"What happened?" Decker asked. "How did the house catch on fire?"

"The lantern fell over," Strayhorn said.

"Did you get the money?" Decker asked.

"Let's go," Strayhorn said without answering the question.

The three rode away, while behind them the Butrum house, now entirely involved with fire, roared as flames climbed up the walls and leapt up from the roof. A pillar of smoke and hot air carried thousands of sparks into the sky, scattering red stars among the blue.

When he first saw him, he gasped, for he thought that the man had no nose and he wondered if it had been cut off. When the man came to sit at the table with him, though, he saw that he did have a nose, it was just mashed so flat that it was almost even with his face.

"My name is Nelson," the man said. "I got a message to meet someone here, at this table, at eleven o'clock. Would that be you?"

"Yes."

Nelson sat down. "Some folks call me No Nose, but I don't know why." As soon as he said it, he began wheezing through his misshapen nose as he laughed at the joke he had just told on himself. "Do you get it?" he asked.

"Yes, I get it."

"I got 'n a fight with my brother when I was a kid and he

smashed me in the face with an ax handle, broke my nose so that it's like this," No Nose said. "Can't do nothin' about it, so I joke about it."

"Indeed."

"I didn't get your name," No Nose said.

"My name isn't important."

"It's important to me, mister, if we're going to do business together," No Nose said.

"Very well, my name is Smith."

"Is that your name?"

"I have a proposition for you," Smith replied without answering.

"A what?"

"A . . . suggestion," Smith explained. "A suggestion as to how you might be able to make a lot of money."

"A suggestion," No Nose repeated.

"Yes. If you are interested."

"I might be. You say it could make me a lot of money. How much money are we talking about?"

"Oh, I assure you, we are talking about a great deal of money. For both of us."

"So you say."

"Yes, so I say. And I am in a position to know what I am talking about. Are you interested? Because if you aren't interested, I can always get someone else."

"No, no, I'm interested," No Nose said. "What is this great idea?"

"Before we proceed, I must tell you that what I am proposing, though it will be extremely profitable, is against the law. You could go to prison if caught."

No Nose laughed. "Mr. Smith, I don't reckon you would have even got in touch with me if this was legal. I ain't afraid of doin' somethin' illegal. Most ways of making a lot of money is against the law anyway."

"It will also require a few more people who are equally willing to violate the law. Do you have access to such men?"

No Nose laughed. "Do I have access?" he mimicked. "Yes, I have . . . access."

"How many men do you have?"

"How many do I need?"

"At least four, I would think. Maybe more."

"I can get them."

"You can get them? Or you have them?"

"Look, what is it with all the questions here? Do you have an idea of how to make a lot of money or not? Because if you don't, then there ain't no need in us talkin' anymore," No Nose said.

"Yes, I have an idea. I was just making certain you understood that we would need more men in order to do the job effectively."

"I've got them," No Nose said. "Now, what is this job you have in mind?"

Chapter Seventeen

Hennessey and Taylor had ridden south from Denver for four days, and were having breakfast at a café in the small town of Clermon. Hennessey was reading a newspaper that had been left on the table. Taylor was buttering a biscuit.

"Well, well, well, what do you know?" Hennessey said aloud.

"What do I know about what?" Taylor asked as he added jam to the biscuit.

"Listen to this," Hennessey said. He began reading. "Colorado Springs is pleased to have as a visitor Matt Jensen. Mr. Jensen, recently honored by Governor John Long Routt, is a true hero of Colorado, having risked his life to save a train from sure disaster. A modest man, Mr. Jensen declines to think of himself as a hero."

"Yeah, yeah, we know all that. We was in Denver, remember?"

Putting the paper down, Hennessey looked across the table toward Taylor. "You are missing the point," he said.

"What is the point?"

"The point is Jensen was in Denver. Now he is in

Colorado Springs. That's only fifteen miles from here. I think we should pay him a visit."

"What are you talking about?" Taylor asked. "Why would we want to visit him?"

"Why? Because we're going to kill the son of a bitch, that's why," Hennessey answered.

Colorado Springs

Matt was a guest in the Del Rey Hotel, staying there not to "take the waters," as did so many who came there, but merely to enjoy a few days in a nice hotel that was known for good service and excellent food. He was not normally given to such affectations, but the recent windfall of five hundred dollars made this little interlude possible.

From the window of his third-floor hotel room, he had an excellent view of the Pikes Peak. He could also look out onto the street, scarred as it was with wagon ruts and dotted with horse droppings. The railroad station was halfway down the street, and he saw a train just pulling away. Just down the street from the hotel was the Second Chance Saloon.

Because the saloon was on the same side of the street as the hotel, Matt couldn't actually see it from his window, but he could hear laughter and piano music. It all seemed very inviting to Matt, so after supper he planned to go into the saloon to see if he could find a poker game.

Half an hour later, bathed and shaved, Matt went into the dining room downstairs, only to learn that it was too late because they had quit serving lunch.

"You got any idea where I could go to get something to eat?" Matt asked.

"You might try down the street at the Second Chance,"

the maitre d' suggested. "They don't have that big of a menu, but the food isn't all that bad."

"Thanks," Matt replied.

Leaving the hotel, he walked down the street to the middle of the block. The street was filled with mid-afternoon commerce as wagons, surreys, carriages, and horses created a busy flow of traffic. Reaching the saloon, he pushed through the batwing doors and went inside. About half-a-dozen tables were filled. Stepping up to the bar, he ordered a beer, but just before he took out his money, a nickel was put on the bar.

"Uh-uh, your money's no good here. I'm buyin'," a man said, coming up beside him. When Matt turned, he saw a middle-aged man wearing a sheriff's badge. The sheriff stuck out his hand. "You'd be Matt Jensen, wouldn't you?"

"Yes."

"I don't reckon you remember me, Matt, but I met you several years ago when I was sheriffin' down in Meeker. You was just a pup then."

Matt smiled. "Sure I remember," he said. "That was when Smoke shot Bodine and Colby. You're Sheriff Adams."

Sheriff Adams chuckled. "You've got a good memory, friend," he said. "But then, for a boy your age to see something like that, I reckon it would stick in your memory. And, from what I hear, you are every bit as good as Smoke."

Matt shook his head. "I wouldn't say that," he said. "But I am grateful to Smoke for teaching me what skills I do have."

The bartender picked up the sheriff's nickel, then sat a mug of beer in front of Matt. Matt hefted it, blew off the suds, then held it out toward Sheriff Adams. "I'm obliged," he said.

Sheriff Adams nodded. "You say Smoke Jensen taught you everything, but I doubt that even Smoke taught you how to crawl across the top of ice-covered train cars doing sixty miles an hour in order to stop a runaway train."

"You've heard of my little bout of foolishness, have you?"

"Who hasn't heard?" Sheriff Adams replied. "You are a hero all over the state. What brings you to Colorado Springs? You're a long way from home, aren't you?"

"Nothing in particular brings me here, Sheriff," Matt said. "And since I move around a lot, I'm never any further from home than the nearest hotel."

"Ahh, the joys of youth," the sheriff said. "There was a time when I thought it would be nice to be like tumbleweed, just wandering around from place to place."

"What kept you from doing it?"

"Well, the war stopped me," the sheriff said. He chuckled. "Oh, don't get me wrong. I traveled during the war— Shiloh, Antietam, Chancelorsville, Franklin—but it wasn't quite the kind of traveling I had in mind. Then, after the war, I came out here from Ohio. But that's about as far as my wanderin' got me, because the next thing you know I had me a wife and a houseful of kids. That's when I started into this line of work. I was a city sheriff, then a deputy, then a sheriff back in Meeker. Then, Millie, that's my wife, took the lumbago and we figured to come here for the waters. It's done wonders for her."

"Oh, say, Mr. Jensen," the bartender said. "I almost forgot, but the mail clerk dropped a letter off for you today. It came general delivery, but he figured the best way to get it to you would be to leave it here. Just a minute, I'll get it for you."

A moment later, the bartender handed the letter to Matt.

"Thanks," Matt said. He pointed to an empty table. "Think you could bring me something to eat?"

"Ham, beans, cornbread?" the bartender suggested.

"Sounds good," Matt agreed as he took the letter to the table.

Matt didn't even look at the letter until he sat down, then he smiled when he saw the return address.

> *Layne McKenzie*
> *C/O Governor John Long Routt*
> *Governor's Mansion*
> *Denver, Colorado*

Opening the letter, Matt saw a little tuft of raven-black hair, tied with a piece of green yarn. There was also a slight essence of lavender, reminding him of the perfume that Layne wore.

Dear Mr. Jensen:

If you are surprised to be receiving this letter, believe me, you are no more surprised than I am with myself for writing it. I know that it is very forward of me, and probably very foolish as well, but God help me, because I can't help myself.

I hope you don't mind, Mr. Jensen, but I have researched your background. I know that Smoke Jensen is not your actual brother, but rather someone who took you in when you were still quite young. I know too that you assumed his name out of a sense of gratitude. To do such a thing speaks very highly of you. It shows a

*strong sense of obligation and loyalty, excellent traits
in anyone.*

*That does not surprise me, so readily did you risk
you life to save others. You have attempted to pass your
exploits off as non-heroic, by claiming that you were just
saving your own life. But that is merely because of your
self-deprecating nature.*

*I enjoyed our brief meetings, on the train, at the
Firemen's Charity Ball, and again at the reception
where you were honored by the state. I confess to hoping
our meetings would have been more frequent, but you
are a man who is careful of the feelings of others, and
you understood what I did not. You knew that your
nomadic life would not lend itself to encumbering
relationships, and that to do any less would be to trifle
with my feelings.*

*I understand that, Matthew Jensen. I know that
there can never be anything in the nature of a romantic
connection between us. Indeed, the conditions of my
employment with the school board of Cairo, Illinois,
would preclude that. However, I do believe that, even if
we never see each other again, I can set apart this brief
moment when our lives converged, and hold that dear
to my memory in all the years to come. I do hope that
sharing this bit of information with you does not
burden you with the unwanted attention of an
admiring female. May your life be filled with blessings
is the prayer I shall say for you for the rest of my days.*

> *Sincerely,*
> *Layne McKenzie*

"Are you Mr. Jensen?" someone asked.

Looking up, Matt saw an old man, unkempt and poorly dressed.

"Trumbo, what are you doin' in here?" the bartender called out angrily. He pointed at the man who had addressed Matt. "I told you not to come in here anymore begging for drinks."

Trumbo pulled himself up with as much dignity as he could muster.

"I ain't in here cadging drinks," he said. He held up a coin. "I got money for my own drink. All I'm a'doin' is talkin' to Mr. Jensen."

"You got no business talking to him," the bartender said.

"Yes, I do," Trumbo insisted. "Where do you think I got this here money? I was paid to give him a message."

"What message is that?" Matt asked.

"There's a fella out in the street told me to tell you to come out to meet him," Trumbo said.

"He's out there now?" Matt asked.

"Yes, sir. He's a'standin' right out there in the middle of the street. Said he'll be a'waitin' for you."

"What does he want with Mr. Jensen?" Sheriff Adams asked.

"Well, sir, he didn't tell me that," Trumbo said. "But if you was to ask me, I don't think he's plannin' on greetin' him like an old friend."

Sheriff Adams walked over to look out through the window. Although moments before the street had been busy, now it was deserted, except for one man, who was standing in the middle of the street about one hundred feet away. It was easy to see why the street had become deserted, because the man was holding a gun in his hand, pointing it toward the saloon door. He was obviously prepared to fight.

"Trumbo is right," Adams said. "Whoever that fella is, he's standing out there holding a gun."

"Jensen!" the man in the street called. "Matt Jensen, I'm callin' you out!"

Matt walked over to look out as well. "I'll be damned," he said. "It's Al Hennessey."

"Al Hennessey? Are you sure?"

"Yes."

Adams sighed, then loosened his pistol in his holster. "You stay here, Matt," he said. "Hennessey is a wanted man. This'll be my business, I reckon."

Matt shook his head. "No, it's my business," he said. "It's me he wants. I'm the one that brought him in to hang."

As Matt continued to look outside, he saw that though the street had emptied, men and women could still be seen scurrying down the sidewalks, stepping into buildings, or behind them, to get out of the line of fire while taking up positions in the doors and windows so they wouldn't miss anything. Even the horses had been moved off the street as nervous owners feared they might get hit by a stray bullet.

"You don't have to do this yourself, you know," Sheriff Adams said. "I could go out through the back door, then sneak around and come up on him from the other end of the street. I think if he saw the two of us, he might give up."

"No, I thank you, Sheriff," Matt said. "But this is my fight. I'm going to have to fight it my way."

"The thing is, Matt, your way might get someone killed."

"That's true," Matt said. Pulling his pistol, he checked the loads, then dropped the pistol back in the holster before stepping outside. "I just intend to make certain it isn't you, me, or some innocent person from town."

"Jensen, you comin' out?"

Matt stepped through the batwing doors.

"I'm here, Hennessey," he said.

"Well, we meet again," Hennessey said. "Only this time, you don't have the drop on me. We meet even."

"Not entirely even," Matt replied. "You already have your pistol drawn."

Hennessey smiled, a slow, evil smile. "Yeah," he said. "I do, don't I?"

Even as he was finishing his comment, Hennessey pulled the trigger. His bullet slammed into the front wall of the saloon, right beside Matt. Matt dived off the porch and into the street, rolling to his left and drawing his gun as he did so. Hennessey managed to get off a second shot.

The second bullet crashed harmlessly into the wooden front stoop of the Second Chance Saloon. From his prone position on the ground, Matt fired at Hennessey and hit him in the knee. Hennessey let out a howl and went down, but he was still firing, and Matt felt a bullet tear through the crown of his hat. Now Matt took slow and deliberate aim and pulled the trigger. He hit Hennessey in the temple, and saw a little pink mist of blood spray up from the impact of the bullet.

Hennessey was stopped instantly and, for a moment, there was deadly quiet. Matt stood up and started walking toward Hennessey, when all of a sudden there was another gunshot. This time, the bullet hit the ground right beside Matt, then ricocheted down the street with a high, keening whine.

Looking up, Matt saw a puff of gun smoke drifting from behind the false front of the hardware store that was right across from the saloon. He ran toward the side of the street, then dived behind a watering trough just as a second shot was fired.

By the sound of the shot, Matt knew that his adversary was using a rifle. The fact that he had a rifle, as well as elevation, cover, and concealment, gave him an advantage over Matt's position. Matt fired at the false front where he saw the last puff of smoke, but it was more to see what kind of reaction he would get than anything else. He had no real target.

"Is Hennessey dead?" a voice called down from the roof.

"Yes," Matt answered.

"I figured he was."

"Coleman was killed when you escaped," Matt said. "Boone was hanged, and Hennessey is lying here in the street. That means you must be Taylor."

"I'm Taylor."

Taylor was quiet for a moment, then he called down again. "I'm the only one left."

"You want to come down?" Matt called. "Give yourself up?"

"No, I don't reckon I want to do that," Taylor said. "I done been sentenced to hang. I got nothin' to gain by givin' myself up."

Matt raised himself up just far enough to peer over the top of the water trough. As soon as he did so, Taylor fired, and the bullet hit in the water so close to him that it got his face wet.

"Nearly got you that time," Taylor said.

"Yeah, you did," Matt said, wiping the water from his face.

"Taylor, are you part Indian?"

"What? No, why do you ask?"

"Was Hennessey?"

"No," Taylor said. He fired again, and his bullet hit

the ground by the edge of the watering trough, then ricocheted into the front stoop behind.

Matt lay there for a moment longer. Then he took off a boot and slipped it over the point of his other foot, then put his hat on it. Lifting his leg so that the boot and hat were above the trough, he leaned out around the end and looked up toward the false front. He saw Taylor step to the side of the false front and raise his rifle to his shoulder, aiming at Matt's hat.

Matt fired, and saw a puff of dust fly up from Taylor's shirt. Taylor dropped the rifle and slapped his hands over his chest. Then he tumbled forward off the roof of the hardware store.

Matt slipped his boot back on, then ran across the street to check on him.

"Damn," Taylor said, breathing hard. "Damn, that hurts." He chuckled. "I guess it beats hangin', though, don't you think?"

"Yes," Matt replied. "I'm pretty sure it beats hanging."

"If you look at it like that, I sort of came out ahead in this, didn't I?"

Matt didn't answer. Taylor drew a couple more gasping breaths, then he stopped.

"So there were two of them, were there?" Sheriff Adams said, coming up behind Matt then.

Matt nodded.

"I should've suspected that. Don't know how many men would actually call you out to a fair fight. Damn, you don't think there are any more, do you?" Adams began looking around.

"Not from this bunch," Matt said, putting his pistol away. "Taylor was the last of them. But I do have someone else after me."

"I'm not surprised, son," Adams said. "Whenever a man gets himself a reputation like you have, men are going to be crawling out from under rocks just to get a crack at your. They all want to be known as the man who killed Matt Jensen. But hell, I don't need to be telling you that."

"I've run into such men," Matt said. "But this isn't what I'm talking about." Matt took from his pocket one of the bullets and the piece of paper with which it had been wrapped. He showed them to Sheriff Adams.

"What is that?" Adams asked.

"According to Smoke, it is a Hopi death symbol."

"You ever run across any Hopi?" Adams asked

"Yes, but they have all been peaceful," Matt answered.

Adams shook his head. "Apparently not all," he said.

Chapter Eighteen

Dorena

Strayhorn was sitting in the corner the saloon nursing a glass of green whiskey that had been colored with rusty nails and flavored with a few drops of kerosene. It had been three weeks since he, Teech, and Decker had conducted their raid on the Butrum Ranch and, once again, he found himself short of money.

A whore came over to smile down at him. The smile was not her most attractive feature because it disclosed a mouth of missing and broken teeth, the result of too many drunken and violent men. And though Mabel Franklin was probably no older than thirty, the dissipation of her profession made her look much older. She was compensating for her loss of looks by showing more of her body, and the dress she was wearing was scooped so low as to show almost all of her breasts.

She pushed back an errant strand of mousy brown hair.

"Honey, they tell me you spend a lot of your time down in the adobes with the Mex whores," she said. "Is that right?"

Strayhorn looked up at her. "What is it to you?"

The woman grabbed her breasts and lifted them so that both nipples were clearly visible. "I just thought maybe you'd like to come back to your own kind now, to see what you've been missin' out on," she said.

"You offererin' for free, are you?" Strayhorn asked.

Mabel laughed. "You are a funny man," she said.

"Then go away, I ain't interested," he said, making a dismissive wave with his hand.

The smile left Mabel's face and, summoning what dignity she could, she shrugged her shoulders, turned, and walked away.

Strayhorn heard a man's laughter and looking up, saw No Nose Nelson looking toward him. Nobody who ever met No Nose had to ask how he got his name, for broken cartilage had pushed his nose so far in that it was practically even with the rest of his face.

"Damn me if I don't think you hurt Mabel's feelin's there," No Nose said.

"Whores ain't got no feelin's," Strayhorn replied derisively.

Although he wasn't invited, No Nose came over to Strayhorn's table, bringing his bottle and glass. He refilled Strayhorn's glass. "On me," he said.

"Thanks."

No Nose lifted his glass and held it toward Strayhorn. Strayhorn lifted his own and returned the gesture, then both men drank. No Nose refilled both glasses.

"What is it, No Nose?" Strayhorn asked. "We ain't such good friends that you'll buy me drinks just to be nice."

No Nose chuckled. "You're a pretty smart man, ain't you? Yep, you've got me pegged all right."

"So, what is it? Someone you want me to kill? What?" Strayhorn asked.

"Someone I want you to kill?" he asked. No Nose laughed out loud this time. "Hell, no, Strayhorn. Anybody I want killed, I'll do it myself. You know that."

"Then what do you want?"

"I figured maybe me'n you might go in on a deal together," No Nose said.

"Why would I want to go in on a deal with you?"

No Nose took a swallow of his whiskey before he responded.

"I don't know," he answered. "Why would you? Maybe because nothin' you've tried recently has worked out for you?"

"I'm doin' all right," Strayhorn said.

"How much money did you get from holding up the train?"

"What train?"

No Nose laughed. "Strayhorn, there ain't a man or whore in Dorena but what ain't laughin' at the mess you made with that train robbery. You managed to get four good men killed and you came away with how much money? Oh, wait, I can answer that. You came away with none."

"A problem came up," Strayhorn said.

"Yes, and I know who problem was," No Nose said. "It was Matt Jensen, the same one that killed Hennessey and Taylor."

Strayhorn face registered surprise. "Wait a minute, are you tellin' me Hennessey and Taylor are dead?"

"You didn't know that?"

"No."

"They was killed by Matt Jensen," No Nose said. "Happened in Colorado Springs a couple of weeks ago."

Strayhorn shook his head. "I hadn't heard anything about that," he said. "You sure that's true?"

No Nose nodded. "Yeah, I'm sure. Pauley Moore rode in this morning with the news," he said.

"And you believe him?"

"It ain't just what he said. He brought a newspaper with the story."

"I'll be damn." Strayhorn took another swallow of his whiskey and thought for a moment before he spoke again. "Well, the dumb sons of bitches wanted to go off on their own," he said. "So I reckon what happened to 'em ain't none of my concern."

"That's the way I look at it," No Nose said. "So tell me. Would you like to team up with me on a job?"

"What is the job?"

No Nose shook his head. "No, I'm not ready to tell you that yet. Not until you agree that we are going to work together."

"Well, if you have the idea for a job, why do you even need me?" Strayhorn asked.

"Because this job needs more than one person," No Nose said. "And you've got Teech and Decker with you."

"So, what you are saying is, you don't just want me, you want all of us."

"Yes."

"Is there enough money for that?"

"How much money does the governor of Colorado have?"

Strayhorn shook his head. "How much money does the governor of Colorado have? What the hell does that have to do with anything? What are you talking about?"

"I'll tell you all about it when you agree to come in with me."

"All right," Strayhorn said, nodding his head. "Let me hear it."

Denver

The Denver depot was teeming with activity as trains arrived and departed, their whistles and bells augmenting the chugging sound of steam engines in operation. Out in the car shed, smoke and steam swirled between the several trains before drifting up to gather in little clouds under the high roof. The shed was heavy with the aroma of smoke and expended steam, as well as various prepared foods being offered by the many peddlers who were working the crowd.

Inside the main building, scores of people were scurrying about, buying tickets, or making arrangements for their baggage. The wooden floor of the depot vibrated slightly with the arrival or departure of every train, thus creating the illusion that the very building was alive.

Millie St Cyr, Norma Jean Proudy, Sue Kendal, and Annie Jones had come to see Layne McKenzie off, but a moment earlier Millie had disappeared. Now she came back, holding an artificial flower.

"I saw this in the little shop when we came in," Millie said as she began pinning the flower to Layne's blouse. "And I knew I had to get it for you."

"Oh, how lovely," Layne said, running her fingers lightly through the colorful silk. "I shall wear this on the very first day I teach school."

"And think of Denver and all your friends out here," Millie said.

"I will," Layne promised. She embraced all of them. "I will never forget any of you, and I will think of all of you often."

"I am so glad your uncle invited you to come to Denver," Norma Jean said.

"Yes, I am too. It has been a wonderful summer," Layne said. "I hate going back East."

"You wouldn't have to go back," Millie said. "Your uncle is the governor of Colorado. I know he could get you a job teaching school here in Denver."

"It's tempting," Millie said. "It really is. But I've been out here for almost five months now, and I'm anxious to see my mother and father. Also, it wouldn't be fair to the Cairo school system if I left now. They are counting on me to take the job I contracted for."

"I know," Millie said. "It's just that we have become such good friends that I don't want to see you go." Suddenly, a large smile spread across her face. "Oh, I know something that might change your mind. Think about this. If you stay here, you will probably see Matt Jensen again."

Layne laughed. "As if that meant anything," she said.

"I know, your contract says you must stay single. But you have to admit you probably won't find another man like Mr. Jensen back in Cairo, Illinois."

"Nor anywhere back East," Sue added.

"It doesn't matter what my contract says about getting married," Layne said. "It is quite obvious that Mr. Jensen has his own life to live. And quite frankly, so do I. So, I'm afraid that using Matt Jensen as an incentive to keep me out here won't work."

"Well, you can't say I didn't try," Millie said, and the others laughed with her.

"Ladies and gentlemen!" someone shouted through a set of stand-mounted megaphones. "The train to Mountain Springs, La Junta, Dodge City, Wichita, and all points east will be boarding on track number seven in fifteen minutes."

"That's my train. I guess I had better be boarding," Layne said.

"What about your luggage?" Millie asked.

"Uncle John took care of that for me," Layne said. She looked around at the crowd. "Oh, I wonder where he is. I certainly don't want to leave without telling him good-bye and thanking him for such a wonderful summer."

"Here he comes," Annie said, pointing to the musta-chioed governor, who was working his way through the crowded floor of the depot.

"Is it true that he is trying to get the right to vote for women?" Norma Jean asked.

"That is what he told me," Layne said.

"He is certainly a forward-thinking man. You are so lucky to have him as your uncle."

"I agree," Layne said. She embraced her uncle as he came up to her. "Oh, Uncle John, I'm glad you are back. I was afraid I might have to leave before telling you good-bye."

"You needn't have worried about that. I wasn't about to let that happen," Governor Routt said. "Come along, I'll show you your car."

"Oh, I don't want to board until I have to," Layne said. "I'm still visiting with my friends."

"They can come too," the governor said. "They can come onto the car with you."

"Oh, we would just be in the way of the other passen-gers who are boarding," Millie said.

The governor chuckled. "No, you won't," he said. "Trust me."

Puzzled as to what mystery her uncle was concealing,

Layne and her friends followed him out of the depot into the car shed. They moved along the platform at the end of the tracks, passing trains that had been backed into position until they reached Track Number Seven. There were a few porters standing there, and when they saw the governor they smiled.

"Right this way, Governor," one of them said. "Your car is all ready for you."

"Your car?" Layne said. "Uncle John, what is he talking about?"

"You'll see," the governor replied, merely adding to the mystery.

They walked practically the full length of the train, passing day coaches, sleepers, and Wagner Parlor cars. Then they reached the first car just behind the baggage car. Beautifully varnished, the car glistened. It differed in appearance from the other cars because there were fewer windows, and the windows it did have were larger, and had curtains.

"Here you go, my dear," the governor said.

"What is this? I don't understand?"

"This is my private car," Governor Routt said. "I've made arrangements for you to be able to use it all the way to Cairo."

"But can you do that?"

"Of course I can," the governor replied. "This car belongs to me personally, not to the state of Colorado. All it requires is that I make arrangements with the various railroad companies to pull it. And those arrangements have all been made."

"Oh!" Layne said. "Oh, my!"

"Can we see the inside of it?" Millie asked.

"Yes, that's why I invited all of you to come see her

aboard," the governor replied. He held out his hand in invitation. "Climb aboard," he offered.

Layne had never seen anything as lush as the interior of the car. The walls were painted red and liberally hung with red drapery. A red overstuffed sofa sat on one side of the car, while two red-cushioned, white-wicker chairs flanked a marble-topped desk on the opposite side. At the back of the car was a separate room, with walls of walnut. Inside this room, which could be completely closed off, was a bed.

"Oh, it is absolutely beautiful!" Layne said.

"I thought you might enjoy it," the governor said. He took an envelope from his pocket. "And ladies, if you would like, you can ride as far as Pueblo with her. Here are tickets for your return trip."

"Oh," Millie said. "I wish I had known this earlier so I could tell my family."

The governor chuckled. "I have already spoken to your families, and they have all given their permission."

The young women squealed in delight.

A young black man, dressed in white, came into the car then.

"Governor, the train is going to pull out in five minutes," he said.

"Thank you, Travis," the governor said. "Ladies, this is Travis. He is the porter who is assigned especially to this car. He will deliver your meals to you and take care of anything you might need."

The engineer gave two short whistles then, and Governor Routt, with a final wave, stepped down onto the long, narrow brick path that stretched between this train and the train on Track Number Six. He stayed there until the train pulled out, while the girls moved to the windows to wave good-bye.

Ten minutes later, the train was on the main track, picking up speed as it left the city of Denver behind.

"Are one of you ladies Miss Proud?" Travis asked.

"Yes, I'm Miss Proud," Norma Jean said.

Travis held up a box. "This was delivered to the train just before we left," he said. "The man said it came from your mama."

"Oh!" Norma Jean said as a broad smile spread across her face. "It's my tatting! And there is enough here for all of us to do!"

Excitedly, the young women went through the box, then accepted the shuttles and pieces of work from Norma Jean.

"Oh, no," Layne said, holding out her hand. "I would just make a mess of it."

"Oh, tish tosh, you can do it," Millie said. "We'll help."

For the next three hours, the young women tatted and talked. Layne tried to keep up with them, but was able to do so only because one of her friends would always take her work from her to get her through difficult spots.

At noon, Travis came into the car pushing a cart on which there were four covered trays. Travis set the table with elegant china, sparkling crystal, and shining silver. Then he lifted off the covers to present the meal of baked ham, glazed carrots, creamed Swiss chard, and a dessert of chocolate cake.

"Oh, my, what a feast!" Norma Jean said.

After a long and leisurely lunch, the girls spent the remaining two hours in conversation, laughing at stories they shared from their youth and reminiscing over the summer just passed.

"Ladies," Travis called after a while. "We're comin' in to Pueblo."

"Oh, dear," Millie said. "This is where we get off."

Quickly, they gathered up the tatting work and put it back into the box. Norma Jean started to pick it up, but Travis reached out to take it from her.

"No need for you to have to carry something that heavy," he said. "I'll find someone to handle it for you."

"Thank you, Travis," Norma Jean said. "Oh, wait," she said. Reaching down into the box, she took out the handkerchief with the tatting Layne had done. "Something to remember us by," she said.

"Ha!" Layne replied. "It's just that I did such a poor job with it that you don't want to keep it."

The girls laughed. Then they embraced, exchanged tearful good-byes, and extracted a promise from Layne that she would return for another visit next summer.

Layne watched them through the window, waving at them as they hurried to catch a train back to Denver.

"Oh, don't I have to change trains here?" Layne asked Travis.

"No, ma'am," Travis replied. "All we have to do is just stay put. A switch engine will come pick us up directly and take us over to another track, where we'll be hooked on to a train going East."

"Oh," Layne said with a smile. "That certainly makes traveling easy, doesn't it?"

"Yes, ma'am, it truly does," Travis replied.

A moment later, Layne felt the bump as the car was picked up by a switch engine, then moved to another track. A short while after that, they were hooked onto a new engine and, as dark was falling, they pulled out of the station.

Chapter Nineteen

After the others left the train, Layne settled down to make the rest of the trip by herself. She had to admit that the car was luxurious; if she had been traveling in one of the regular coaches, she might be uncomfortable, but at least she would have someone to talk to. In this car, especially now that all her friends had left, she was all alone.

There were a couple of books to read, but she found that reading while riding made her nauseous. She tried to entertain herself by looking at the scenery through the window, but the eastern half of Colorado offered little in the way of interest.

She had thought that perhaps she could meet someone over lunch or dinner, but to her chagrin, Travis delivered the meals to her. By the time it was nine o'clock, Layne was ready to go to bed, not so much because she was tired as because she was bored. She had Travis turn down the bed for her, then slipped in between the sheets and, with the rhythmic clacking of the wheels providing a soothing background noise, fell into an early slumber.

* * *

Mustang Creek

No Nose Nelson, Strayhorn, Teech, Decker, and Pauley Moore waited in the dark alongside the track.

"What makes you so sure the train is going to stop here?" Teech asked.

"The train has to have water, don't it?" No Nose replied.

"I reckon so," Teech answered.

No Nose pointed to the water tower that stood alongside the railroad tracks.

"Well, there's the water. That means the train will stop."

Strayhorn climbed up the rock-covered berm and stood on the track, looking north. "I sure wish the moon wasn't so bright."

A full moon hung in the eastern sky, making the twin ribbons of steel gleam softly.

"Don't worry none about the moon," No Nose said. "Once we have what we've come for, we'll be able to ride out of here with no problem. There won't be nobody followin' us."

"The money, you mean," Strayhorn said.

"What?"

"You said once we have what we come for. You're talkin' about money, right? This train is carryin' a lot of money?"

"I don't know," No Nose replied.

"You don't know? What do you mean, you don't know?" Teech asked. "What the hell are we doin' here, if you don't know whether or not the train is carryin' any money?"

"'Cause we ain't here for the money," No Nose said.

"That's it," Teech said angrily. "I ain't standin' out in the middle of nowhere, in the middle of the night, waitin' to rob a train that ain't carryin' no money."

"Teech is right, No Nose," Strayhorn said. "You said

you would tell us what you had in mind when the time came. Well, seems to me like the time has come."

In the distance, the men heard the long, lonesome wail of a train whistle.

"Here it comes," No Nose said. "You men get in position, and stay out of sight until I give the word."

"What are we doin' here, No Nose? If we ain't robbin' this train, what are we doin' here?" Teech demanded.

"I'll tell you this," No Nose said. "Just go along with me, and there will be more money than you can imagine."

Strayhorn looked at the others, then back at No Nose. "All right," he said. "We've come this far, we may as well see it through. But if this turns out to be nothin', you don't have to worry about the law comin' after you, No Nose, 'cause I'll kill you my ownself."

"Damn, I can hear it, but I still don't see no train yet," Decker said.

"You will. Just keep looking that way," Strayhorn said.

They heard the whistle a couple more times before they saw it. And even then, they didn't see the train, but they did see the headlamp, a gas flame behind a glass, set in front of a mirrored reflector. The reflector gathered all the light from the gas flame, intensified it, and then projected it forward in a long beam that stabbed ahead, picking up insects that gleamed in the light.

The train whistled again, and this time they could hear the puffing of the steam engine as it labored hard to pull the train though the night.

"Remember, nobody makes a move until I give the order," No Nose said. "We don't want to take a chance on being seen."

No Nose walked up onto the track and stayed there until all the others were in position. He looked to see if any of them could be seen from the approaching train; then, satisfied that they could not, he ran back down to join them. He watched the train approach, listening to the puffs of steam as it escaped from the pistons. He could see bright sparks embedded in the heavy, black smoke that poured from the flared smokestack. More sparks were falling from the firebox, leaving a carpet of orange-glowing embers lying between the rails and trailing out behind the train, glimmering for a moment or two in the darkness before finally going dark themselves.

The train began squeaking and clanging as the engineer applied the brakes. It got slower, and slower still, until finally it approached the water tower. The engineer brought his train to a stop in exactly the right place. By now, the fireman was already standing on the tender, reaching for the line that hung down from the curved mouth of the long water spout.

For a long moment, the area was very quiet, the solitude interrupted only by the sigh of escaping steam and the snapping and popping of bearings and fittings as they cooled. The fireman grabbed the water spout, then swung the spigot down and guided it to the open mouth of the tender. He pulled on the valve rope, and the water started thundering into the cavernous tank.

"Now," Strayhorn shouted, and all five men rushed toward the engine.

The engineer, who was leaning out the cab window, saw the men approaching and jumped back with a start.

"Who are you? What do you want?"

"We want you to climb down from that engine," No Nose said. He pointed his pistol at the fireman, who was standing on the tender, taking on water. "'Cause if you don't, we're goin' to kill your fireman."

"No," the engineer said. "Don't shoot him, I'm comin' down."

The engineer climbed down onto the ground alongside the track and stood there beside the huge engine as it continued to vent steam through its relief valve.

"Fireman," Strayhorn called. "Get yourself some water and douse that fire."

"Are you serious? If I put the fire out that way, it'll take two or three hours before we can get steam up to run again. We've got trains comin' up behind us, it could cause a wreck."

"That's your problem, not ours. Douse the fire like I said, or we'll kill you and do it ourselves," No Nose demanded.

"All right, all right," the fireman said. "I'll do it, I'll do it."

"I don't know why you stopped our train," the engineer said as the fireman got a bucket from the cab, then filled it with water. "We aren't carrying any money."

There was a loud hissing noise as the fireman tossed water into the firebox.

"I know you ain't carryin' no money," No Nose said. "That ain't what we're after."

The engineer shook his head in confusion. "Then, I don't understand. What are you after?"

No Nose pointed to the first car behind the baggage car. "We're after the person that's in that private car," he said.

"Are you serious? There's nobody in that car but one young woman," the engineer said.

"Yeah," No Nose replied with a broad grin. "The governor's niece."

"The governor's niece?" Strayhorn asked. "That's what we come here for?"

"Yeah."

"Why?"

"Think about it," No Nose said. "Remember when I asked you how much money the governor has?"

"Yes."

"Well, we're about to get some of it. I figure the governor is going to be willing to pay a lot to get her back."

When the train made the stop for water, Layne, who was asleep in the bedroom of the governor's private car, was only vaguely aware. She was too comfortable and too tired from all the packing and the preparation for her return to Cairo to pay too much attention to it.

Rolling over in bed, she pulled the covers up and listened to the bumping sounds from outside as the fireman lowered the spout from the trackside water tower and began a flow of water into the tank.

Layne thought of the fireman standing out there in the in the middle of the night and, by contrast, it made her own condition seem even more comfortable. She was not aware of the drama being played out just outside the train. Even as she was drifting back to sleep, No Nose, Strayhorn, and Teech were climbing onto the private car. The car was dimly lit by two low-burning gimbal-mounted lanterns, one on either side. The lanterns illuminated the luxuriousness of the car, the plush sofa, the overstuffed chairs, and a table on which sat a silver tray of pastries.

"Damn, would you look at this?" Teech said, helping himself to a pastry. "You ever see a railroad car like this before?"

"No," Strayhorn said. "Pay attention to what you're doin'."

Suddenly, a porter appeared from a small corridor at the back of the car.

"What's goin' on here? What are you men doin' on this car?" he asked.

"Where's she at?" Strayhorn asked.

The porter picked up a knife that was lying on the table. "Get off this car," he ordered.

Strayhorn drew his pistol and fired, his bullet hitting the porter in the neck. The porter's eyes grew wide and he dropped the knife, then clutched at his throat. Blood spilled through his fingers as he fell to the floor.

Inside the small bedroom, Layne was awakened by the loud sound of the gunshot. She sat up in her bed.

"Oh! What is it? What is going on?"

Suddenly, the door to the bedroom compartment was jerked open. She opened her mouth to scream, but one of men stuck the barrel of his gun in her mouth.

"If you scream, I'll pull the trigger," he said in a low, gruff voice.

Layne stared at him with eyes that were open wide with fear, but she made no sound.

"That's a good girl," the man said. "Get up."

"I ah ess I ill iow," she mumbled, unable to talk because of the gun in her mouth.

"What did you say?" Strayhorn asked as he pulled the gun out.

"I said I'm not dressed. I'm still in my nightgown."

"Well, get dressed," No Nose said. "We'll wait."

"I'll have to take my nightgown off."

"Then do it."

"But I don't have anything on under my nightgown."

No Nose smiled an evil smile. "Good," he said.

Layne hesitated, and No Nose pointed his pistol at

her, then cocked it. "Do it, or I'll shoot you here and now," he ordered.

Trying hard to hold back her tears and shaking uncontrollably, Layne pulled the nightgown over her head, exposing her nudity.

"Damn, Strayhorn, lookit that," Teech said. "I ain't never seen nothin' like that."

"You've seen naked women before," Strayhorn said.

Teech shook his head. "All I've ever seen was whores. I might'a thought I'd seen naked women before, but I tell you true, I ain't never seen nothin' like this."

Finally, with every inch of her skin burning in embarrassment, Layne got dressed. She looked at the men who were ogling her.

"What now?" she asked.

No Nose made a motion with his pistol. "Now, you come with us," he said.

"Hey, No Nose, seein' her naked like that has got me all excited here. Are we goin' to get to have us any fun with this woman?" Teech asked as they led Layne off the train.

"It all depends," No Nose replied.

"Depends on what?"

"Whether or not the governor pays what we're goin' to ask him," No Nose said.

The outlaws followed Mustang Creek south to a small cabin that was no more than two miles from where they had removed her from the train. Layne had ridden on the horse in front of Decker, who was selected because he was the smallest. Once they reached the cabin, they tied her up, then tied her to a bed that had a dirty mattress but no sheets or blankets.

Layne's back and legs were cramped, and the ropes were beginning to rub blisters on her wrists. She had no idea where she was, nor did she know why they had taken her. She just knew that she had never been so terrified in her life.

"You want something to eat?" Strayhorn asked.

Layne now knew their names because she had heard them addressing each other. She was very careful not to let them know that she knew their names, though, because she was afraid that if they knew she knew, they might kill her just to keep her quiet.

"I'm not hungry," Layne said.

"You got to eat somethin'," Strayhorn said, offering her a plate of very unappetizing-looking beans. "You ain't et nothin' since we brung you here."

"I'm not hungry."

"Here, try to eat somethin'," Strayhorn said, holding a spoon toward her mouth.

Keeping her mouth tightly shut, Layne turned her face away.

"Goddamnit woman, eat!" Strayhorn demanded.

"Leave her alone," No Nose said. "If she don't want to eat, she don't have to eat."

"She's got to eat sometime," Strayhorn said. "We ain't goin' to get nothin' from the governor if she starves herself to death."

"You aren't going to get anything from the governor?" Layne said. "Is that what this is all about? You think the governor is going to pay you to get me back?"

"Do you think he ain't?" No Nose asked. "What father wouldn't pay to get his daughter back unharmed?"

"He's not my father, he's my uncle," Layne said.

"I know that. But father, uncle, it don't make no difference. He's goin' to pay us a lot of money to get you back."

"That is, as long as she is alive," Strayhorn said. "That's why I'm trying to feed her."

Layne felt a bit better after hearing that. She was not as frightened for her life as she was, since it was obvious that they would need to keep her alive in order for their scheme to work.

"I'm not hungry now," Layne said, softening her tone somewhat. "Maybe later."

"That's all right by me," Strayhorn said. "If you don't want to eat, I ain't goin' to beg you. It ain't no skin off my ass, that's for sure," he said. "I'll just eat 'em myself."

He put the spoon of beans in his own mouth.

Chapter Twenty

Colorado Springs

"Extra! Extra! Governor's niece taken from train!" the newspaper boy shouted. "Extra! Extra!"

Matt was walking up from the hotel when he heard the newsboy, and he held up his hand to summon him.

"Boy, I'll take a paper," he said.

"Yes, sir, Mr. Jensen," the boy said, his eyes wide with wonder. Since the showdown in the street with Hennessey and Taylor, Matt Jensen's name was on everyone's lips, and the newsboy recognized him at once.

Matt gave the boy a quarter.

"It ain't but a two cents is all the cost it is," the boy said.

"That's all right. You can keep the quarter."

"Yes, sir!" the boy said excitedly. "Thank you, Mr. Jensen!"

Matt took the paper into the saloon, then found an empty table and sat down to read.

No Leads on Missing Woman.

Porter Foully Murdered.

The fate of Miss Layne McKenzie, niece of Governor John Long Routt, is still unknown. The engineer, fireman, and conductor of the Flyer reported that the young lady was taken from the governor's private car shortly after midnight on the 8th instant, when the train stopped at Mustang Creek to take on water.

That Miss McKenzie was the target of their scheme is not in question, as the engineer stated that they knew she was on the train and had no other purpose in mind but to take her.

"I don't know how they knew it," Paul Cephus, the engineer, reported. "But they knew from the moment they stopped the train that she was a passenger."

Travis Smith, the porter who was assigned to the governor's car, came to the young lady's defense and was murdered for his efforts.

"We are very concerned about this and are doing all we can do to bring about a safe recovery of Miss McKenzie," General William Jackson Palmer, President of the Denver and Rio Grande, said to this newspaper. "We are asking that anyone who has any information on Miss McKenzie's whereabouts please contact the authorities. The railroad is offering a

reward of one thousand dollars to
anyone who can offer assistance in
the safe recovery of Miss McKenzie."

"Damn," Matt said, folding the paper and putting it
on the table. "Damn."

"Something wrong, Mr. Jensen?" one of the bar girls
asked, seeing the expression on his face.

"Yes," Matt said. He pointed to the paper. "A young
woman that I know, the governor's niece, was abducted
from the train."

"You know the governor's niece?" the bar girl asked,
her eyes wide with wonder.

Matt nodded. "Yes, I know her."

The bar girl picked up the paper and began reading
the article. "Oh, how frightened she must be," she said.

"I was told that I could find Matt Jensen in here," a
man's voice said rather loudly.

The tone in the voice of the inquisitor alerted Matt,
and instantly, he was ready for a confrontation. He
dropped his hand to his pistol, though as he was still sitting at the table, that move wasn't apparent to all.

"I'm Matt Jensen," Matt called out.

"Oh, am I glad to have found you," the man said. He
started toward Matt.

"That's far enough," Matt said, holding up his left
hand to stop the man.

"I beg your pardon?" the man asked, confusion evident in his face.

"Who are you, and why are you looking for me?"

"Oh. My name is James Cornett, Mr. Jensen. I repre-
sent the Denver and Rio Grande Railroad. And I have a
message for you from the governor."

Matt relaxed and nodded. "Come ahead," he said.

The man, unaware that he had just been tested and passed, came the rest of the way across the floor, removing a folded piece of paper from his jacket pocket as he did so.

"This is from the governor," he said, handing the paper to Matt.

Matt took the message from Cornett, unfolded it, and began to read.

Matt Jensen,

Matt, can you return to Denver soonest? As you may have heard by now, my niece, Layne McKenzie, was taken from my private car by armed men while she was returning home. I have received a ransom demand of ten thousand dollars. I can meet the demand, but would have no guarantee of the safe return of my niece.

I urgently request that you make a personal effort to find and rescue my niece. If you would agree to undertake this assignment, I can furnish you with a state commission that will give you legal authority in any county in the state. In addition, the Denver and Rio Grande Railroad will provide you with a very generous reward.

If you agree to the proposal, please accompany Mr. Cornett, the bearer of this message, back to the depot, where a private train awaits you.

> *Sincerely,*
> *John Long Routt*
> *Governor of Colorado*

When Matt and Cornett reached the station, Matt saw an engine with steam up, a tender, the governor's private car, and a stock car. The side door of the stock car was open, and a ramp ran from the door to the ground.

The engineer was standing beside the engine, looking at his watch.

"Are you all ready to go, Mr. Jensen?" he asked.

"Yes, soon as I get my horse onto the train," Matt said, leading Spirit up the ramp and into the car. He put him into one of the stalls, and reached up to rub him behind the ears.

"You know what this is all about, don't you, boy?" he said. "You've ridden the train more than most people."

With Spirit secure, Matt stepped back outside as a crew took down the ramp and closed the door.

"How long do you think it will take us to get there?" Matt asked the engineer.

"The railroad has cleared the tracks for us between here and Denver," the engineer replied. "And I have no speed limit. I expect we'll be doing better than fifty miles to the hour, Mr. Jensen, which means we'll be there in about an hour and a half."

"That's fast," Matt said.

"Yes, sir, I'll say it's fast," the engineer said, smiling broadly. "Our regular train service allows four hours between the two cities. Why, if we had wings, we'd be flying," added. "Tim!" he called up to the engine cab.

The fireman stuck his head through the window.

"Is the steam pressure up?"

"We're ready to go, Burt," Tim replied.

"All right, gents, climb aboard and let's get under way," Burt said.

Matt looked around at the plush car, then shook his head and clucked. "Are there really people who travel like this?" he asked.

"Yes, sir," Cornett replied. "You'd be amazed at how many private cars we move every day."

"Probably not very many private trains, though," Matt suggested.

Cornett chuckled. "No, sir, not that many private trains," he agreed.

Even as Matt settled into one of the overstuffed chairs, the train started forward. Within minutes, the train was traveling faster than Matt ever had, and the trees and shrubbery that were adjacent to the track were whipping by so fast as to be a blur.

The train made the passage from Colorado Springs to Denver in one hour and twenty-two minutes. When the abbreviated train pulled into the station, Matt was greeted by George Highgate, who Matt remembered was a member of the governor's staff.

"Mr. Jensen," Highgate called out to him.

Nodding his acknowledgment, Matt started toward him.

"The governor is in the mansion and has asked me to take you to him as soon as you arrive. Have you had lunch?"

"No, I haven't," Matt replied.

Highgate nodded. "The governor anticipated that, sir. He will have lunch waiting for you."

"Mr. Jensen, I'll take care of your horse," Cornett said. "Would you like me to bring him down to the Governor's Mansion?"

"Yes, thank you," Matt said. "And thanks for coming to Colorado Springs to get me."

"It was my honor, sir," Cornett replied.

Highgate led Matt out to the governor's carriage, a yellow and black phaeton, highly polished and with pleated yellow leather seats. The vehicle was so beautifully suspended that it negotiated the cobblestone and brick-paved streets of Denver as if it were gliding on air.

The Governor's Mansion was a two-story, red-brick Victorian house, reached by a curved driveway that passed through a black, wrought-iron picket fence.

Governor Routt met Matt in the foyer. "Thank you for coming, Matt," he said. "Please, join us in the dining room so we can discuss some business."

"All right," Matt answered.

When Matt stepped into the dining room, he saw two other men.

"Matt, this is General Palmer, President of the Denver and Rio Grande."

Palmer was a fastidiously dressed man, clean shaven and with dark hair. He had commanded the 15th Pennsylvania Cavalry during the Civil War, and his experiences as the commander of a daring and highly successful group of cavalrymen had provided him with the kind of background he needed to be a scout for the Kansas-Pacific Railroad in its expansion to the West. But when the Kansas-Pacific decided to use a route other than the one Palmer had recommended, he left the company and started a railroad of his own. The Denver and Rio Grande was the result.

General Palmer, always a personable man, met Matt with an extended hand.

"Mr. Jensen, it's good at last to meet you, sir. I've heard many good things about you," he said.

"Often things get exaggerated in the telling, General," Matt said.

Palmer chuckled. "I appreciate your self-deprecating nature, young man," he said. "But I have heard too many stories from too many sources to doubt them. I'm glad you accepted the invitation."

"And you have met my private secretary, Mr. Highgate."

"Yes, I have," Matt said, shaking Highgate's offered hand.

"This is awful," Highgate said. "Simply awful."

"Matt, as I said in the letter, this is all about my niece. I want you to find her, and I am prepared to offer you a position of state investigator, which will give you absolute legal authority in any county in the state. And, of course, pay a salary that is commensurate with that position."

"And I am prepared to offer you a position as consultant to the railroad," General Palmer added. "With a one-time fee of fifteen hundred dollars."

"That's very generous," Matt said.

"That is payable whether you find the young lady or not," General Palmer said. "If you do find her, and return her safely, I will also pay a bonus of an additional fifteen hundred dollars."

"That is exceptionally generous," Matt said.

"Just tell me that you will do it," Governor Routt said. He pinched the bridge of his nose and closed his eyes. "I cannot bear to think that I, in some way, might be responsible for this."

"How can you hold yourself responsible for it, Governor?"

"I invited her out here."

"John, don't be foolish," Palmer said. "You are in no way responsible. On the contrary, you are taking every action possible to see to her safe return."

"Providing it is not too late for that," Routt said. "I just pray that she is still alive."

"Governor, I believe I read in your letter that you had received a ransom demand?" Matt said.

"Yes, for ten thousand dollars," the governor replied.

"Then I'm sure she is still alive," Matt said. "They need her in order to extract that money from you."

"Believe me, I would pay it in a minute if I could be sure it would guarantee her safe return. But I just don't know how well I can trust these people."

"I have suggested that the governor pay it," Highgate said.

"You have? Why?"

"Why? Isn't it obvious, man? Paying the ransom will assure her safe return."

"I don't know," Matt said. "I think the governor's instinct is correct. Anyone who would do something like this is probably not very trustworthy. It's not good to sit back and wait for things happen; it's better to make them happen."

"I suppose there is some merit to what you are saying," Highgate said. "But they were very specific when they spoke to me. They told me that if the governor paid the ransom, they would release Miss McKenzie unharmed. But if we tried anything, such as calling in the law or trying to bring about a rescue, they would kill her."

Matt looked at Highgate with some surprise. "When they spoke to you?"

"Yes," Governor Routt said. "That is how I learned of the ransom demand. They approached Mr. Highgate."

"Why would they approach you?" Matt asked.

"I suppose because I am the governor's private secretary," Highgate replied. "They knew that I had the ear of the governor."

Matt nodded. "That's true, I suppose," he said. He

chuckled. "I must say that what surprises me is to think of someone like that even knowing there was such a position as secretary to the governor, let alone who it would be."

"Yes, sir, I must admit I was surprised as well," Highgate said. "And somewhat frightened."

"Why were you frightened? Did they threaten you?"

"No, not what you might all a direct threat," Highgate said. "But they were—rather desperate-looking men—certainly not the kind of people I would normally encounter."

Chapter Twenty-one

The outlaws' cabin

"Beans again," Decker growled as he stared down into the pot. "Damn, I'm sick of beans."

"They wouldn't be bad if we had some bacon to go with 'em," Teech said.

"Yeah, well, we ain't got no bacon," Decker said. "We ain't go no onion, nor peppers, nor nothin'."

"Eat your beans or don't eat 'em, I don't give a damn," Strayhorn said. "Just quit your bitchin'."

Teech laughed.

"What are you laughin' at?" Decker asked.

"How many cows have we done stole in our lifetime?" he asked. "I know damn well we've rustled enough beef to start a full-sized stampede, but we ain't got so much as a mouthful of meat to lay alongside our beans."

"And you think that's funny?" Decker asked.

"Yeah, I do. Look, if you want meat, you can always go back to punchin' cows for thirty a month and found. We purt' near always had meat then. But we didn't ever have no chance of gettin' ahold of some real money, though, did we?"

"Maybe you ain't noticed it, Teech, but we ain't exactly been gettin' a lot of money lately neither, have we?" Decker replied. "In fact, it's been quite a while since we've so much as put one dollar in our pocket."

"Yeah, you do have a point there," Teech said. He turned to Strayhorn, who had been eating his own beans in silence. "What about it, Strayhorn? Accordin' to No Nose, all we had to do was take this here girl off the train and money would be fallin' in our laps." Teech pointed to Layne, who was sitting on the bed with her wrists and ankles bound. "Well, we took her, and we ain't got no money yet."

"No Nose has gone into town now to make all the arrangements," Strayhorn said. "I expect when he comes back, he'll have the money."

"Then what?" Decker asked.

"What do you mean, then what? We'll have the money," Strayhorn said.

"No, I mean, then what about the woman? What are we going to do with her?"

"We'll cross that bridge when we come to it," Strayhorn said.

Layne gasped. "You said you would let me go," she said.

"Yeah," Strayhorn said. "And we will, if there is no trouble."

"What do you mean, no trouble?"

"Well now, missy, just think about it for a minute," Strayhorn said. "It ain't very likely they're goin' to just hand over the money like they was buyin' a horse or somethin'. More'n likely, they're goin' to be thinkin' about tryin' something so's they can get you back and keep their money too. So, until we've got the money, and we know they ain't tryin' to pull no fast one on us, I reckon the best thing to do would be just to keep you for a while."

"Someone's comin'," Teech said, and he, Strayhorn, and Decker took out their pistols, then moved to the windows to look outside.

"It's No Nose," Strayhorn said.

"I hope he's got the money," Decker said.

"He ain't likely to have it with him," Strayhorn said. "But maybe he's got it worked out how we can get it."

No Nose dismounted, then came into the cabin.

"Did you get the money?" Decker asked right away.

No Nose glared at him.

"Well, did you?"

"Any food left?" No Nose said.

"Some beans," Strayhorn said.

No Nose picked up a plate from the table. It had been Strayhorn's plate, and though he had eaten all the beans, the plate itself was still dirty. No Nose paid no attention to the fact that the plate was dirty. Instead, he walked over to the little potbellied stove and began spooning out beans.

"You ain't answered," Decker said. "Did you get the money or what?"

"No, I didn't get no money," No Nose replied.

"What happened?"

"The governor's called in Matt Jensen."

"Matt Jensen?" Teech said.

"Yeah, he's made him a state policeman," No Nose said.

Strayhorn shook his head. "What is a state policeman? I've never heard of such a thing."

"It's like a sheriff, only he ain't restricted to just one

county. That means he can go anywhere in the state he wants."

"That's bad," Strayhorn said.

"Yeah? How bad can it be?" No Nose asked. "He's only one man."

"How bad? We've already lost five good men to that son of a bitch," Decker said. "Is that bad enough for you?"

"Seven if you count Boone and Clay," Teech said. Then he laughed. "Only Boone and Clay weren't no-count anyhow, and neither was Hennessey or Taylor if you want my way of thinkin' about it, which means we only lost three that was worth anything."

"It don't seem right that one ordinary man could do that," No Nose said.

"Well, Matt Jensen ain't exactly what would you call an ordinary man," Teech said.

"What do you mean?"

"He's more like a ghost than a regular man. I mean, no matter where we go, seems like he's there comin' in as silent as smoke, raisin' hell, then goin' away without so much as a scratch for all the shootin'."

"I guess he's been pretty lucky all right," No Nose said.

"Lucky, hell. Luck ain't got nothin' to do with it," Teech said. "I'm here to tell you, Matt Jensen ain't no ordinary man."

"You've run into him, Strayhorn. Teech says he's no ordinary man. What do you think?" No Nose asked.

Strayhorn spooned some beans onto his folded tortilla, then took a bite and chewed thoughtfully before he answered. "What do I think? I think we need to kill the sonofabitch. That's what I think."

"Easy enough to say—not so easy to do. From the way

you been talkin', don't sound to me like Matt Jensen will be the kind of man that dies easy," No Nose said.

"Bullshit. Put a bullet in his hide and he'll die just like ever'one else," Strayhorn growled.

"Then how come we ain't been able to kill him?" Teech asked.

"'Cause there ain't nobody gone about it right," Strayhorn said. "First you had Clay, but that don't count for much because he was a blowhard who thought he was better than he was. Then there was Hennessey and Taylor, and they were damn fools. If you do it right, Jensen can be killed just like any other man."

"What are you tellin' us, Strayhorn?" Decker asked. "Are you sayin' that *you'd* be willin' to go up against him?"

"Hell, no," Strayhorn answered. "I ain't willin' to go up against him. And far as I'm concerned, anyone who would go against him is a fool."

"I thought you said he needed killin'."

"He *does* need killin'," Strayhorn said. He smiled. "But what does goin' up against him have to do with it? Look here, we don't need to make no sportin' contest out of this. We ain't like Clay, tryin' to be known as the 'fastest gun.' All we want is for the son of a bitch to be dead, and we don't care how he is killed, or who kills him."

"All right, so, how are we goin' to do it?" Teech asked. "Sneak up on him and shoot him in the back? I'm not sure you can even sneak up on someone like Matt Jensen. That son of a bitch has eyes in the back of his head."

"Yeah, how are we goin' to get close enough to him to kill him?" No Nose asked.

"We ain't," Strayhorn said.

No Nose looked confused. "What do you mean? I thought you said he needed killin'."

"He does need killin'," Strayhorn said. "Only, we ain't goin' to do it. We're goin' to hire it done. That's where you come in."

"Me?" No Nose said, sputtering. "Wait a minute! What do you mean me?"

"We're all in this together, ain't we?" Strayhorn asked. "I mean, if Jensen is really comin' after us, he's comin' after ever'one of us, right?"

"Yeah, I guess so," No Nose replied. "But that still don't tell me why I'm the one that has to do it. And all alone."

"Don't worry, I don't mean you have to kill him. But you are goin' to have to fix it so we can kill him."

"How'm I supposed to do that?"

"First thing is, you've got to go back and see the man who helped us set up this kidnapping in the first place."

"Won't do no good to see him. He ain't got money."

"Didn't you say he works for the governor?"

"Yeah, he said he does. I don't know if he actually does or not, though." No Nose chuckled. "You ought to see him. He's a real funny-lookin' fella. Kind'a tall, bald-headed, wears one of the pointy beards and those funny little glasses that just perch on your nose." No Nose laughed. "Ain't the kind I could wear, that's for sure."

"Oh, my God," Layne said. "You're talking about Mr. Highgate."

"Who?" Strayhorn asked.

"Mr. Highgate. He's the governor's private secretary. But, no, I can't believe he would be a party to something like this."

"Highgate, huh?" No Nose said. "That's good to know."

"If this fella Highgate is the governor's private secretary, he ought to be able to get the money without any trouble," Strayhorn said.

No Nose shook his head. "He ain't got five hundred dollars. He told me he wouldn't be doin' this if he didn't need the money so bad." No Nose looked over at Layne. "That's why he also wants to make sure the girl don't get hurt."

"Yeah, we know how much he cares about the girl," Strayhorn said derisively. "I tell you what. Don't worry none about him not havin' the money. In for a penny, in for a pound. He'll find some way to come up with it."

"All right, suppose I can get the money from him. Then what?"

"Then we'll put out the word that we're paying five hundred dollars to anyone who kills Matt Jensen. And we don't care how they do it."

"Damn," Pauley said. "I know somebody in Dorena who would do it."

"Who?" Strayhorn asked.

"That half-breed. I can't think of his name, but you'll know him if you ever see him. He's a short, bandy-legged fella with a face that's so ugly, it would make a train take five miles of dirt road."

"You talkin' about Goneril?" Strayhorn asked.

"Yeah, Goneril, that's his name. Word is, he'll kill anyone if you pay him."

"Hold it," Decker said. "Are you sayin' this fella Goneril is good enough to go up against Matt Jensen?"

Pauley laughed. "Good ain't got nothin' to do with it," he said. "Like as not, Jensen will never even see him."

"What do you think he would charge us?" Strayhorn asked.

"He once took out a U.S. marshal for two hundred dollars," Pauley said. "I'm sure he'd go after Jensen for five hundred dollars."

"Maybe we ought to talk to him," Strayhorn said.

"A lot of good that will do," Teech said.

"What do you mean?"

"Well, how long do you think folks have been trying to kill this Jensen fella anyway? If they haven't done it up to now, this half-breed you're talkin' about ain't likely to get it done either."

"We don't lose nothin' by him tryin'," Strayhorn said. "Besides which, we got us an edge."

"What sort of edge?" Decker asked.

Strayhorn pointed to Layne.

"We got the girl," he said. "Jensen will be comin' after her. All the breed has to do is stay between the girl and Jensen. He'll get his shot."

"Good idea," No Nose said, nodding his head in acquiescence.

"I got a question," Teech said.

"What?"

"I thought this whole thing was to get money for the girl. Now you say we're usin' her for bait. Where does the money come in?"

"Oh, we'll get the money all right," Strayhorn said. He smiled. "And you just give me an idea."

"What's that?"

"No Nose, when you go talk to this Highgate fella, you tell him to tell the governor that since he didn't listen to us, since he sent someone to kill us, the cost of getting his niece back alive has just gone up."

"You mean ask him for more money?" No Nose said.

"Yes."

"How much more?"

"I'd say double what we are asking now," Strayhorn

said. "Instead of ten thousand dollars, we'll ask for twenty thousand."

"Oh, I don't know," No Nose said.

"What do you mean, you don't know?"

"Highgate is sure that ten thousand is all we could get. I mean, he was pretty certain about that."

"We were going to ask for ten thousand, and he was going to keep half of it, right? Five thousand dollars?"

"Yes."

Strayhorn laughed. "That's fine. He can still have five thousand. Only now, we'll keep fifteen thousand."

No Nose looked skeptical for a minute, then he broke into a big smile. "Yeah," he said. "Yeah, I like the way you think."

Denver

"Mr. Highgate?"

Highgate was sitting at his desk in the small office that was adjacent to the governor's larger office. He looked up as his name was called.

"What is it, Mr. Collins? Can't you see that I am busy?" Highgate said, irritated at having been interrupted by one of the clerks that worked at the Capitol Building.

"I'm sorry, Mr. Highgate, but a gentleman asked me to give you this note. He said it was very important and you would know what it was about."

Highgate removed his glasses and began polishing them. "He said I would know what it is about?"

"Yes, sir."

"I have no idea what it is about," Highgate said. "And whatever it is, it can't possibly be more important than the assignment I am carrying out for the governor."

"Yes, sir, that's why I told him that he couldn't see you.

But he was very insistent that I deliver this note to you, and to be honest, he was a very frightening-looking man, what with no nose and all."

Highgate looked up quickly.

"What did you say?"

"I said he was very insistent that I deliver this note to you."

"No, not that," Highgate said, waving the comment aside. "I mean about no nose."

"Oh. Well, he actually does have a nose, of course," Collins said. "But it is mashed so flat against his face that it looks as if he doesn't have one. As I say, he presents a very frightening visage."

"Give me the note," Highgate said.

Collins handed the note across the desk. He made no attempt to leave after Highgate took the note.

"Why are you standing there?" Highgate asked.

"I thought perhaps you might want to answer him."

"Where is he now?"

"He is in the entry hall, sir."

Highgate nodded, then opened the note to read.

Mr. Highgate, we have to talk, now. Meet me tonight at nine o'clock in the Bucket of Blood Saloon.

Nelson

Highgate wrote something on the paper and handed it back to Collins.

"Give this to him," he said.

"Very good, sir," Collins replied, taking the note.

Highgate had written that he would meet with Nelson tonight at the time and place of Nelson's choosing.

When he and Nelson had entered into their arrangement, he had established a regular schedule for a brief, weekly meeting, at which time Nelson would provide him with information upon the well-being of the governor's niece, and he could provide Nelson with information regarding the status of the governor's willingness to pay the ransom.

The time and place of this meeting tonight was unscheduled, and Highgate intended to give Nelson a piece of his mind. He simply would not put up with changes in this very carefully planned operation.

Chapter Twenty-two

The Bucket of Blood Saloon was in a seamier part of Denver. Highgate had agreed to it as a meeting place because he had never been there before and he was quite sure that he would not be recognized. He realized almost immediately, though, that he should have changed clothes before coming there. Although everyone else was in denims and work clothes, Highgate was wearing a suit. That made him stand out like a rose in a cabbage patch, and everyone in the saloon stared at him.

Feeling extremely self-conscious, Highgate surveyed the room until he saw what he was looking for. No Nose Nelson was sitting at a table alone, in the far corner of the room.

"Good evening, Mr. Highgate," No Nose said.

"First of all, I thought it was clearly understood that we would have absolutely no contact other than that which we have already scheduled," Highgate said. "Now you come to me with this request for an unscheduled meeting. That is against the rules that we made, and I have little use for anyone who can't follow rules."

"Well, somethin' has come up," No Nose said. "And we figured we had better talk to you about it."

"And another thing. How did you know my name?" he asked.

"That is your name, ain't it?"

"Yes," Highgate said. "How did you find out?"

"It don't matter how I found out. I know. That's all you need to know."

"What has come up? Has Miss McKenzie been harmed in any way?"

No Nose laughed, a wheezing, snorting laugh. "You are the one who set this up, and you are worried about whether or not she has been harmed?"

"I am in this for the money," Highgate said. "I do not want anyone hurt."

"I'll be sure and tell her that you asked about her," No Nose said.

"No! You mustn't! Don't you understand? She must never know that I am a part of this. If word gets back to the governor that I was involved in her abduction, I—I don't know what would happen."

"If she found out? Why, you—" No Nose started, then stopped in mid-sentence, deciding for the moment that it might be better that Highgate not realize that Layne knew.

"What?" Highgate asked. "What were you going to say?"

"I was just going to say that I'm glad that you understand what might happen if the governor found out about you. Because that is exactly what will happen if you cross me now." No Nose punctuated his comment with a drink of his beer.

"Cross you? I have no intention of crossing you," Highgate said. Nervously, Highgate drummed his fingers on the table. "Why are you here, Mr. Nelson?"

"I'm here to get some money."

Highgate shook his head. "The governor has not authorized payment yet. I'm trying to convince him, but I'm not having any luck."

"He has sent Matt Jensen after us, hasn't he?"

"You know about that?"

"I know about it."

"I didn't have anything to do with that," Highgate said. "I tried to talk him out of it."

"Yes, well, now you can deliver the governor a new message," No Nose said.

"What is that?"

"Tell the governor that we are very disappointed that he didn't accept our first offer. Tell him that the offer has changed. Now, we want twenty thousand dollars, instead of ten thousand."

"Twenty thousand dollars?" Highgate repeated with a gasp. He said the words so loudly that some of the closer patrons turned to look at him. "No, you have no authority to change the amount. In case you have forgotten, I am the one who set this entire operation up. It was my idea and my plan. And I arrived at just the correct figure after very careful consideration. Ten thousand is the most we can reasonably expect to get for this. And as long as I am in charge of this operation, that will continue to be the amount we seek."

No Nose chuckled. "Well, that's just it, Highgate, You ain't in charge no more. I am. And the amount I'm asking for is twenty thousand. But the rest of our deal remains the same. You will still get five thousand for your share."

"Why would that be? If, by chance, we could get more money, then my share should be proportionate."

"Proportionate? What does that mean?"

"It means that if your share goes up, mine should go up as well."

No Nose laughed. "Proportionate. I'll give you this. You sure are a high-toned talker. Now, what I want you to do is go back to the governor and tell him the cost of getting his niece back unhurt is now twenty thousand dollars. Tell him that's because he brought Matt Jensen in. Also, and this is from you, I'll need five hundred dollars in cash right away."

"What?" Highgate gasped. "I don't have five hundred dollars!"

"Get it."

"Where am I supposed to get it?"

No Nose shook his head. "I don't know and I don't care. That's your problem, not mine. I'll be here the same time tomorrow night. You be here with the five hundred dollars."

"But no, that's impossible," Highgate said. "Where am I supposed to get five hundred dollars?"

"Like I told you, I don't care. But if you aren't here tomorrow night with five hundred dollars, the governor is going to find out about your part in snatching his niece from the train."

"No, dear God, no!" Highgate said. "You can't do that! I—I would go to prison."

"Yeah, you would," No Nose said with a smile.

"I wouldn't survive prison."

"No, you wouldn't," No Nose said.

"What—what am I to do?"

"You're to get five hundred dollars, that's what you are to do," No Nose said. "And if I were you, I'd get started right away."

* * *

"Twenty thousand dollars?" Governor Routt replied when Highgate informed him of the new demand.

"Yes, sir, that is what they are asking for now," Highgate replied.

"Why did they up the price?"

"I was told it is because you brought in Matt Jensen," Highgate said. "Governor, you will forgive me for saying this, but you might remember that I advised you to pay the ten thousand dollars. If you had done so when I first asked, no doubt your niece would be safe now and it would be over with.

"As it stands now, Miss McKenzie is still in danger, and the price for guaranteeing her safety has gone to twenty thousand dollars."

Governor Routt held up his finger and shook his head. "No, George, that is where you are wrong. If I thought I could guarantee her safety, I would have paid the ten thousand. But it wouldn't matter if they lowered the price to five thousand or raised it to one hundred thousand. Men like these cannot be trusted. No, sir. I am convinced that the best possible course of action is to let Matt Jensen find these heartless and evil wretches and rescue Layne."

Highgate closed his eyes and pinched the bridge of his nose. Once, when he was a child, he had climbed a tree in order to reach a bird's nest. When he got even with the bird's nest, he started out on a limb after it. The farther out on the limb he climbed, the more frightened he became until he realized two things. One—he couldn't get back from the limb, and two—he was going to fall.

That was exactly where Highgate was right now. He was out on the limb with No Nose and his nefarious allies, and there was no coming back. He had no choice but to go all the way with them now.

"I need five hundred dollars," Highgate suddenly blurted out.

"I beg your pardon?" Governor Routt said, startled by the sudden announcement.

"Five hundred dollars," Highgate repeated. "I need five hundred dollars."

"George, that is a rather substantial sum. What on earth do you need it for?"

"The—gentleman—and I use that word loosely, who has been relaying information to me about the status of Miss McKenzie, says that he can find out where she is for five hundred dollars."

"Do you think he can?"

"I believe he can, yes."

Governor Routt stroked his chin. "I don't know," he said. "I am not inclined to trust such people." He shook his head. "I think no."

"But Governor, surely you want what is best for Miss McKenzie?" Highgate said.

Governor Routt frowned at his private secretary. "Are you questioning my concern for my own niece?" he asked.

"No, sir, no, sir, of course not," Highgate said, dissembling. "It's just that, well, were I in your condition, I would do everything I could to guarantee her safe return."

"And I am," Governor Routt said. "But I will not be swindled or cheated by the kind of men who would take advantage of something like this to line their own pockets. And my experience tells me that this is what your contact person is trying to do. Tell him thanks, but no, thanks."

Highgate's head began spinning, and he had to sit down to keep from passing out. What was he going to do? If he didn't get the five hundred dollars, Nelson was going to tell the governor about his own involvement in this.

"Don't be so glum, George," Governor Routt said in a friendly tone of voice. "I'm right about this. You'll see. Why, I believe we will have Layne back, fit as a fiddle, in no time."

"Yes, sir," Highgate said. His voice sounded high and tinny.

When Highgate returned to his own office, he saw one of the state legislators waiting for him.

"Yes, can I help you?" he asked.

"Please remind the governor that he is supposed to have lunch today with the House Committee for Mining," the legislator said.

"All right, wait here, I'll be right back."

Returning to the governor's office, Highgate passed on the information.

"Oh, yes, I had nearly forgotten that," Governor Routt said. "Thank you." He looked around at his desk. "Ahh, my desk is a mess."

"I'll take care of it for you, Governor. You can go to your lunch."

"Thanks," Governor Routt said.

Highgate watched the governor leave, then heard him say heartily, "Hello, Michael. So good of you boys to invite me to lunch today."

"We've got a lot to talk about on this new bill, Governor. I hope you are up for it."

"Well, it never hurts to talk, does it? I think everyone who knows me says that's what I do best," Governor Routt teased, and Highgate could hear the receding laughter as the two men walked away from the offices.

Highgate felt a hollowness in the pit of his stomach, and a spinning sensation in his head. What was he going to do?

Part of him wanted to flee, to leave Denver, to leave

Colorado, and never come back. But what would he do then? How would he make a living?

Highgate had just finished clearing away the governor's desk when he saw a letter from the governor, written on stationery with an official letterhead. At that moment, he saw a solution to his problem.

"Yes!" he said aloud. Taking one sheet of stationery, he returned to his own desk. Over the last few years as the governor's private secretary, Highgate had learned many things. He knew which state accounts the governor could draw money from, he knew which of these accounts were subject to frequent use, which accounts were rarely used and thus rarely audited. He also knew how to sign the governor's name in such a way that even those most familiar with his signature would not be able to tell the difference.

Returning to the governor's desk, he borrowed the governor's pen and ink. That would make the document all the more authentic.

State of Colorado
Office of the Governor

To Disbursement Officer, Miscellaneous Accounts:
Pay to the bearer of this note five hundred (500) dollars in cash.

                              John Long Routt
                                  Governor

"Will twenty-dollar bills be all right?" the disbursement officer asked.

"Twenty-dollar bills will be fine," Highgate answered.

Highgate was amazed at how easy this had been. The document was paid without question, and he had not been recognized. As he left the disbursing office, he was struck with the irony of it all. Had he figured out how to do this in the first place, he would not have needed to put himself in danger by entering into an alliance with No Nose Nelson and the men who had taken Layne McKenzie.

When Highgate returned to the Bucket of Blood that night, he had his hand down in his jacket pocket, wrapped securely around the envelope containing the money.

"Did you get the money?" No Nose asked.

"Is that the way you greet someone?"

"Did you get the money?" No Nose repeated.

"Yes, I got the money."

"Give it to me."

"Before I give you this money, I need some guarantees from you," Highgate said.

Highgate heard a clicking sound from under the table. He wasn't sure what the sound was, but it was frightening.

"Here is your guarantee," No Nose said. "I've got a gun under this table, and it is pointing right at your gut. If you don't give me that money right now, I guarantee that I will shoot you."

"You wouldn't dare shoot me in a public place like this," Highgate said.

No Nose laughed. "Look around, Highgate," he said. "Why, there isn't a person in here that I couldn't get to slit your throat for five dollars. Do you think anyone would blink twice if I shot you? That's why I chose this place."

Highgate looked around at the saloon patrons. Never in his life had he seen such a repulsive-looking group of men and women. Gulping, he put his finger to his collar and pulled it away

"All right, alright, here's the money," Highgate said, removing the envelope from his pocket and passing it over to No Nose.

No Nose put his pistol away, then took the money out of the envelope and began to count it.

"It's all there," Highgate said. "Five hundred dollars."

No Nose nodded, smiled, then put the money into his own pocket.

"There now, do you see what you can do when you put your mind to it? You didn't think you would be able to come up with the money."

"This was easy compared to asking the governor for twenty thousand dollars. I'm telling you, he isn't going to go through with that."

"He'll go through with it." No Nose finished his drink, then stood. "I'll see you around," he said.

Highgate stayed behind for a few minutes after No Nose left.

"Honey, you want to go upstairs?"

Looking toward the sound of the voice, Highgate saw an overweight and underdressed woman.

"I beg your pardon?" Highgate replied.

"I asked if you wanted to go upstairs with me."

"Why would I want to do that?"

"Oh, honey, don't you want some of this?" the woman asked, putting her hands on her crotch and thrusting it forward.

"No!" Highgate said, standing up so quickly that he knocked over the chair in which he had been sitting.

Several others, seeing what was going on, laughed out loud.

Highgate suddenly realized that he was alone in the saloon and while he did not enjoy the company of No

Nose, strangely enough, he felt safer in here with No Nose than without him. Now he was frightened.

"I—uh—must go," Highgate said, starting quickly toward the door.

"I'd run too, if I were you, mister," one of the customers shouted to him. "That there thing of Lucy's is like a snappin' turtle. Why, if you was to get yourself caught in that—it wouldn't let go of you till it thunders."

The shouted mockery elicited laughs from everyone in the saloon, including Lucy's high-pitched chortle, and Highgate could still hear them laughing as he hurried away, summoning the first hack he saw.

"Where to, mister?" the driver said.

As the governor's private secretary, Highgate had a room in the Governor's Mansion, and he started to give that address, then thought better of it.

"To the Denver and Rio Grande depot," he said.

The driver snapped the reins against the back of his team and the cab moved quickly through the streets of Denver. Not until they were several blocks away did Highgate breathe easily.

Then, getting out at the depot, he waited for a few minutes before summoning another cab to take him back home.

As he rode in this cab, he began thinking about the governor's niece, and he hoped that she was all right. He had a terribly guilty conscience about what he had done, but there was nothing he could do about it now. The fat was in the fire.

Chapter Twenty-three

Because his birth had been the result of his mother having been raped, he was not given a name at birth. He was referred to only as "Boy," or "White Eyes," until he was old enough to be enrolled in the Indian school. There, one of the teachers who had a passion for Shakespeare gave him the name Goneril after a character in *King Lear*.

Goneril grew up half-white and half-Indian, not living in both worlds, but trapped between the two worlds. When his mother died, he lost all connection with his Indian heritage, and the fact that he was a half-breed kept him apart from white society.

The abnormal environment in which Goneril grew to adulthood created a being who, for all intent and purposes, was totally dysfunctional. But, in a perverse way, it provided him with a persona that was both unique and deadly. Goneril had learned that such a character trait, while off-putting to normal society, could be a valuable asset to those who wanted his services. He became a killer for hire.

Goneril was a man who could kill without compunction. The life of a human being was as unimportant to him as was the life of a cockroach. It made no difference to him who his target was, or why they were being killed. The only thing that mattered to him was the money he was paid for the job. He was totally dispassionate about those he killed, except for one.

Early in his life, Goneril learned the identity of his father and made a vow to find him and kill him for what he had done to his mother. By the time he found him, though, Clyde Payson was literally standing at death's door, about to ascend the steps to the gallows where he was to be hanged by the neck until dead.

Payson did not recognize Goneril, but there was no reason he should have. He had never seen Goneril, and didn't even know he existed. Payson learned that he was a father only in the last second of his life, hearing Goneril shout the news to him, even as he was falling through the open trapdoor.

Frustrated by events beyond his control, Goneril altered his plan. If he could not kill his father, he would kill the person who had thwarted that goal. He would kill the man who was responsible for his father's death. And so it happened that the one thing that had been Goneril's greatest asset, dispassion, was cast aside in this quest.

Goneril was obsessed with the task of killing Matt Jensen. He had tried, and failed, on several previous occasions. Each time he failed, the compulsion grew, until now it totally dominated him. As a result, he now had an almost debilitating determination to kill the man he deemed responsible for his father's death.

He had not put aside his intention to kill Matt Jensen, but he was running out of money and was going to have to get back to business. That's why when Pauley Moore asked him if he would meet with someone who might want to hire his services, he agreed.

The meeting place was the saloon in Dorena. Goneril was sitting alone at a table as he waited. He was always alone, partly because he was a half-breed, but mostly because people were uncomfortable around him. And that suited him fine because, over the years, he had become very uncomfortable around others. He looked up as someone approached his table.

"Your name Gonner?" the man asked.

"Goneril."

"Yeah, Gonner, that's what I said. My name's Strayhorn. I got a job for you, if you're interested."

"Sit down," Goneril offered.

"It pays five hundred dollars," Strayhorn said as he sat.

Goneril nodded. "Must be a big job," he said.

"It is," Strayhorn said. "But I ain't goin' no higher'n five hundred, so you can take it or leave it."

"Who is it?"

Strayhorn chuckled. "I like that," he said.

"You like what?"

"I like that you said 'who' is it, rather than 'what' is it."

"You want me to kill someone, don't you?"

"Yeah."

"Who is it?"

"Remember, it's five hundred dollars," Strayhorn repeated. "Not a penny more."

Goneril drummed his fingers on the table and stared at Strayhorn with such intensity that Strayhorn cleared his throat self-consciously.

"It's Matt Jensen," he said.

Goneril fought hard to resist the urge to smile. Could he

actually be this lucky? Was someone actually willing to pay him to kill the very man he was determined to kill anyway?

"You ever heard of him?" Strayhorn asked.

"Yes, I have heard of him."

"He's a hard man to kill."

"Yes."

"But," Strayhorn said, smiling and holding up his finger, "we got somethin' that might make it just a bit easier."

"What's that?"

"We've got somethin' he wants. I figure we can use it as bait to draw him out. You don't have to go up against him or anything like that. We don't want you to prove anything, we just want you to kill the son of a bitch."

"That's what I will do," Goneril said. He held his hand out. "As soon as you give me the money."

Strayhorn shook his head. "No, sir," he said. "You'll get the money after Jensen is dead."

"Then get yourself someone else."

"What?" Strayhorn asked, surprised by the response. "Wait a minute, are you telling me you aren't going to take the job?"

"I'm telling you that I will do it only if you give me the money in advance."

"What if we give you the money and you don't get the job done?"

"You don't have to worry about that. If I tell you I'm going to kill him, then you can be sure that I will do it."

"How about if I give you half now, and half after you kill him?" Strayhorn suggested.

Goneril drummed his fingers on the table for a moment, then he nodded.

"All right, half now, half when it's done."

Strayhorn gave Goneril half the money, then put the rest back in his pocket.

"Don't go spending my money now," Goneril said, pointing to the pocket. "Because after this job is done, when I come for it, I don't intend to wait. If you don't have every penny of what you owe me, I will kill you."

"Don't you be worryin' none about that," Strayhorn said. "It'll be here."

"It better be. Now, what is this you say you have that he wants?"

"We snatched a girl—the governor's niece. Jensen is comin' after her."

"Where is she now?"

"We've got her hid away in a cabin up on Mustang Creek."

"This is the governor's niece, you say?"

"Yes."

"Why did you take her?"

"It ain't really none of your business why we took her," Strayhorn replied. "The only business you got to concern yourself with is killin' Matt Jensen."

"Fair enough," Goneril said. "Where did you snatch the girl?"

"What do you need to know that for?"

"You're usin' her as bait to draw Jensen to you, right?"

"Yes."

"He's goin' to know where you snatched her, so he'll start there. All I need to do is put myself somewhere between there and the girl."

"Yeah," Strayhorn said. "Yeah, I see what you mean. All right, we took her off the train when it stopped for water at Mustang Creek."

"You took her off the train at Mustang Creek, and you are keeping her in a cabin on Mustang Creek?"

"Yes."

"That's all I need to know."

The cabin at Mustang Creek

"You mean he didn't come back with you?" Teech asked when Strayhorn returned to the cabin.

"No."

"That son of a bitch has just run off with our money is what he done."

Strayhorn shook his head. "No, I don't think so," he said. "I think he is going to do the job."

"Maybe he will and maybe he won't. But I tell you true, I don't intend to wait for him," Teech said.

"What do you mean?"

"I mean I intend to kill the son of a bitch myself."

"Ha!" Decker said. "You're wantin' the rest of that money for yourself, ain't you?"

"I hadn't thought about it like that," Teech said. "But why not? If I kill him, I have as much right to the money as Goneril."

"Wait a minute, is that right?" Decker asked. "If Teech and I kill Jensen, we'll get the money?"

"What do you mean, you and me?" Teech asked.

"I'm comin' with you," Decker said. "That is, if we really will get the money. What do you say, Strayhorn?"

"I don't care who kills the son of a bitch, as long as someone does," Strayhorn said.

"What about it, Teech? Do you care if I come with you?"

"I guess with someone like Jensen, it wouldn't hurt to have someone along," Teech replied. "So if you want to go with me, come along."

"You won't kill him," Layne said.

"What do you mean we won't kill him?"

"Matt Jensen is more of a man than all of you put together. You can try, but you won't kill him."

"We'll just see about that, girlie," Teech said. "We'll just see about that."

A railroad water tower at Mustang Creek

When the train stopped for water at Mustang Creek, Matt got off. He was standing alongside the track as Spirit was brought down from the stock car. The man who had been the conductor on the train the night that Layne was taken, pointed.

"The moon was pretty bright that night," he said. "So I watched them leave. There were five of them, and they stayed very close to the creek until I could no longer see them."

"Which side of the creek?"

"They were on the right side for as long as I was able to see them."

"Did they have a horse for the girl?" Matt asked.

The conductor shook his head. "No, sir, they did not. As I recall, they put her up on a horse in front of one of them."

"You've been very helpful, thanks," Matt said.

"I wish I could tell you more."

"This is a start."

"Here's your horse, Mr. Jensen," the stock handler said, leading Spirit over to him."

"Thanks," Matt said, swinging into the saddle.

"He's a good-lookin' horse."

"He's about as good a horse as a man could ask for," Matt said.

The engineer gave a short toot on his whistle, and the conductor and stock handler hurried back to the train as Matt started up the right side of the creek. He picked up the kidnappers' trail right away, identifying it by the fact that there were five sets of prints, one of which indicated that the horse was carrying double.

After about a mile, he saw something hanging in a bush and riding up to it quickly, he leaned down to retrieve it. It was a tatting-trimmed handkerchief. Holding it to his nose, he smelled the hint of lavender that was her signature perfume. He wadded it up in his hand, then stuck it in his shirt pocket. It was obvious that Layne was doing all she could to help him.

"Good girl, Layne," Matt said quietly. "You just hang on, I'm coming for you."

Matt slapped his knees against Spirit's sides and the horse responded.

"Spirit, if they have hurt that girl in any way . . ." Matt said. He didn't finish the sentence. He didn't have to.

"He'll have to come this way," Teech said. "So I figure all we have to do is find us a good place to wait. Then, when we see him, we open up on him."

"If he don't see us first," Decker replied.

"Are you worried?"

"I just keep thinkin' about Hennessey and Taylor, and how they thought they was goin' to kill him, but they didn't."

"Yeah, but you heard what Pauley said. That dumb son of a bitch Hennessey called Jensen out. We ain't goin' to do nothin' like that," Teech insisted.

"Yeah, I guess you're right," Decker said.

Because they were approaching the crest of a ridge, neither Teech nor Decker had any idea that Matt was just on the other side, coming toward them. Matt couldn't see them either, but he heard them talking. And because they were close enough that he could hear them quite clearly, it also meant they were close enough for him to confront. Matt slapped his legs against the side of his horse and crested the ridge. There, no more than twenty yards in front of him, he saw Teech and Decker.

"Why don't you fellas just hold it right there?" he called.

"What the hell? Where'd you come from?" Teech hissed, startled by Matt's sudden appearance.

"Where I came from isn't your problem," Matt said. "Your problem is that I'm here. Now, drop those guns and lead me to the girl."

Suddenly, there was an angry buzz, then the "thocking" sound of a heavy bullet tearing into flesh. A fountain of blood squirted up from Spirit's neck and the animal went down on its front knees, then collapsed onto its right side. It was almost a full second after the strike of the bullet before the heavy boom of a distant rifle reached Matt's ears.

The fall pinned Matt's leg under his horse. He also dropped his pistol on the way down, and now it lay just out of reach of his grasping fingers.

"What the hell? Who's that shooting?" Decker shouted, pulling hard on the reins of his horse, which, though not hit, was spooked by the sight of seeing Matt's horse go down. "Is it one of our men? Who is it?"

"Who the hell cares?" Teech shouted back. "Look at him! Jensen is pinned down. Now's my chance to kill the son of a bitch!" Teech raised his gun and fired at Matt. Although Matt's right leg was still pinned, he was able to flip his left leg over the saddle and lay down behind his horse, thus providing him with some cover. Teech's bullet dug into his saddle and sent up a little puff of dust, but did no further damage.

"Come on, Teech!" Decker shouted. "Let's get the hell out of here while the getting is good!"

"I ain't leavin' till I put a bullet in that bastard!" Teech said angrily. "I still owe the bastard for what he did to Loomis, Kale, and Malone! Only thing is, I can't get him from here."

Teech slapped his legs against the side of his horse and moved around to get a better shot at Matt.

Matt made one more desperate grab for his pistol, but it was still out of reach. His rifle, however, was in the saddle sheath on the side of the horse that was on the ground, and Matt could see about six inches of the stock sticking out. He grabbed it, and was gratified to see that the weapon could be pulled free. He jerked it from the sheath and jacked a shell into the chamber, just as Teech came around to get into position to shoot him. "Say hello to my friends when you get to hell," Teech said, raising his pistol and taking careful aim. The smile left his face as he saw the end of Matt's rifle raise up, then spit a finger of flame. The .44-40 bullet from Matt's rifle hit Teech just under the chin, then exited the back of his head along with a pink spray of blood and bone as Teech tumbled off his horse.

"Say hello to them yourself," Matt said.

"He got Teech!" Decker shouted as he galloped away. "Jensen got Teech!"

Decker rode away hard now, not even bothering to look back to see what happened to Teech.

In the meantime, another bullet whistled by from the distant rifle. When Matt located the source of the shooting, he saw, at the crest of the next hill beyond the little valley, a mounted man with one leg thrown casually across his saddle. Using that leg to provide a stable firing platform, the shooter raised his rifle to fire again. There was a flash of light, the man rolled back from the recoil, then the bullet whizzed by so close to Matt's head that it made his ears pop. All this before the report of the rifle actually reached him. With a gasp of disbelief, Matt realized that this man was firing from at least one thousand yards away! Matt fired back, not with any expectation of actually hitting his target, but merely to show his enemy that he wasn't completely helpless.

In a way, Matt was running a bluff, because he *was* practically helpless. He was still trapped under his horse and he knew if he didn't get himself free soon, whoever was shooting at him would be able to change locations and catch Matt in an exposed position. He tried again to pull his leg free, but he was unable to do so. Then he got an idea. He stuck the stock of the rifle just under Spirit's side and grabbed the barrel. Using the rifle as a lever, he pushed up and wedged just enough space between the horse's flesh and the ground to allow him to slip his leg free.

His first fear was that his leg might be broken, but as soon as he pulled it out, he knew that it wasn't. The blood circulation was cut off, however, and when he tried to stand, he promptly fell back down again. As it was, that turned out to be a blessing, for another bullet whistled by at that very moment, at the precise place where his head would have been had he been standing. Crawling on his belly, Matt slithered and twisted his way back up to the crest of the ridge. He reached the crest, just as another bullet plowed into the dirt beside him. Matt twisted around behind the crest and looked back toward the place where the shots were coming from. With the crest providing him with cover and a rifle in his hands, he was no longer an easy target. Whoever was after him realized this as well, for Matt saw him put his rifle back in the saddle sheath, then turn and ride away as casually as if he were riding down Main Street. And why not? There was no way Matt was going to hit him at this distance, at least not with a .44-40 Winchester.

After the rider was gone, Matt managed to capture Teech's horse, which had trotted away during the shooting but afterward, had wandered back to begin cropping grass. Matt led the horse back to Spirit, then stood there for a moment, looking down at the horse that had served him so well for so long.

He recalled the day Smoke had given Spirit to him.

"Come on, I think it's time we went out to the corral to pick out your horse," Smoke said.

"*My* horse?"

"Yeah, your horse. A man's got to have a horse."

"Which horse is mine?" Matt asked.

"Why don't you take the best one?" Smoke replied. "Except for that one," he added, pointing to an Appaloosa over in one corner of the corral. "That one is mine."

"Which horse is the best?" Matt asked.

"Huh-uh," Smoke replied, shaking his head. "I'm willing to give you the best horse in my string, but as to which horse that is, well, you're just going to have to figure that out for yourself."

Matt walked out to the small corral that Smoke had built and, leaning on the split-rail fence, looked at the string of seven horses from which he could choose.

After looking them over very carefully, Matt smiled and nodded.

"You've made your choice?" Smoke asked.

"Yes."

"Which one?"

"I want that one," Matt said, pointing to a bay.

"Why not the chestnut?" Smoke asked. "He looks stronger."

"Look at the chestnut's front feet," Matt said. "They are splayed. The bay's feet are just right."

"What about the black one over there?"

"Huh-uh," Matt said. "His back legs are set too far back. I want the bay."

Smoke reached out and ran his hand through Matt's hair.

"You're learning, kid, you're learning," he said. "The bay is yours."

Matt's grin spread from ear to ear. "I've never had a horse before," he said. He jumped down from the rail fence and started toward the horse.

"That's all right, he's never had a rider before," Smoke said.

"What?" Matt asked, jerking around in surprise as he stared at Smoke. "Did you say that he's never been ridden?"

"He's as spirited as he was the day we brought him in."

"How'm I going to ride him if he has never been ridden?"

"Well, I reckon you are just going to have to break him," Smoke said, passing the words off as easily as if he had just suggested that Matt should wear a hat.

"Break him? I can't break a horse!"

"Sure you can. It'll be fun," Smoke suggested.

Smoke showed Matt how to saddle the horse, and gave him some pointers on riding it.

"Now, you don't want to break the horse's spirit," Smoke said. "What you want to do is make him your partner."

"How do I do that?"

"Walk him around for a bit so that he gets used to his saddle and to you. Then get on."

"He won't throw me then?"

"Oh, he'll still throw you a few times," Smoke said with a little laugh. "But at least he'll know how serious you are."

To Matt's happy surprise, he wasn't thrown even once. The horse did buck a few times, coming down on stiff legs, then sunfishing, and finally galloping at full speed around the corral. But after a few minutes, he stopped fighting, and Matt leaned over to pat him gently on the neck.

"Good job, Matt," Smoke said, clapping his hands quietly. "You've got a real touch with horses. You didn't break him, you trained him, and that's real good. He's not mean, but he still has spirit."

"Smoke, can I name him?"

"Sure, he's your horse, you can name him anything you want."

Matt continued to pat the horse on the neck as he thought of a name.

"That's it," he said, smiling broadly. "I've come up with a name."

"What are you going to call him?"

"Spirit."

"You were a good horse and a good companion, Spirit," Matt said as he took the saddle from Spirit and put it on Teech's horse. "And you deserve better than to be left out here like this. But I'm pretty sure you would understand. We started on this job together, and I aim to finish it for both of us."

Once Matt was mounted, he rode down into the little valley, then to the top of the distant ridge to the spot where the shooting had come from. He wanted to have a look at the place where the gunman had been. A flash of sunlight led him to the first sign. When he picked it up, he saw that it was the brass casing of a .50-caliber shell. He had seen such rifles and knew that, when fitted with a telescope, they could be fired accurately at ranges up to one thousand yards.

He also saw something else. A .50-caliber bullet with a little piece of paper wrapped around it. He wasn't surprised by what he saw when he unwrapped the paper.

Chapter Twenty-four

Layne was wearing gray cotton trousers, a white shirt, and a vest, all belonging to Hodge Decker. She was also wearing a hat, which concealed her full head of hair so that her sex could be determined only if someone studied her closely. She was not bound or restricted in any way, but Strayhorn let it be known that if she tried to get away from them, he would kill her.

They stopped at the edge of town and Strayhorn pointed to the sign.

"You see this?" he asked.

YOU ARE ENTERING
DORENA

We've got our own Law.
We don't need none of yours.

"I see it," Layne replied.

"This here is what as known as an open town," Strayhorn said. "Some folks might call it an outlaw town. What that means is, there ain't no sense in you tryin' to tell anyone here that you are our prisoner, 'cause it won't do you no good. Fact is, it'll prob'ly be worse for you 'cause if someone else gets ahold of you, well, more'n likely they won't be as nice to you as we been."

"Do you call the way you've treated me nice?" Layne asked.

Strayhorn chuckled and nodded. "Oh, yeah," he said. "You don't have no idea what some of the folks in this town would do to you if they got you. Fact is, if it wasn't for keepin' you from bein' all marked up so's we can get the full amount of money for you, why, we would'a already had our own fun with you. If you know what I mean."

Layne shivered. "I know what you mean," she said.

"Good. Then you'll believe me when I tell you it's best for you if you don't say nothin' to nobody. Don't let nobody even know you're a woman. You understand?"

Layne nodded. "I understand."

"I still think it wasn't smart to bring her here," No Nose said.

"You'd rather stay out there at the cabin and wait on Jensen, would you?" Strayhorn asked.

"We wouldn't have to stay there. We could'a gone somewhere else."

"Where?" Strayhorn asked. "No matter where we might go, Jensen would track us. So, let him track us here. I figure here we'll outnumber him about one hundred to one. Even if he finds the girl, there won't be nothin' he can do about it."

"I think Strayhorn is right, No Nose," Pauley said.

"Maybe," No Nose said. "We'll see."

The four rode on into town, and to those on the street, there was nothing remarkable about them. It was just four more riders coming into town, at least three of whom they recognized.

When they stopped in front of the saloon, Strayhorn, No Nose, and Pauley dismounted easily, but Layne stayed in the saddle.

"Get down off that horse," Strayhorn ordered.

"I can't," Layne said. "The only way I've ever ridden before this was sidesaddle. I don't know how to get off."

Strayhorn pointed to the left stirrup. "Just stand in this stirrup, throw your right leg over, and get down," he said. "And do it quick, 'cause I ain't goin' to help you."

Layne did as Strayhorn directed, only instead of throwing her leg over behind, she brought it around in front, then slid down, as if dismounting from a sidesaddle.

"I hope to hell nobody seen you do that," Strayhorn said irritably.

Someone did see it. When the four riders arrived, Mabel Franklin saw everything. Unlike the whores who lived in rooms over the top of the saloon, Mabel had her own crib, and she was there now, standing at the window, watching the four riders come in. She recognized Strayhorn, No Nose, and Pauley, and because she recognized the clothes on the fourth rider, she thought it was Decker.

As they passed close by her crib, though, she realized that it wasn't Decker, and she wondered who it was. Her curiosity intensified when she saw the way the rider dismounted. Pulling the curtain to one side, she watched as the four stepped up onto the porch, then passed out of view.

Her curiosity as yet unsatisfied, Mabel left her crib and walked up the alley to go into the saloon through the back door. Stepping into the back of the saloon, she stood the shadows so as not to be noticed.

"Do you want some food?" Mabel heard Strayhorn say to the person in Decker's clothes.

Mabel couldn't hear the reply, but from Strayhorn's response, it was in the negative.

"In the whole time you been with us, you ain't hardly eat enough to keep a bird alive," Strayhorn said. "You ain't worth nothin' to us if you starve yourself to death. How about some whiskey? You want some whiskey?"

This time, Mabel could hear the answer.

"Could I have some water?"

"Water? All right, I'll get you some water."

Mabel waited until Strayhorn left to get the water, then, putting on a practiced smile, she walked over to the table, as if soliciting business.

"Hello, boys," she said. "I haven't seen you in a while."

"Did you miss us, Mabel?" Pauley asked.

"Oh, honey, you know I did," Mabel said. She walked over and pushed his hat back, then ran her hand through his hair, all the while trying to get a good look at the quiet one who had ordered only water.

"And who is this handsome fella?" Mabel asked, looking at the one in Decker's clothes. "How about it, honey? Would you like Mabel to show you a good time?"

"What?" Layne gasped, looking up at Mabel.

"Here, you, get away from that table!" Strayhorn shouted angrily, coming back from the bar.

"I was just—" Mabel began, but Strayhorn interrupted her.

"You was just nothin'," Strayhorn said. "Now, get away from her before I knock out what few teeth you have left."

"Get away from her?"

"Him," Strayhorn corrected. "Get away from him. Get away from all of us, now."

"All right, honey, all right," Mabel said. "You don't have to get yourself into a piss soup over it. I was just tryin' to be friendly is all."

"We don't need you to be friendly," Strayhorn said. "If we want any whores, we'll find someone that's a lot better-lookin' than you."

"Mabel, you know better than to bother the customers," the bartender called to her. "If they don't want you botherin' 'em, don't bother 'em."

"All right, all right," Mabel said. "I'm sorry."

With a great show of indignation over being so summarily rejected, Mabel left.

Never, in her life had Layne been in a place like this. All around her she heard men laughing and talking loudly, using language that she knew was vulgar, even though she didn't even know what some of the words meant.

It was the women in the saloon who were the most shocking. She couldn't even look at them, so scandalous were they. The woman who had come to the table to talk to her was wearing a dress that was cut so low in front that her breasts spilled over. And yet, she was one of the more modest ones. There were at least half-a-dozen other women in the saloon who made no effort at all to cover their breasts. Even though Layne was well read, she had no idea that such places even existed, and she could feel her cheeks flaming in embarrassment.

* * *

Mabel left the saloon, then hurried down the alley to her crib. Her crib was a small, one-room house that served as both her home and a place to which she could bring her customers. She had a strong suspicion about something, and she wanted to check it out. Stepping inside, she located the newspaper she had brought back to her crib the day before, when someone had left in the saloon.

The story she was looking for was on the very first page of the paper.

No Leads on Missing Woman.

Porter Foully Murdered.

The fate of Miss Layne McKenzie, niece of Governor John Long Routt, is still unknown. The engineer, fireman, and conductor of the Flyer reported that the young lady was taken from the governor's private car shortly after midnight on the 8th instant, when the train stopped at Mustang Creek to take on water.

Mabel read the entire article until she came to the part she was looking for.

"The railroad is offering a reward of one thousand dollars to anyone who can offer assistance in the safe recovery of Miss McKenzie."

Mabel had heard talk of some big job that No Nose Nelson and Marcus Strayhorn had planned. She knew about the botched railroad robbery, and assumed the big job she had heard people talk about would be another robbery attempt.

But she knew now that it wasn't a robbery at all. They had taken a girl from the train, and she would bet anything in the world that the person wearing Decker's clothes was that girl.

Mabel looked at the newspaper again, rereading the last line in the article.

> "The railroad is offering a reward of one thousand dollars to anyone who can offer assistance in the safe recovery of Miss McKenzie."

With one thousand dollars, Mabel could leave this place and buy a small house somewhere. She could start over, maybe take in some sewing or washing. With that much money, she would never have to be "on the line" again.

And there was something else, something that had nothing to do with the reward money. She felt sorry for the girl, and if there was any way she could help her escape, she was going to do it.

Mabel returned to the saloon, and even though she was carefully avoiding Strayhorn's table, she continued to watch it from wherever she was in the room. She had no specific plan in mind, but she needed to be alert for any opportunity that might come her way. She moved about the saloon, engaging in banter with the customers, sometimes refilling their glasses for them, but always keeping an eye on the person in Decker's clothes, the person that Mabel was convinced was the governor's niece.

"Here comes the half-breed," Mabel heard someone say and, looking toward the front door, she saw Goneril.

Mabel had never been with Goneril, had never drunk

with him, and had never so much as spoken to him. In a town that had more than its share of robbers and murderers, she found Goneril to be particularly frightening. The only good thing was that he seemed as disinterested in Mabel and the other whores as they were frightened of him.

Goneril looked neither left nor right, but walked directly to Strayhorn's table. Mabel moved close enough to be able to overhear the conversation.

"Hey, Strayhorn," Pauley said. "I thought you hired Goneril to take care of Jensen."

"I did," Strayhorn replied.

"Then what's he doin' here in Dorena?" Pauley nodded toward the man who was coming toward them.

Goneril didn't wait for a greeting, but began talking right away. The tone and timbre of his voice reflected his anger.

"What's the idea of sending Teech and Decker after Jensen?" Goneril asked angrily.

"Did they kill him?" Strayhorn asked.

"No, they didn't kill him. And their being in the way kept *me* from killing him."

"That sounds to me like it's between you and them," Strayhorn said.

"Not any more, it isn't."

"What do you mean?"

"They're dead. Both of them."

"Jensen killed them?"

"Jensen killed Teech," Goneril said. "I killed Decker."

"You killed Decker?"

"Yes."

"Why?"

"You hired me to kill Jensen. I didn't want the competition."

"Teech and Decker were a couple of hotheads," Strayhorn said. "I tried to keep 'em from going after Jensen. But they went out on their own anyway. Don't worry, nobody else is going to try."

Goneril pointed at Strayhorn, then looked at all of them. "I killed Decker, and I will kill anyone else who gets in my way. Do I make myself clear?"

"Pretty clear," Strayhorn said.

Goneril stared at them for a moment longer, then he turned and left the saloon.

"Teech and Decker," Strayhorn said after Goneril was gone. "They were so cocksure of themselves."

"Teech had been with you for a long time, hadn't he, Strayhorn?" Pauley asked.

"Yeah, Teech was my cousin, but after his ma run off and his pa got hisself kilt, my ma brought him in and raised him like one of her own. So Teech was more like a brother than a cousin."

"Well, I'm sorry about that."

Inexplicably, Strayhorn looked at the other two and smiled. "Hell, far as I'm concerned, it just means that we only have to split the money three ways now. That's five thousand dollars apiece, boys."

"If the governor pays," No Nose said.

"He'll pay," Strayhorn said. He looked at Layne. "He better pay."

"Mr. Strayhorn, I need to—uh—" Layne began, but she didn't finish her sentence.

"You need to what?"

"I need to—uh—the water," Layne said, pointing to

the glass. She cleared her throat. "I have to . . . ," She couldn't finish the sentence.

No Nose laughed. "What the hell," he said. "I think the little lady's tellin' you she needs to take a piss."

"There's an outhouse out back," Strayhorn said.

"Are you just goin' to let her go by herself?" Pauley asked.

"Where the hell is she going to go?" Strayhorn replied. "She knows what would happen if anyone else in this town got hold of her."

Overhearing the conversation, Mabel moved quickly to step out the back door. She was waiting, just out of sight, as Layne came into the alley. She saw Layne stop and stare at the odiferous outhouse in obvious dismay over its condition and her situation.

She hesitated.

"It don't get to smellin' no better by you a'waitin', honey," Mabel said.

"Oh!" Layne gasped, startled by Mabel's sudden and unexpected appearance.

"Go ahead, honey, I'll keep an eye open for you," Mabel said.

"What?"

"I said I'll keep an eye open for you," Mabel repeated. "You bein' a woman and all, I don't reckon you'd be wantin' any men to come in on you while you are takin' care of your business now, would you?"

"No, I . . . ," Layne paused in mid-sentence. "You know I'm a woman?"

"Honey, I not only know *what* you are, I know *who* you are," Mabel said. "You're the governor's daughter, ain't you?"

"I'm his niece."

"I knew it," Mabel said. "Strayhorn and them others snatched you from the train, didn't they? And they're holdin' you till they get some money from the governor."

"Who are you?" Layne asked.

"I'm just a whore, honey," she said. "But even whores know right from wrong, and what they're doin' with you is wrong."

Layne's eyes welled with tears, which then began sliding down her cheeks as she nodded. "I'm so afraid," she said.

"Yeah, well, don't you worry none, honey, 'cause I'm goin' to get you away from them," Mabel said.

"What is your name?" Layne asked.

"My name is Mabel. Mabel Franklin."

"Mabel, I know you mean well, but you mustn't help me," Layne said. "Strayhorn told me what would happen if I try to escape. And if you help me, it will be just as dangerous for you."

Mabel made a little motion with her hand. "Take care of your business," she said. "And leave the rest to me."

When Layne came out of the privy a few moments later, Mabel was still standing there.

"Come with me," Mabel said.

"Where? Strayhorn told me that everyone in town was an outlaw."

Mabel chuckled. "Honey, not ever'one in town is an outlaw. Fact is, we used to be a pretty nice town till people like Strayhorn moved in. They killed off the law we had and took over. "They's some good folks in the town. They're just scared to do anything, that's all. Come with me."

"Where are we going?"

"Someplace where you will be safe," Mabel answered.

Mabel started up the alley with Layne. They had gone

no farther than twenty yards or so when two men came around the corner.

"Oh!" Layne said.

Mabel grabbed Layne and pulled the young woman against her. She leaned against the back wall of the dry-goods store, then lifted one leg and wrapped it around Layne. Grabbing Layne's hand, she put it on her bare thigh, then pulled Layne's head down to her neck. When Layne tried to fight her, she tightened the hold with her leg.

"Damn, Mabel, you got one that can't even wait to get you into your crib?" one of the men asked.

"Honey, if he's got the money, he can have me any-where he wants," Mabel answered.

Both men laughed, then continued on up the alley.

Mabel waited until they turned a corner before she lowered her leg.

"I'm sorry, honey," she said.

"No, that's—that's all right," Layne said. "I didn't un-derstand what you were doing at first."

"Come on, we've got to hurry before Strayhorn comes searching for you."

When they reached the end of the alley, Mabel crossed the street and went down into the Mexican quarters.

"I have a friend here who will help us out," she said.

Going up to one of the little adobe houses, Mabel knocked on the door. The Mexican woman who an-swered the door looked surprised.

"Señorita Franklin?" she said.

"Frederica, I need help," Mabel said. "Please, let us in."

"*Sí*, come, come," Frederica said, stepping back to allow both to come in.

"This is Frederica Arino," Mabel said to Layne.

As soon as Layne stepped into the house, she took off the man's hat she was wearing and let her hair fall.

"*Oh, mi, usted es una mujer!* You are a woman!" Frederica said, repeating it in English.

"Yes, she is a woman, and she needs your help," Mabel said. "We must not let Strayhorn find her."

"Strayhorn," Frederica said with a snarl. She looked over at her daughter, who looked away in shame. "*Strayhorn es un bastardo. Escupí sobre él.* Yes, I will help your friend. I will help anyone to hide from Strayhorn."

"*Gracias, Señora Arino. Estoy en su deuda,*" Layne said.

"You speak Spanish?" Mabel asked in surprise.

"I studied Spanish in school," Layne replied.

"Oh, this is going to be so easy!" Mabel said. "Frederica, you can—"

"*Sí,*" Frederica interrupted, smiling broadly. "I know what to do."

A younger version of Frederica came into the room then, accompanied by a young boy.

"This is my daughter, Maria, and my son, Esteban," Frederica said. "She will help me."

"*Maria, soy* pleased *hacer su conocimiento,*" Layne said.

The young girl made a slight curtsy. "*Y yo usted,*" she said.

"Esteban, go to the house of your aunt Carmelita."

"But I want to stay here, Mama."

"Do as I tell you," Frederica said in a more demanding tone. "And don't come back until I come for you."

"*Sí,* Mama," Esteban said, leaving reluctantly.

"Well," Mabel said. "I had better go as well. I should be back before I am missed. I would not want anyone to find me over here."

"Mabel, I don't know how to thank you," Layne said.

"You just do what Frederica says and you'll be fine," Mabel said, patting Layne on her hand.

Mabel started out the front door.

"No, this door," Maria said quickly, taking her to the back door. She pointed. "This way, then you will come out behind the *farmacia.*"

"The drugstore, yes. Yes, good idea. I'll buy some belladonna. That will be my reason for being gone from the saloon."

Half an hour later, with the help of Frederica and Maria, Layne had undergone a complete transformation. Gone were the men's clothes, replaced now by a bright yellow dress with black lace around a low-cut bodice. It was cinched tight at her waist. Her hair hung in long black tendrils secured with a tortoise-shell comb. Her skin had been slightly darkened with a tea made from onion skins, her cheeks were heavily rouged, her lips painted red, and her eyes accented with a dark shadow.

Suddenly, they heard shouts, curses, and gunshots from the street. Looking through the window of Frederica's small house, Layne could see Strayhorn walking up and down in the middle of the street. Strayhorn fired his pistol into the air again.

"Layne McKenzie!" Strayhorn was yelling. "I know you ain't left town! If you know what's good for you, you'd better get out here now! If you don't show yourself in one minute, I'll kill you when I find you! Do you understand that, you bitch? Money or no money, I will kill you if I have to come find you! Get out here now!"

Layne shivered in fear.

"I'll give one hundred dollars in cash to any man or

woman who brings that bitch back to me!" Strayhorn shouted. "And don't be fooled! She's wearin' a man's clothes!"

"Do not worry, he will not find you." Frederica gave Layne a basket. "Here, we will go to market now."

"What?"

Frederica pointed to the market, which was right across the street. Strayhorn was standing in front of the market.

"We will go to market now."

"No!" Layne said. "Strayhorn is out there! He will see me!"

"No, Señorita," Frederica said. She moved Layne over to stand in front of a mirror. "This is what he will see. You are no longer Layne McKenzie, you are my younger sister, Juanita Arino."

"I am afraid," Layne said.

"Señorita, he will not see you," Maria said.

With a deep breath and a squaring of her shoulders, Layne accepted their assurances, and agreed to go out with them.

"Speak to me only in Spanish," Frederica said as the three of them left her house and started toward the market.

Seeing Frederica, Strayhorn came toward them. Layne felt her stomach draw tight in fear.

"Hey, you, Frederica!" Strayhorn said to Frederica. "I'm looking for an American woman who ran away from me. Have you seen her?"

"What does she look like?" Frederica asked.

"What does she look like? Hell, she looks like an American," Strayhorn answered. "Only, she ain't like one of the ugly American whores, she's prettier than that. If you seen her, you would know she was someone new."

"I have not seen such a person."

"What about you?" Strayhorn asked Maria.

"I have seen no one, *Señor*," Maria answered.

"What about you, girlie? Have you seen a gringo woman?" Strayhorn asked, looking directly at Layne.

"She does not speak English," Frederica said. "I will ask for you."

Turning to Layne, Frederica said, in Spanish.

"Usted ha visto a una mujer estadounidense hermosa?" Frederica asked.

"Señor, he visto nada," Layne replied.

"She says she has seen nothing," Frederica said.

"I know damn well that bitch is somewhere," Strayhorn said. "If you see her, I will give you one hundred dollars to bring her to me."

"May we go to market now?" Frederica asked.

"What? Yes, yes, go on, get out of here," Strayhorn said. "Layne McKenzie, it is too late for you now!" he shouted as Frederica, Maria, and Layne walked away. "When I find you now, I am going to kill you!"

"He didn't recognize me," Layne said quietly as they walked away. "He looked right at me, but he didn't recognize me."

"You are safe with us," Frederica said.

Chapter Twenty-five

After a full day of looking for Layne McKenzie without success, Strayhorn came back to the saloon.

"You lose your girlfriend, did you?" Mabel teased.

"Shut up."

"You didn't have to bring in your own girlfriend. I told you, anytime you want a real American woman, I'll take you to my crib," Mabel said.

"I'd rather be with a goat," Strayhorn said.

"We like to please here in beautiful Dorena," Mabel said. "If you prefer goats, I'm sure we can accommodate you."

Everyone in the saloon laughed.

"Get out of here!" Strayhorn shouted angrily.

"Sure, honey, whatever you say," Mabel said, walking away from the table. She had baited him only to see if he suspected her in any way of arranging for Layne to disappear. She was confident now that he did not.

Strayhorn ordered steak and eggs from the kitchen, and when it was put on the table in front of him, he reached for the steak and picked it up in his hands.

"Strayhorn, you really need to work on your table

manners," Matt said. "Haven't you ever heard of a knife and fork?"

Gasping, Strayhorn looked up to see that the person who had just delivered his food was not the bartender, but Matt Jensen.

"You!" Strayhorn said in surprise.

"Go ahead, take a bite," Matt said. "I wouldn't want to send a man to hell on an empty stomach."

Strayhorn held the piece of meat just in front of his mouth, staring wide-eyed at Matt. "Where did you come from? How did you get here?"

Matt shook his head. "That's not how it works," he said. "I ask the questions, you answer them. Where's the girl?"

Strayhorn suddenly dropped the steak and made a mad grab for his pistol, but Matt was quicker on the draw. Instead of shooting Strayhorn, though, he brought his pistol down hard on Strayhorn's head. Strayhorn fell facedown in his food.

Matt bent down to take Strayhorn's pistol. Then he dragged Strayhorn's limp, unconscious form over to one of the supporting posts, where he propped him and, putting one arm to either side, handcuffed him to the post.

All conversation had come to a stop when Matt knocked Strayhorn out. Most of the other patrons looked on in curiosity, making no comment until they saw Matt put on the handcuffs.

"Hey, what the hell you doin' there? Are you a lawman, mister? 'Cause if you are, you got no jurisdiction here," one of the others said.

Matt looked up at the speaker. "Who are you?" he asked.

"The name is Murdoch. Jess Murdoch, and I'm the

man that's goin' to teach you better than to come into Dorena to serve paper. Who the hell are you?"

"My name is Jensen. Matt Jensen."

"Jensen?" someone said in a high, choked voice.

"They say he's kilt more'n twenty men," another added in a harsh whisper.

The man who had challenged Matt began shake.

"Listen, don't pay me no never-mind, mister," he said in a frightened, quivering voice. "I was just funnin' you is all. You go on about your business."

"Obliged," Matt replied. He walked back over to the table where Strayhorn had been sitting. The untouched steak had fallen back onto his plate, and Matt cut off a generous piece of it and stuck it into his mouth. He picked up the pitcher of beer and took several swallows before he set it back down. The rest of the saloon continued to watch him in silence.

"I hear tell nearly everyone in Dorena is an outlaw," Matt said. "Whether you are, or you aren't makes no difference to me. I'm not here after anyone except Strayhorn and whoever was with him when he took a young woman from the train. And I'm also looking for that young woman."

"You ain't the only one lookin' for her," the bartender said.

"What do you mean?"

"The girl got away from Strayhorn sometime this mornin'," the bartender said. "He's been looking for her all day."

"So she is still alive?" Matt asked, feeling a sense of relief.

"As far as I know, she is. Leastwise, she was this mornin'."

Matt looked over at Strayhorn. "Who else was with him?" he asked aloud.

"Mister, you're crazy if you think you can come in

our town and get one of us to squeal on our own," Murdoch said.

Matt pulled his pistol and shot, doing it so fast that everyone was caught by surprise. His bullet clipped off the fleshy bottom part of Murdoch's earlobe, and even as Murdoch was putting his hand to his bloody ear, Matt put his pistol back in his holster.

"Who else was with him?" Matt asked again.

"No Nose Nelson and Pauley Moore," Murdoch said quickly.

"You know where they are?"

"No, no, I don't know."

"How about you?" Matt asked the bartender. "Do you know where they are?"

"Mister, I can't answer that," the bartender replied. "My life wouldn't be worth a plug nickel if I did." Even as he was refusing to speak, however, the bartender flicked his eyes up.

"All right," Matt replied. "I'll find them myself."

Upstairs in one of the rooms, in the bed of a whore, No Nose heard the gunshot. Then the saloon suddenly grow strangely quiet. He stopped.

"Are you finished, honey?" the girl asked.

"Shut up," No Nose hissed.

"What?" the girl asked, surprised by No Nose's harsh command.

"I said shut up!" No Nose hissed again, putting his hand over her mouth. When he was sure she wouldn't speak again, he pulled his hand away. The girl took a long, gasping breath.

No Nose sat up and swung his legs over the side of the

bed, then reached for his pistol. It was still deathly quiet below. "Don't you hear that?" he asked.

"I don't hear anything," the girl answered in a quiet, whimpering voice.

"Yeah, that's just it," No Nose said. "Neither do I."

Still holding his pistol, No Nose began slipping back into his pants. As he was pulling on his boots, he kept his eye on the doorknob. He had just got them on when he saw the doorknob move ever so slightly.

Raising his pistol, No Nose began firing, punching a pattern of six bullets through the door in such a way that one of them was sure to be fatal for whoever was on the other side.

With an angry shout, No Nose rushed across the room and kicked open the door. He ran out onto the landing just outside the door.

Matt had jiggled the doorknob, then stepped to one side, no more than a second before the fusillade of bullets. He stood on one side of the door with his back to the wall, watching the spray of splinters as the bullets came through. Then he heard No Nose's loud, angry shout as the outlaw dashed across the room. When No Nose appeared on the landing, Matt brought his pistol crashing into the back of No Nose's head. The blow, plus the momentum of No Nose's rush, carried him through the banister, causing him to crash headfirst onto one of the tables in the room below.

Matt looked down at him, then realized he didn't have to hurry. No Nose was dead.

* * *

"He's here!" Pauley said. "He's in town, now."

Goneril, who was sharing a stall with his horse, was sitting in the corner, eating beans from a can.

"Where is he?" he asked, wiping some bean juice away from his mouth with the back of his hand.

Pauley pointed. "He's in the saloon. He's already kilt No Nose, and he's got Strayhorn chained up to a post."

Goneril laughed. "Trussed up like a pig goin' to market, is he?"

"What are you goin' to do?" Pauley asked.

Goneril stood up, then walked over to his saddle and tack. He pulled the Remington rolling-block rifle from from its sheath, picked up a little cloth bag of .50-caliber shells, then started toward the ladder that led to the loft of the livery barn.

"I'm goin' to kill the son of a bitch, is what I'm going to do," Goneril said.

"What do you want me to do?" Pauley asked.

"I don't care what you do," Goneril called back over his shoulder as he climbed into the loft.

Pauley watched the half-breed until he could no longer see him. Then it dawned on him that if shooting started between Goneril and Jensen, the livery barn would not be the safest place to be. He left the barn, and stepped into the billiards parlor next door.

Up in the loft of the livery, Goneril prepared for his target. Cocking the hammer on his rifle freed the pivoted breechblock. Then he thumbed the rolling block backward and down to expose the chamber. Pulling a .50-caliber shell from the little cloth bag, he inserted it into the chamber, then rolled the block upward and forward to again seal the breech. After loading, he eased the hammer forward to the half-cock position, got down behind a bale of hay, and looked up the street toward the saloon. He aimed at the front door of the saloon, then waited.

Back at the saloon, Mabel had watched the drama unfold, culminating with No Nose crashing through the upstairs banister and breaking his neck when he fell. Several of the saloon patrons gathered around the body, looking down at it with morbid curiosity.

"You all seen that!" Strayhorn shouted from his postion on the floor, handcuffed to a supporting post. "He kilt No Nose in cold blood. Same as he tried to kill me!"

"Where's the girl?" Matt asked.

"Even if I knew where the bitch was, I wouldn't tell you," Strayhorn said.

"I know where she is," Mabel said.

"Where is she?" Matt asked.

"According to a story I read in the paper, there is a thousand-dollar reward to anyone who finds her. Is that right?"

"How is the girl?" Matt asked.

"She is fine. What about the reward?"

"Yes, there is a reward. And I will see that you get it," Matt said.

"You bitch!" Strayhorn shouted to Mabel from his position on the floor. "You know where she is and you didn't tell me?"

"I not only know where she is, I'm the one who took here there," Mabel said.

"Whore, your life ain't worth a plug nickel," Strayhorn growled.

"Yeah? What are you going to do to me, chained up to the post like you are?"

"I got friends in this town," Strayhorn said.

"You've got no friends," Mabel said.

"Where is the girl?" Matt asked.

"Like I told you, she is safe. I took her over to the house of a friend, Frederica Arino."

"The Mexican whore?" Strayhorn said. "You took her over to that . . ." Strayhorn stopped in mid-sentence. "Wait a minute! Yes, I saw her!" he said. "That was her! Frederica told me it was her sister, and I believed her because I didn't recognize her. But I know now that it was the McKenzie bitch!"

"Where is this place?" Matt asked.

"Come with me, I'll show you," Mabel said.

"You don't need to be worryin' none about no reward!" Strayhorn shouted as Mable and Matt start toward the front door. "Do you hear me, bitch! Neither one of you will get out of this town alive!"

At the far end of the street, in the loft over the livery barn, Gonreil saw the front door of the saloon open. Pulling the hammer back, he rested the rifle on a stanchion, then looked through the sights.

There he was! Matt Jensen stepped through the door and was standing on the front porch, a perfect target!

As Mabel started to step down from the stoop, she caught her foot on a loose board and nearly tripped. In order to regain her balance, she stepped in front of Matt.

Just as Goneril squeezed the trigger, he saw the whore move in front of Jensen.

"Careful," Matt said, reaching out to keep Mabel from falling. That was when he heard the angry buzz of a bullet.

"Uhnn!" Mabel said.

Matt was holding her, and he felt her slump in his arms as the heavy bullet plunged into her chest.

"Oh!" Mabel said. "What happened?"

"You've been shot," Matt said.

"Shot," Mabel repeated. It wasn't a question, it was an observation, and there was more a sense of awe than fear in her voice.

Looking up, he saw a plume of gun smoke drifting away from the open window of the loft of the livery barn.

"Shit!" Goneril said aloud when he realized that he had hit the woman instead of Jensen.

Pulling the hammer back again, he opened the breechblock. The extractor did not eject the empty cartridge, but it did pull it up for enough for him to be able to remove it by hand. Quickly, he slipped another shell into the chamber, closed the block, and looked down the sights for a second shot.

Goneril had not intended to shoot the whore. But having shot her, he expected to get a second attempt at Jensen. But Jensen wasn't there, and neither was the woman.

"What the hell? Where did they go?"

Matt dragged Mabel back into the saloon, then knelt down beside her.

"I probably wouldn't have made it anywhere else anyway," Mabel said. She coughed, and flecks of blood appeared on her lips. "Once a whore, always a whore." She tried to laugh.

"You were trying to help an innocent woman," Matt said. "That had nothing to do with being a whore."

"Promise me you'll get her back home safe," Mabel said.

"I promise," Matt replied.

Mabel nodded. "That's good," she said. "That's good." Mabel died.

"Well, now, that was just real tender," Strayhorn said from the floor where he was handcuffed to the post. "Yes, sir, that just brought tears to my eyes."

Matt stood up and looked down at Mabel for a moment, then started toward the back door of the saloon.

"You goin' to buy flowers for the whore's funeral, are you?" Strayhorn called out to him. Strayhorn laughed, a high-pitched cackle. "Yeah, I belive that's what you're goin' do do all right. You goin' to—*unh!*"

The grunt came from a kick in the face, rendered by Matt as he walked by him. Matt said nothing to him, nor did he even look back. It was just a kick in passing, but it was enough to leave Strayhorn bleeding from the nose and lips.

"I'll kill you, for this!" Strayhorn shouted as Matt started through the back door. "Do you hear me? I'm going to kill you!"

"Strayhorn, if I was you, I'd shut up about now," the bartender said.

Strayhorn glared at the bartender, but said nothing else.

Once outside behind the saloon, Matt darted down the alley, not toward the livery barn, but away from it. When he reached the far end of the alley, he saw a wagon coming up the cross street. Matt got on the side of the wagon away from the livery barn and, shielded by the wagon, crossed the main street unseen.

"What's goin' on?" the wagon driver asked.

"Nothing," Matt said. "Just keep going."

When Matt drew even with the alley on opposite side of the street, he started up the alley toward the livery barn.

At the sound of Goneril's shot, Pauley left the billiards parlor, ran across the street, darted up alongside the leather-goods store, then started up the alley. He saw Matt leaving the back of the saloon and, gasping, he jumped back behind the corner of the leather-goods store to avoid being seen. When he looked around again, he saw Matt slip around behind a wagon and duck down to use it as concealment.

Pauley ran up the alley to the saloon, then went inside.

"Strayhorn! Strayhorn, you still here?" he called.

"Where the hell else would I be?"

"Damn, what happened to you?" Pauley asked when he saw Strayhorn's face.

"Never mind what happened to me. Just get me loose from here."

"How the hell am I goin' to do that?" Pauley asked. "I don't have the key."

"You don't need a key," Murdoch said. Murdoch was the one who had had part of his ear shot away by Matt. The ear was no longer bleeding, but he was still cutching a bloody handkerchief.

"What do you mean, you don't need a key?"

"All you need is a nail or something to stick down inside the cuff there. Push the clasp out of the way, and you can open it."

"Where the hell am I goin' to get a nail?"

"This'll do it," Murdoch said, opening the little shell-extracting ramrod on his pistol. In less than a minute, he had Strayhorn free.

Strayhorn stood up and rubbed his wrists for a moment. "Come on," he said to Pauley. "I intend to put a few bullets in Jensen's carcass."

"He's goin' after Goneril," Pauley said. "Like as not, he'll be dead by the time we get there."

"Then I'll put bullets in his dead body," Strayhorn said angrily.

Matt moved into the barn through the back door. He had to stand there for just a moment to allow his eyes to adjust to the sudden shadows. As he stood there, he heard a slight movement from above, and looking up toward the loft, he saw a few bits of straw fluttering down through a shaft of sunlight.

Putting his pistol in his holster, Matt started up the ladder, climbing up very slowly.

* * *

Goneril heard someone coming up and he smiled, then turned and leveled the big buffalo rifle at the top of the ladder. The top of the hat appeared then the crown, and finally the entire hat.

Goneril pulled the trigger and the rifle roared loudly within the confines of the loft. A huge cloud of smoke rolled out from the end of the barrel, and the hat went flying.

"Hah! I got you!" Goneril shouted.

Suddenly, and to Goneril's complete shock, Matt's head and shoulders appeared above the top of the ladder.

"No, you got my hat," Matt said.

Matt had both hands on the top of the ladder, which showed Goneril that he wasn't armed.

"You son of a bitch!" Goneril shouted. He made a wild, desperate grab for his pistol, drawing it and firing, just as Matt came over the top of the ladder and rolled across the floor of the loft. Goneril managed to fire a second time before Matt was in position to draw his gun. Matt only shot once, but it was enough. His bullet hit Goneril right between the eyes. He walked over to look down at Goneril's body, then, on impulse, searched through his pockets until he found the little piece of paper he was looking for. He wrote something on the paper, then stuck it in Goneril's mouth.

This is for my horse, Spirit.

"Matt! You came for me!" Layne said when Frederica opened the door to Matt's knock. "I knew you would!"

She threw herself into his arms, embracing him and kissing him. Matt didn't push her away. After the effusive greeting, and a heartfelt expression of gratitude to Frederica and Maria, Matt and Layne stepped back outside.

"Well, now, lookie here," Strayhorn said. "Looks like you found my girl for me."

Strayhorn, Pauley, and Murdoch were all three standing about ten yards in front of Frederica's house, and all three had their pistols drawn.

"How did you get here?" Matt asked.

Strayhorn chuckled. "Well, you know what they say, Jensen. You can't keep a good man down." Strayhorn looked at Layne and made a lateral motion with his pistol. "You," he ordered. "Get over there."

"Do it, Layne," Matt said. "I don't want you anywhere near me right now."

"Good thinking, Jensen, because we're about to shoot you dead," Strayhorn said. "Frederica, you whore!" Strayhorn called. "You come out here too. Do it now, or I'll kill this bitch where she stands!"

"No, Señor, don't shoot, I will come," Frederica said.

"Don't come out, Frederica!" Layne called. "He's going to shoot me whether you come out or not."

From behind him, Matt heard Frederica come out of the house. She moved over to join Layne.

"Now, Jensen, you—"

Whatever Strayhorn was about to say was interrupted by the roar of a shotgun. Strayhorn's face was turned to a bloody pulp by a load of double-aught buckshot.

Before Pauley or Murdoch could react, or even know

they were in danger, Matt's pistol was in his hand, and it barked twice. Both men went down with fatal wounds.

From behind him, Frederica's daughter, Maria, came out of the house, carrying a smoking shotgun. Walking over to Strayhorn's body she kicked him, then spit upon him.

"You will never rape a young girl again," she said.

Denver

Matt, Layne, and Governor Routt were having coffee and cake in the parlor of the governor's mansion.

"Another piece of cake, Matt?" the governor asked.

"Thank you, but no," Matt said. "The piece I had was very good, and very generous."

Governor Routt laughed. "That's my fault, I'm afraid. I have trained by kitchen staff not to be parsimonious when it comes to serving dessert. What about you, my dear? Would you like another piece?" the governor asked Layne.

"No, I couldn't eat another bite. Why, you've fed me so now that I won't need to eat a bite for the entire train trip back home."

"You are sure you don't want to use my private car?"

"No, thank you. I'll be just fine."

"Well, I can't say as I blame you," Governor Routt said. "Getting back on that car would have to bring up unpleasant memories for you. I'm so sorry that your visit with us had to wind up so disastrously."

"Nonsense, I loved my visit here," Layne said. "I met several wonderful friends, and it was very exciting." She laughed. "All right, maybe a little too exciting, but I will certainly have stories to tell for the rest of my life."

"You will at that, won't you?" the governor replied.

"Well, you will be pleased to know that I have sent some people into Dorena to run out the riffraff and to restore law and order to that town. It isn't right that an entire town should be stolen from the people as Dorena was."

"I'm glad," Layne said. "I'm so glad you paid the reward to Señora Arino," Layne said.

"She deserved it," Governor Routt said. He hugged his niece again. "And I'm thankful to Mr. Jensen for bringing you safely back to your family."

"I hope Frederica can make a new life for herself," Layne said.

"I believe she will," Matt said.

"I just wish Mabel had lived long enough to collect the reward as well. She and Frederica were very brave women."

"So was Maria," Matt said.

"Yes, so was Maria," Layne agreed. "It's just that I think of her as more of a little girl than a woman."

"She grew up," Matt said.

"I guess she did." Layne sighed, then looked at her uncle. "What's going to happen now to Mr. Highgate?"

"Mr. Highgate is going to spend a very long time in prison," Governor Routt said.

"The funny thing is, I believe him when he said that he didn't really want any harm to come to me. I believe him when he says he regrets his part in all this."

"Yes, well, he will have a long time to contemplate those regrets," the governor said.

The clock chimed two.

"Oh, heavens, it's two o'clock already," Layne said. "The train leaves at three. I had better get ready to go to the depot."

"I'll have the carriage brought around and go to the depot with you," the governor said.

"I had better get going as well," Matt said. "Miss McKenzie . . ." he began.

"Surely, you've earned the right to call me Layne by now," Layne told him.

Matt smiled and nodded. "Layne," he said. "You are a remarkable young lady. The boys and girls in your classroom will be very lucky to have someone like you as their teacher."

"Thank you, Matt," Layne said. She smiled. "Are we never to meet again?"

"I wouldn't say that," Matt said. "Never is a very long time."

Although he could have left Denver by train, Matt preferred to ride away on his new horse, a spitting image of Spirit, bought for him by the Denver and Rio Grande Railroad.

"I've given you a good name," Matt said, patting the animal on his neck. "It is a noble name, a name I hope you can live up to. I'm going to call you Spirit."

As the bustling city of Denver fell behind him, Matt studied the country before him. Somewhere, on the other side of the next range of hills, just over the horizon, there would be more towns to see, more world to explore.

It was already getting on into fall, and a chill wind blew down from the north. There would be snow in the higher elevations soon.

Maybe he would go south.

Turn the page for an exciting preview of

THUNDER OF EAGLES

by William W. Johnstone, with J. A. Johnstone

Coming in May 2008
Wherever Pinnacle Books are sold

Chapter One

Jefferson Tyree lay on top of a flat rock, looking back along the trail over which they had just come. He saw the single rider unerringly following them.

"Is he still there?" Luke Bacca asked.

"Yeah, he's still there," Tyree answered. Tyree was a short man, lean as rawhide with a thin face and a hawk-like nose.

Jefferson Tyree and Luke and John Bacca were on the run. Just over a week earlier, they had raided a ranch just outside MacCallister, Colorado. Waiting outside the house until sunup, they surprised the Poindexters at breakfast, killing Sam Poindexter and his sixteen-year-old son Mort. They also raped, then killed Poindexter's wife Edna.

They took particular pleasure in raping Poindexter's fifteen-year-old daughter Cindy, leaving her alive, though not through any act of compassion. They stabbed her, then rode off, leaving her lying in a pool of her own blood, thinking that she was dead.

Before they left the Poindexter ranch, they stole fifty head of prime beef and moved them up to the railhead at Platte Summit, where the cattle were sold at thirty dollars a head for shipment back East.

"Who'd you say that fella was that's trailin' us?" Luke asked.

"His name is MacCallister. Falcon MacCallister," Tyree said.

"Damn!" John Bacca said, his face showing his fright. "Are you sure it's Falcon MacCallister?"

Tyree got up from the rock, knocked the dust off his pants leg, then worked up a spit before he answered. "Yeah," he said. "I'm sure."

"Son of a bitch! Why did he get involved?"

"Who is Falcon MacCallister?" Luke asked.

"You mean you ain't never heard of him?" John asked.

"No."

"Well, that's 'cause you been in prison for the last ten years. But he's—"

"Nobody," Tyree interrupted. "He ain't nobody."

"The hell he ain't nobody. They write books about him, is all," John Bacca replied. "I don't think they'd be writin' books about nobody."

"They ain't real books," Tyree said. "They're dime novels. Hell, they make near 'bout all that stuff up."

"You ain't never had one wrote about you, have you?" John challenged.

"What are you, some kind of idiot?" Tyree challenged. "Why the hell would I want books wrote about me? I ain't exactly in the kind of business where it's good to have ever'body know who you are."

Luke pointed back down the trail. "This here MacCallister may be nobody, but I'll say this for the son of a bitch. Once he gets his teeth into you, he don't give up. We've tried ever' trick in the book to shake him off our tail, and he's still there."

Jefferson Tyree knew who Falcon MacCallister was, but what he did not realize was that the Poindexters had lived very close to Falcon MacCallister's ranch, which meant that Falcon considered them friends, as well as neighbors. And though Falcon was not a lawman or a bounty hunter, he'd taken a personal interest in this case. Having himself deputized, he'd made it his personal mission to track down the perpetrators.

"So, what are we goin' to do about that son of a bitch? We can't shake him off," John Bacca growled.

"We're goin' to kill 'im," Tyree said.

"All right. How are we goin' to do that?"

Tyree looked around. "We're goin' to ambush him," he said. He pointed to a draw that cut through the mountain range. "Let's go up through this draw; it's got two or three good places in there where we can hide. All we got to do is let him follow us in there, then ambush him."

"What if he don't come in?" John asked.

"He's after us, ain't he? He has to come in, or figure we went on out the other side."

"Tyree's right," Luke said. "Seems to me like the thing to do is just kill this MacCallister fella and get it over with."

"He ain't goin' to be that easy to kill," John protested.

"You think if we shoot him, the bullets will just bounce off of him?" Tyree asked.

"Well, no, but—"

"No, but nothin'," Tyree said, interrupting John. "Come on, I know a perfect spot."

* * *

The man called Falcon MacCallister stopped at the mouth of the canyon to take a drink from his canteen as he studied the terrain. Falcon had a weathered face and hair the color of dried oak. But it was his eyes that people noticed. Deeply lined from hard years, they opened onto a soul that was stoked by experiences that would fill the lifetimes of three men.

Falcon MacCallister had been here before, and he knew this would be a perfect spot to set up an ambush. The question is, did they do that, or did they go on through?

Pulling his long gun out of the saddle holster, Falcon started walking into the canyon, leading his horse. The horse's hooves fell sharply on the stone floor and echoed loudly back from the canyon walls. The canyon made a forty-five-degree turn to the left just in front of him, so he stopped. Right before he got to the turn, he slapped his horse on the rump and sent it on through.

The canyon exploded with the sound of gunfire as the outlaws opened up on what they thought would be their pursuer. Instead, their bullets whizzed harmlessly over the empty saddle of the riderless horse, raised sparks as they hit the rocky ground, then sped off into empty space, echoing and reechoing in a cacophony of whines and shrieks.

Falcon chuckled. "I guess that answers my question," he said aloud.

From his position just around the corner from the turn, Falcon located two of his ambushers. They were about a third of the way up the north wall of the canyon, squeezed in between the wall itself and a rock outcropping that provided them with a natural cover. Or, so they thought.

The firing stopped and, after a few seconds of dying echoes, the canyon grew silent.

"Tyree, do you see him? Where the hell is he?" one of the ambushers yelled, and Falcon could hear the last two words repeated in echo down through the canyon: ". . . *is he, is he, is he?*"

Falcon studied the rock face of the wall just behind the spot where he had located two of the ambushers; then he began firing. His rifle boomed loudly, the thunder of the detonating cartridges picking up resonance through the canyon and doubling and redoubling in intensity. Falcon wasn't even trying to aim at the two men, but was instead taking advantage of the position in which they had placed themselves. He fired several rounds, knowing that the bullets were splattering against the rock wall behind the two men, fragmenting into whizzing, flying missiles. It had the effect that he wanted, because the two men who had thought they had the perfect cover were exposed. Yelling and cursing, they began firing at Falcon.

It took but two more shots from Falcon to silence both of them.

For a long moment, the canyon was in silence.

"Luke, John?" Tyree called.

"They're dead, Tyree," Falcon replied. "Both of them."

Tyree's voice had come from the other side of the narrow draw, halfway up on the opposite wall.

"How do you know they're dead?"

"Because I killed them," Falcon said. "Just like I aim to kill you."

"The hell you say," Tyree replied.

Falcon changed positions, then searched the opposite canyon wall. There was silence for a long time; then, as he knew he would, Tyree popped up to have a look around.

"Tyree," Falcon shouted. And the echo repeated the names. *"Tyree, Tyree, Tyree."*

"What do you want? . . . *want, want, want?"*

"I want you to throw your gun down and give yourself up," Falcon said.

"Why should I do that?"

For his answer, Falcon raised his rifle and shot at the wall just behind Tyree, creating the same effect he had with the Bacca brothers. The only difference was that he shot only one round, but he placed it accurately enough to give a demonstration of what he could do.

"Son of a bitch!" Tyree shouted.

"I can take you out of there if I need to," Falcon said.

"How the hell did you know who we are?" Tyree asked.

"Hell, the whole country knows who you are!" Falcon replied. "You don't have anywhere to go."

Falcon was bluffing. All the time he had been trailing them, he had not known who they were. The names Tyree, John, and Luke he had gotten from the men yelling at each other across the canyon.

"Come on down, Tyree," Falcon said. "I don't want to have to kill you."

"You go to hell," Tyree shouted back down. The echo said, *". . . hell, hell, hell!"*

Falcon waited a few minutes, then he fired a second time. The boom sounded like a cannon blast, and he heard the scream of the bullet, followed once more by a curse.

"By now you've probably figured out that I can make it pretty hot for you up there," Falcon said. "If I shoot again, I'm going to put them where they can do the most damage. You've got five seconds to give yourselves up or die."

Falcon raised his rifle.

"No, wait! . . . *wait, wait, wait!*" The terrified word echoed through the canyon. "I'm comin' down! . . . *down, down, down!*"

"Throw your weapons down first."

Falcon saw a hand appear; then a pistol and rifle started tumbling down the side of the canyon, rattling and clattering until they reached the canyon floor.

"Put your hands up, then step out where I can see you," Falcon ordered.

Moving hesitantly, Tyree edged out from behind the rocky slab where he had taken cover. He was holding his hands over his head.

"Come on down here," Falcon invited.

Stepping gingerly, Tyree came down the wall until, a moment later, he was standing in front of Falcon. Falcon handcuffed him.

"What are you takin' me?" Tyree asked.

"I'm going to take you back to MacCallister to stand trial," Falcon explained.

Two weeks later

The trial of Jefferson Tyree started at nine in the morning, and by lunchtime was over but for the closing arguments. Court recessed for lunch, but by one o'clock everyone was back in place, awaiting the closing arguments.

There was a constant buzz among the spectators in the gallery, but it stilled when the bailiff came into the room.

"Oyez, oyez, oyez, this court in and for the county of

Eagle is now in session, the Honorable Thomas Kuntz presiding," the bailiff called.

Wearing a black robe, Judge Thomas Kuntz entered the courtroom from a door in front, stood behind the bench for a moment, then sat down.

"Be seated," he said.

Kuntz picked up a gavel and banged it once. "This court is now in session. Mr. Bailiff, if you would, please, bring the jury into the courtroom."

The bailiff left the room for a moment, then returned, leading the twelve men who were serving on the jury. They were a disparate group consisting of cowboys, farmers, store clerks, draymen, and businessmen. Quietly, they took their seats.

"Counsel for defense may now present closing arguments," Kuntz said.

Tony Norton, the court-appointed attorney for Tyree, stood and looked at the jury for a moment before he approached the jury box.

"Gentlemen of the jury," he said. "Mine is a very difficult task. I am duty bound to provide Mr. Tyree with the best defense I possibly can." He looked back at Tyree. "It is difficult because Tyree is not a man whose character I can defend. Therefore, I will make no attempt to defend him by his character, but I can, and I will, defend him by the law.

"In order to find Jefferson Tyree guilty of the heinous crime of murdering the Poindexter family, you must be convinced, beyond the shadow of a doubt, that he did it." Norton looked over at Tyree.

"And while every instinct in your gut may tell you he is guilty, this is the United States of America. And in

America, we do not find guilt by gut instinct. We find guilt by evidence, and by eyewitness accounts.

"Gentlemen, the only evidence we have that connects Tyree with the Poindexter ranch is the fact that he sold fifty head of Poindexter's cattle. He could have stolen those cattle from some remote corner of the Poindexter ranch without ever setting foot in the house, or even seeing any member of the family. Because the truth is, we have no physical evidence to put him in the Poindexter family home on that fateful day, and we have no witnesses who have testified that they saw him there.

"The prosecution," he said, looking toward the prosecutor's table, "has told us that young Cindy Poindexter lived long enough to give a description of the three men who attacked her family. One of the men she described as being short."

Norton looked over at Tyree. "Mr. Tyree is short. But so are you, Mr. Blanton. And you, Mr. Dempster." He was specifically referring to two of the men who were seated in the jury box. "And so are you, sir," he said to a man in the gallery, "and, if you will excuse me, so is His Honor the Judge.

"She also said that he had a big nose." Norton pointed toward the prosecutor. "So does Mr. Crader. For that matter, so do I." Norton rubbed his own nose.

"Tragically, young Cindy Poindexter died of her wounds, so she is not here to be able to provide direct eyewitness testimony. And without any physical evidence, and without eyewitness testimony, you cannot, by law, find my client, Mr. Tyree, guilty of murder."

The prosecutor stood up then and stared for a long, pointed moment at Tyree. He stared for so long that the judge cleared his throat.

"Mr. Crader, are you going to honor us with your closing? Or must we somehow discern what you plan to say?" Judge Kuntz asked.

"Sorry, Your Honor," Crader replied. He stepped over to the jury box, standing exactly where Norton had been standing but a few moments before.

"Tragically, young Cindy Poindexter died of her wounds," Crader began. "These are the exact words that Mr. Norton used in his defense of this murderer. Tragically, she died, so she is not here to provide direct eyewitness testimony.

"Gentlemen, Cindy may not be here in person, but she is here in spirit. With her dying breath, she gave the sheriff a description of the short, big-nosed man who seemed to be the leader. Tyree is a short, big-nosed man.

"'There were three of them,' Cindy said. And when Mr. MacCallister tracked Tyree down, there were three of them.

"I remind you also that Jefferson Tyree and two other men sold fifty head of cattle that bore the Poindexter brand. Perhaps this is circumstantial, and not direct physical evidence, but if you put the circumstantial evidence with the gut feeling that you know Tyree is guilty, you will not let young Cindy Poindexter's last desperate attempt to bring about justice be unrewarded. Bring in the verdict that will allow the souls of Cindy and her family to rest in peace. Bring in the verdict that will allow us to hang this monster."

"Damn right!" someone said from the gallery.

"Hang the son of a bitch!" another added.

Judge Kuntz brought his gavel down sharply. "Order," he said.

Having finished his closing, and with the case

now presented, the judge released the jury for their deliberation.

They were back within an hour.

"Mr. Foreman, has the jury reached a verdict?" Judge Kuntz asked the foreman.

"We have, Your Honor."

Kuntz turned toward the defense table. "Would the defendant and attorney please stand?"

Norton and Tyree stood.

Kuntz turned back toward the foreman of the jury.

"Publish the verdict, Mr. Foreman."

"Your Honor, on the first charge, the murder of the Poindexters in the first degree, we, the jury, find the defendant, Jefferson Tyree . . ." The foreman made a long, direct pause before he finished. "Not guilty."

"What?" someone in the courtroom shouted.

"No! This is a travesty!" another yelled.

The entire courtroom broke out into shouts of derision and disapproval.

"Order!" Kuntz said as he repeatedly banged his gavel. "Order!"

He banged the gavel repeatedly.

"I will have order now, or I will clear this court!" he said.

Finally, the court grew quiet, and Kuntz looked toward the foreman.

"As to the second charge of cattle rustling, how do you find?"

"Your Honor, on the charge of cattle rustling, we find the defendant, Jefferson Tyree, guilty as charged."

"Thank you, Mr. Foreman. Would the defendant please stand?"

At Norton's urging, Tyree stood.

"Mr. Tyree. I can understand the jury's inability to find you guilty of murder due to lack of evidence or the sworn testimony of an eyewitness. Therefore, I cannot sentence you to hang."

Tyree smiled broadly.

"Before you get too happy, Mr. Tryee, let me tell you what I am going to do. I am going to sentence you to life in prison."

"What? For stealing a few cows? You can't do that," Tyree complained.

"That's where you are quite wrong, Mr. Tyree. I can, and I just did," Judge Kuntz said.

Chapter Two

One year later

When Kyle Pollard came on duty as a guard at the maximum security blockhouse of the State Prison at Canon City, Colorado, he settled back in his chair, tipped it against the wall, and picked up the notes that had been left by the previous guard.

"Jefferson Tyree is to go to the dispensary at two-thirty today."

Pollard drummed his fingers on the desk for a moment, then let out a long breath.

"Hey, you, Pollard," one of the prisoners called.

"What do you want?" Pollard called back.

"Is it true Tyree is gettin' out of here?"

"What?"

"Tyree is saying that his sentence has been commuted by the governor. He says he's gettin' out of here today."

"Tyree is full of it," Pollard said. "He's not getting out of here today, or any day, until the day he dies."

"Yeah, well, I didn't think so. But I just thought you'd like to know what he's tellin' everyone."

"So, you've told me."

"Is that worth a chaw of terbaccy?"

Pollard chuckled. "Simmons, you sure you didn't make all this up just to get a little tobacco?"

"No, sir, I didn't make none of it up," Simmons said. "He tole me that he's gettin' out of prison today. He says that's why he's goin' to the dispensary. He says the state needs to show that he wasn't sick or nothin' when they let him go."

"It's nothing of the kind," Pollard replied. "He's goin' to the dispensary to be checked out for cooties, same as ever'one else in the prison."

"I'm just tellin' you what he's tellin' ever'one is all," Simmons said.

"Well, that's not worth anything," Pollard said. "But I do like you keeping me up with what's goin' on, so I guess it's worth a chew."

Pollard opened the outer gate, then stepped up to Simmons's cell to pass a twist of chewing tobacco through the bars.

"Thanks," Simmons said.

Pollard then walked up and down the length of the corridor looking into all the cells. When he reached Tyree's cell about five minutes before he was due at the dispensary, he saw that the prisoner was lying on his bunk with his hands laced behind his head.

"Are you ready to go?" he asked.

"What's there to getting ready?" Tyree replied. "What am I supposed to do, get all the cooties lined up for the doc?" Tyree laughed at his own joke.

"What's this I hear about you telling people you're going to be getting out today?"

Tyree chuckled. "Some folks will believe anything," he

said. "Don't tell me. Simmons reported it to you and you paid him off with some tobacco. Am I right?"

Pollard chuckled as well. "Yeah, I gave him a small twist."

Tyree shook his head. "I can't believe you were dumb enough to fall for that. But then, you are dumb enough to have a job like this, so, I guess it isn't all that hard to believe."

"I'm dumb?" Pollard said. "In a couple of hours, I'll be home with the wife and kids. You'll still be here." Pollard sniggered. "In fact, you'll be for the rest of your life."

The smile left Tyree's face. "So they say," he said.

"So they say," Pollard said with a snort. "You damn right, so they say." He started to unlock the cell, then stopped and looked over at Tyree. "Get up. You know the procedure," he said.

Tyree was well acquainted with the procedure. He had already been in prison for a year, and this wasn't the first time he had ever been incarcerated.

"Come on, Tyree, I'm waiting," Pollard said again, more impatiently than before.

"Yeah, keep your shirt on. I'm movin' as fast as I can," Tyree grunted.

Tyree got out of his bunk, then leaned against the wall. Pollard stepped into the cell then, and cuffed Tyree's hands behind his back. The cuffs were held together with a twelve-inch length of chain.

"All right, Tyree, let's go," Pollard said. "You lead the way, you know where the dispensary is." He pushed Tyree roughly to get him started.

"I'm goin', I'm goin', ain't no need to be a'pushin' me like that."

"Come on, let's go." He jabbed Tyree with his nightstick

again, this time in the small of the back, hard enough to make the killer gasp.

"That hurt."

"Did it now?" Pollard taunted.

They left the cell block and stepped out into the yard. Because of the heat of the day, the yard was empty, and as Tyree checked each of the guard towers, he noticed that none of the guards were looking inward; they were all looking out, away from the prison. Just in front of them, Tyree saw a wagon sitting outside the prison commissary. It had just made the two-thirty delivery. Tyree was expecting to see it—in fact, that was why he arranged to have his nine o'clock appointment traded with one of the other prisoners.

Suddenly Tyree stopped and stooped down.

"What are you doing?" Pollard asked. "Stand up."

"I've got a rock in my shoe," Pollard said.

"Just leave it, you don't have far to go."

"It hurts," Tyree complained. "It'll just take a second to get it out."

"All right, but hurry it up," Pollard said.

"Look up there at the wall. What the hell is Cooper doing, pissing off the wall like that?" Tyree asked. "This may be a prison, but we have to live here, and I don't like it when a guard steps out of the tower and pisses in our yard like that."

"What are you talking about?" Pollard asked, looking toward the wall. "I don't see anybody—unnhg!"

While squatted down on the ground, Tyree had stepped back over the length of chain in order to get his handcuffed hands in front of him. Then, before Pollard knew what was happening, Tyree used the length of chain as a club to knock the guard down.

Tyree fell upon Pollard, hitting him with the chain several more times, until he was sure the man was dead. Quickly, he got the keys and released the handcuffs. Then he dragged Pollard's body over to the well and dropped him down into it. After that, he climbed into the delivery wagon and hid himself under a roll of canvas.

A moment later, the driver and one of the cooks came out of the prison commissary.

"I won't be makin' the delivery next week," the driver said. "I'm goin' down to Yorkville to visit my daughter. She just had a baby."

"Just had a baby, did she? Was it a boy or a girl?" the cook asked.

"Boy."

"Ha! Knowin' you, you'll have him out huntin' with you in a couple of years."

"I may not wait that long," the wagon driver said, and both laughed.

Tyree felt the wagon sag as the driver climbed into the seat, then pulled away from the commissary. The driver stopped at the gate, and Tyree grew tense. This was the critical moment.

"Open up!" the driver shouted. "I just came to deliver groceries, I don't plan to stay here all day."

"Make you nervous, does it, Zeb?" one of the guards called down from the tower. "'Fraid we might keep you in here for a while?"

"Just open the damn door, will you? This place gives me the willies."

"What do you think, Paul? You think we should go down and check it out?" the guard who had been talking to Zeb asked the other.

"Nah, no need to do that," Paul replied. "I can see the wagon from up here. Ain't nothin' in it but a tarp roll. Let 'im out, Clay."

Clay pulled the lever to unlock the gate. "See you on Friday, Zeb," Clay shouted down to him.

Zeb gave the guards a little wave, then drove on through.

Tyree lay very still as the wagon passed through the gate, then proceeded up the road. He counted to one hundred, then very carefully lifted the tarp and looked around. They were on First Street, having just crossed over the railroad. Tyree slipped out from under the tarp and, without being noticed, let himself down from the back of the wagon. He moved quickly off the road into a little stand of trees, and down to the banks of the Arkansas River. He continued along the river, following it west, eventually breaking into an easy, ground-covering lope.

Many escapees, Tyree knew, were recaptured almost immediately, because they really didn't know where they were going. Tyree was different; he knew exactly where he was going. He had planned it all out well in advance. He knew that there was a ranch house just over three miles from the prison. Tyree had seen it when the barred wagon that transported prisoners had brought him to the prison. When Tyree and five other prisoners were transferred to the State Penitentiary, they had been sitting in the back of the wagon, chained to a steel rod that ran the length of the floor. The others were badly dispirited, and they kept their heads down in defeat and disgrace.

Tyree was still defiant, and he studied the area around the prison, already making plans for an opportunity like the one he had seized today. Even then, he had noticed the small ranch and the stable of horses.

And yet, a horse and freedom wouldn't satisfy Tyree's most burning need. That need wouldn't be completely satisfied until he settled a score with the man who sent him up in the first place.

"Mr. Falcon MacCallister," Tyree said quietly. "I'm comin' after you."

Ten miles west of Canon City, Jefferson Tyree saw a rambling, unpainted wooden structure that stretched and leaned and bulged and sagged until it looked as if the slightest puff of wind might blow it down. A crudely lettered sign nailed to one of the porch supports read: FOOD, DRINK, GOODS.

There were no horses tied up outside, which was good. Tyree planned to pick up a few dollars here, and the fewer people in the building, the better it would be.

The interior of the store was a study of shadow and light. Some of the light came through the door, and some came through windows that were nearly opaque with dirt. Most of it, however, was in the form of gleaming dust motes that hung suspended in the still air, illuminated by the bars of sunbeams that stabbed through the cracks between the boards.

There were only two people in the building, a man and woman. The man was behind a counter, the woman was sweeping the floor.

"This your store?" Tyree asked.

"Yes, sir, it is," the man behind the counter replied. "It may not look like much, but it keeps the wife and me workin'. Don't it, dear?"

"Keeps one of us workin' anyway," the woman replied as she continued to sweep the floor.

The man laughed. "The wife has a good sense of humor," he said to Tyree. "Yes, sir, if you can't find a woman that's rich or pretty, then the next best thing is to find one with a sense of humor." He laughed out loud at his own joke. "Now, what can I do for you?"

"You got any pistols?"

"Yes, sir, I do," the clerk said. "I've got a dandy collection of pistols; Smith and Wessons, Colts, Remingtons. Just take a look here."

"I'll need ammunition as well," Tyree said.

The proprietor laughed. "My, you aren't prepared at all, are you?" he said. "Well, before I can sell you any ammunition, I'll need to know what sort of pistol you are going to be buying."

"Tell me about this one," Tyree said, picking up one of the pistols.

"Yes, sir, that's one of our finest," the proprietor said. "It is a Colt single-action, six-shot, solid-frame revolver."

"Solid-frame? What does that mean?"

"It means that the frame doesn't break down to load it. The cylinder is loaded by single rounds. See, you've got a loading gate, located at the right side of the frame. Then, the empty cases are ejected one by one, through the opened loading gate, by pulling back on the ejector rod located under the barrel and to the right."

"What is this, a .45?"

"It's a .44, sir."

Tyree shook his head. "I'm not very good with a gun, I don't know much about them. You'll have to show me how to load it."

"It's very simple, sir," the proprietor said. He took a couple of cartridges from the box and handed them to Tyree. "Open the side gate there."

"It won't open," Tyree said.

"Oh, I forgot to tell you. The gun can be loaded and unloaded only when the hammer is set to half-cock position, like so."

The proprietor set the hammer, then watched as Tyree slipped two rounds into the cylinder.

"Very good, sir," the proprietor said. "Now, will there be anything else?"

Tyree pointed to the black metal cash drawer that set on the counter. "Yes. You can open that cash drawer for me," he said.

"I beg your pardon?" the proprietor said, shocked by the unexpected turn of events.

"I said, open the cash drawer for me," Tyree repeated. "And give me all your money."

Suddenly, and unexpectedly, Tyree felt a blow on the back of his head. The blow knocked him down, but not out, and looking up, he saw the proprietor's wife holding the broom handle.

"You crazy bitch!" Tyree shouted. He shot her, and saw the look of surprise on her face as the bullet plunged into her heart.

"Suzie!" the proprietor shouted.

Tyree shot him as well, then got up from the floor and dusted himself off. Almost casually, he finished loading the pistol, then, moving around the store, he began collecting supplies: a belt and holster, a couple of new shirts, some coffee, bacon, beans, and a hat. After that, he cleaned out the cash drawer, finding a total of sixty-two dollars and fifty-one cents.

Turning southwest, Tyree rode hard for two days, avoiding towns until he reached Badito. Badito was little more than a flyblown speck on the wide-open range. He chose it because it had no railroad and he saw no telegraph wires leading into it, which meant they had probably not heard of his escape yet. Stopping in front of the Bull's Head Saloon, Tyree went inside and ordered a beer. It was his first beer in over a year.

Shortly after Tyree arrived, a young man stopped in front of the Bull's Head. Going inside, he stepped up to the bar. The saloon was relatively quiet, with only four men at one table and a fifth standing down at the far end of the bar. The four at the table were playing cards; the one at the end of the bar was nursing a drink. The man nursing the drink was a fairly small man with dark hair, dark, beady eyes, a narrow mouth, and a nose shaped somewhat like a hawk's beak. He looked up as the young man entered, but turned his attention back to the beer in front of him.

"What'll it be?" the bartender asked.

"Beer."

"A beer it is," the bartender replied. He turned to draw the beer.

"Make it two beers."

The bartender laughed. "You sound like you've worked yourself up quite a thirst."

"Yes, sir, I reckon I have. I went down into New Mexico to have a look around."

"Did you now?" the bartender replied as he put the beers on the bar before the young man. "See anything interesting down there?"

"A lot of desert. It's good to be back to land that can be farmed."

"You like farmin', do you?" the bartender asked.

"Yes, sir, I do. My pa's a farmer, and I was raised on a farm."

"I know some farmers. What's you pa's name?"

"My pa's name is Carter Manning."

"Hmm, I don't know think I know him."

"We live up in a place called Hancock," Manning said. "Well, we don't actually live there. Like I say, we live on a farm outside Hancock. But we get our mail at the Hancock post office."

"I was wonderin' why you smelled like pig shit," Tyree said without looking up from his beer.

"I beg your pardon sir," Manning said. "What did you just say?"

"I said you smelled like pig shit," Tyree said. "You and your old man. As far as I'm concerned, all farmers smell like pig shit."

"I won't hold that against you, 'cause I reckon you are just trying to make a joke," Manning said. "But I don't mind tellin' you, mister, I don't see anything funny about it."

"Well, that's good, 'cause I don't mean it as a joke. You smell like pig shit, just like all the rest of the farmers in the world."

"Mister, looks to me like we're getting off on the wrong foot here. Let me see if I can't change your mind. My name's Manning, John Nathan Manning, and here's to you, Mister . . ."

"My name is MacCallister, Falcon MacCallister," Tyree said. "And I'd sooner drink horse piss than drink with a farmer."

"Falcon MacCallister? You're Falcon Mac-Callister?"

"That's what I said."

"I—I've never met Falcon MacCallister, but I've certainly heard a lot about him. If you are MacCallister, you are very different from anything I've ever heard."

"Boy, that sounds like you're callin' me a liar," Tyree said.

Using the back of his hand, Manning wiped beer foam from his mouth. It was obvious that Tyree had irritated him, and for the briefest of moments, that irritation reflected in his face. But he put it aside, then forced a smile.

"Hell, Mr. MacCallister, if you don't want to drink with me, that's fine. You're the one that butted into this conversation, so why don't we just each one of us mind our own business? I'll keep quiet, and you do the same."

"So now, you not only call me a liar, you tell me to shut up," Tyree said.

"What's the matter with you, mister?" Manning asked, bristling now at the man's comment. "Are you aching for a fight or something? Because if you are, I'll be happy to oblige."

"Easy, son," the bartender said, reaching across the bar to put his hand on Manning's arm. "There's something about this that ain't goin' down right."

Manning continued to stare at Tyree, his anger showing clearly in his face. By contrast, the expression on Tyree's face had not changed.

"I just don't like being insulted by some sawed-off runt of a man who doesn't know when to keep his mouth shut," Manning said. "And I don't care if he's the famous Falcon MacCallister or not."

"Let it go," the bartender said.

"Yeah, sonny, let it go, before you get so scared you piss in your pants," Tyree taunted.

"That's it, mister! I'm going to mop the floor with your sorry hide!" Manning said. He put up his fists.

Tyree smiled, a smile without mirth. "If we're going to

fight, why don't we make it permanent?" he asked. He stepped away from the bar, then turned, exposing a pistol that he wore low and kicked out, in the way of a gunfighter.

"Hold on there, mister," the bartender said to Tyree. "There's no need to carry this any further."

"Yeah, there is," Tyree said. "This young fella here has brought me to the ball, and now I reckon he owes me a dance."

Manning suddenly realized that he had been suckered into this, and he stopped, then opened his fists and held his hands palm-out in front of him.

"Why are you pushing this?" he asked. "What do you want?"

"I want to settle this little dispute between us permanently," Tyree said.

"No, there's no need for all this. This little disagreement isn't worth either one of us dying over."

"Oh, it won't be *either* of us, sonny. It'll just be you dyin'," Tyree said.

"I'm not a gunfighter, mister. I don't have any intention of drawing on you. If you shoot me, you are going to have to shoot me in cold blood and in front of these witnesses."

"What witnesses?" Tyree asked, looking toward the table where the cardplayers had interrupted their game to watch the unfolding drama. "I don't see any witnesses."

Taking their cue, all four men got up from the table, two of them standing so quickly that their chairs fell over. The chairs struck the floor with two pops as loud as gunshots, and Manning jumped. The four cardplayers hurried out the front door.

Tyree turned toward the bartender. "You plannin' on takin' part in this?" he asked.

"Don't do this, mister," the bartender said. "The boy didn't mean nothin'."

"Either get a gun and take part in this, or go outside with the others," Tyree ordered.

A line of perspiration beads broke out on the bartender's upper lip. He looked over at Manning with an expression of pity in his face.

"I'm sorry, boy," he said. "I—I . . ." He couldn't finish.

"Go ahead, Mr. Bartender," Manning said, his voice tight with fear. "I'm just sorry I got you into this. I know this ain't your fight."

The bartender remained a second longer, then, with a sigh, headed for the door.

The saloon was now empty except for Manning and Tyree. Manning's knees grew so weak that he could barely stand, and he felt nauseous.

"Anytime, sonny," Tyree said with an evil smile.

Suddenly, Manning made a ragged, desperate grab for his pistol. He cleared the holster with it, then, as if changing his mind in the middle, he turned and tried to run, doing so just as Tyree fired. As a result, Tyree's bullet struck Manning in the back. Manning went down, took a few ragged gasps, and then died.

Tyree finished his drink, then walked over to look down at Manning's body.

"Son of a bitch, boy," he said. "You made Falcon MacCallister shoot you in the back. Wonder what your pa will think of that?"

Tyree was laughing as he walked by the saloon patrons and bartender, who were gathered just outside.

"I've heard of Falcon MacCallister," someone said as

they watched Tyree ride off. "Never knew he was an evil son of bitch."

"That wasn't Falcon MacCallister, you damn fool," the bartender said. "That was Jefferson Tyree."

A few days later, and from another town, Tyree posted a letter.

Carter Manning
General Delivery
Hancock, Colorado

Dear Mr. Manning,
   I don't know if nobody has told you this yet but your boy has been kilt. I seen it happen and can tell you that it was Falcon MacCallister what shot him in the back.

                    Jefferson Tyree

Chapter Three

Pueblo, Colorado

Rachael Kirby played the opening bars of the music as the curtain opened on stage. There, on stage, were Hugh and Mary Buffington, members of the troupe from the J. Garon production of the play *Squatter Sovereignty*.

When they first appeared on stage, the audience saw nothing unusual. The two moved around from one side of the stage to the other, as if searching for something, and Rachael played the music to accompany their movement.

Then, with a crashing piano crescendo, Hugh turned, so that the audience could see his back.

Hanging from his back was a fish.

The audience roared with laughter.

Hugh reacted as if he had no idea what the audience was laughing at, and he kept whirling about, looking behind him, but of course, as the fish was attached to his back, he never saw it.

Rachael kept time with the antics on stage, the piano music adding to the comedy.

Finally, Hugh reached over his shoulder and, finding

the fish, unhooked it and brought it around so he could see it. He gasped, and opened his mouth and eyes wide as he looked at the fish.

Again, the piano music reflected his reaction.

HUGH: By heavens, that's a *haddock*.

MARY: 'Tis, and was hanging to a *sucker*.

The crowd exploded with laughter.

HUGH: You're only *codding* me.

More laughter.

MARY: What *eels* you?

By now, the laughter was nonstop.

HUGH: I've *smelt* that before.

The crowd's laughter was so loud that for the moment, Rachael had to quit playing the piano.

Throwing the fish into the wings of the stage, Hugh and Mary looped their arms together and marched about singing:

> If you want for information
> Or in need of merriment,
> Come over with me socially
> To Murphy's tenement.
> He owns a row of houses
> In the first ward, near the dock,
> Where Ireland's represented
> By the babies on our block.

Rachael accompanied every act and every song, even playing while the curtain was drawn between acts. Most of her music was light, but as a finale to each show, she would play a piece from one of the old established composers, such as Bach, Beethoven, Vivaldi, or Chopin.

Such music was not foreign to Rachael, who was a classically trained pianist. She had performed on concert stages in New York, Boston, and Philadelphia, as well as in opera houses in London, Paris, and Berlin.

The conclusion of her number was met with thunderous applause, which intensified, and was accompanied by shouts of "Huzzah" when the curtains parted for the final bows of the theater group.

Rachael continued to play until the theater emptied. Then, as a couple of theater employees went around extinguishing the gas lanterns, Rachael gathered her music and went backstage to join the others.

It was always an exciting time after a show, with the energy high and the performers teasing each other over the slightest gaff. Also, after every evening performance, the troupe would go out for a late dinner.

But when Rachael went backstage she found, not the merriment and excitement she expected, but angry expressions and harsh words.

"What is it?" she asked, puzzled the reaction of the players. "What's going on?"

"J. Garon, that's what's going on," Hugh said.

"What about Mr. Garon? Where is he?"

"That's what we'd like to know," Mary said.

"The son of a bitch has absconded with the money," Hugh said.

"You mean tonight's take?"

Hugh shook his head. "No. I mean *all* the money. Everything we've taken in since we started this tour."

"What's worse, he has stuck us with the bill that is due for this theater this week," Mary said.

"Yes, we owe the theater owner two hundred fifty dollars," Hugh explained.

"We owe it? How could we owe it? Garon is the troupe manager."

"Garon's not here and we are," Hugh explained. "The theater manager has already let us know that either we pay what we owe, or he'll take legal action against us."

"Can we come up with two hundred fifty dollars?"

"How much money do you have?" Hugh asked.

"About fifty dollars," Rachael said.

"We can come close."

"But that fifty is all I have. If Garon is gone and we are on our own, I'll need money to live."

"We're all in the same boat, my dear," one of the other players said.

"Maybe we can do another performance tomorrow night," Rachael suggested. "Surely, one more performance will make enough money to get us out of this."

Hugh shook his head. "We've already approached the theater manager with that proposal," he said. "But he has the theater all booked. There's nothing we can do."

"At least, our hotel bill is paid for one more night," Mary said.

"And we have train tickets that will take us back to New York," Hugh said.

"But not enough money to eat on the train," another added. "It's going to be a long, hungry trip."

"The way I see it, we have no choice," Hugh said. "We have to go back to New York."

"I'm not going back," Rachael said, surprising the others.

"What do you mean, you aren't going back?" Hugh

asked, surprised by her statement. "Surely, you don't intend to stay out here in this—this godforsaken West, do you? Don't you want to go back to New York?"

"No, why should I go back?" Rachael replied. "There's nothing for me back there."

"Rachael, it is ridiculous for you to let Edwin Mathias ruin your whole life," Hugh said.

"Hugh," Mary scolded.

"Oh," Hugh said. "Look, I'm sorry, I shouldn't have—"

"Don't worry about it," Rachael said. "I know you are just trying to be helpful."

They debated as to whether they should have dinner at their usual place that night, or save what little money they had in order to get back home. In the end, they decided they would have dinner.

"We may as well have one last dinner together," Hugh said. "For who knows when we will eat again."

"That's Hugh for you," one of the others said. "Laughing as we pass through the graveyard."

The others laughed.

Although the dinner could have been a somber affair, the members of the stranded troupe laughed, and exchanged stories in spite of, or perhaps because of, their situation.

Afterward, Rachael went up to her room at the hotel, then lay in bed, staring up at the darkness. She had very little money, no job, no prospects, and no contacts in the West. But she also had no intention of going back East. Her situation was bleak at best, and a lesser person might have cried.

Rachael refused to let herself cry. She had been through a worse situation than this. She had been through Edwin Mathias.

New York, two years earlier

Unable to sleep after her first performance of the season, Rachael Kirby waited until she was sure that the morning paper was out. Getting out of bed, she went downstairs, and out onto Fourth Avenue to wait by the newsstand until the vendor arrived with a large packet of today's newspapers.

"Good morning, miss," the vendor said.

"Is that today's paper?" Rachael asked.

The vendor chuckled. "It is indeed. Hot off the press, miss," he said. "It's five o'clock in the morning. There must be a story you really want to see."

"The reviews," Rachael said.

"Ahh, the reviews, yes, I understand. You are an actress, are you?"

"I am a musician, and I did my opening show of the season last night," Rachael said, handing the vendor two cents.

"I hope it is a good review for you then, miss," the vendor said as he gave her a folded issue of the paper.

Rachael took the paper over to the corner and stood under the greenish cast from the gaslight in order to read the review.

Beautiful Chamber Music

Mr. Edwin Mathias, Miss Rachael Kirby
Thrill Audience at the Stuyvesant Theater

The opportunities to hear chamber music under satisfying conditions in New York are not frequent, and therefore it is a pleasure to record that Mr. Edwin Mathias and Miss Rachael Kirby gave a violin and piano sonata recital in the first of what is planned to be many performances for the season.

If last night's performance is any indication, they are assured of a very successful season. The performance was in the Stuyvesant Theater, a perfectly excellent auditorium for chamber music. The feeling is the same as if one is in a drawing room.

The additional fact that Mr. Mathias and Miss Kirby are engaged to be married gave the occasion even more of an air of intimacy.

The programme included Brahms' Sonata in A Major, Beethoven's Sonata in G Minor, and a delightful piece by Chopin. Never was music more beautifully played than by these two wonderful musicians.

"Oh, this is wonderful!" Rachael said aloud.

"I beg your pardon?" the vendor said.

Rachael chuckled. "I'm sorry," she said. "I didn't realize that I had spoken aloud."

Clutching the newspaper tightly, Rachael hurried to Edwin's apartment.

Should she wake him up to share the news? They were both worried about how their concert would be received, being as they were only two people playing music that normally was performed by full orchestras. In fact, some of their closest friends told them they were taking an enormous risk.

But Rachael and Edwin had put together a schedule hoping for a successful season that would then give them the opportunity to be married. Then, they would go to Europe to play there.

They had each played in Europe before, but always as part of some larger ensemble, never as individuals, and never together. The idea that they could go to Europe as man and wife would be a dream come true. In fact, there were some who said that a marriage between Rachael and Edwin was ordained in heaven.

Rachael went up the stairs to Edwin's third floor walk-up. She started to knock on the door, but feared that if she knocked loudly enough to awaken Edwin, she might also awaken his neighbors. She not only did not want to be rude enough to awaken his neighbors, she also didn't want his neighbors knowing that she was here at this hour, as it might cause talk.

Suddenly, she got an idea. She would cook breakfast for him. She knew where he hid the extra key and, taking it, she went inside to Edwin's small kitchen. She opened the door to the icebox and took out a slab of bacon and some eggs.

The bacon was snapping and twitching in the pan, permeating the apartment with its rich aroma, when she heard Edwin behind her.

"Rachael, what are you doing here?" Edwin asked.

"Isn't it obvious, silly? I'm cooking breakfast," Rachael said, stepping over to kiss him. She intended to kiss him on the lips, but at the last minute he turned his head, so that she wound up kissing him on the cheek, feeling the stubble of a morning beard against her lips.

"But this is my apartment," Edwin said. "What are you doing here?"

"I told you, I'm cooking breakfast. I couldn't wait. Look!" she said, holding up the newspaper opened to the review page. "We got a wonderful write up! Our season is made, Edwin! It's made! Why, we may not even have to wait until the end of the season to get married. Isn't that wonderful?"

"Edwin, what's going on? Who are you talking to?" a woman's voice asked. The voice was followed by the appearance of a very pretty, and very scantily clad, woman. "Oh, I know you," she said, smiling as she saw Rachael. "You were on the stage with Edwin last night. You were wonderful!"

Rachael was too struck to respond. Instead, she just stared at the young woman.

"Of course you wouldn't remember me, but I was sitting in the front row," she said. "Afterward, I just had to come up and say how much I enjoyed the concert. Then, as Edwin and I began talking, one thing led to another and, somehow, I wound up spending the night here."

"Yes," Rachael said in a quiet, strained voice. "I can see that."

"I know, being in show business, this is probably nothing unusual to you. But I must confess, it's all very new to me, and very exciting."

Rachael turned to go.

"Rachael, wait," Edwin called.

Rachael stopped. "Wait for what?" she asked.

"This—this." He made a gesture with his hands. "I don't know how to explain this, it just happened," he said. He forced a smile. "But you are right, it's wonderful news about the review."

"Good-bye, Edwin."

"Rachael, no, don't go. We can work this out."

"There is nothing to work out," Rachael said. Stepping outside, she forced herself not to cry.

Now, two years later, Rachael lay in bed in a hotel room in Pueblo, Colorado, staring up into the darkness. She had not cried over Edwin, and she was not going to cry now.

She had given twenty-five dollars of her money to help pay for the theater. The troupe had managed to come up with only two hundred eighteen of the two hundred fifty dollars needed, but Joel Montgomery, owner of the theater, had agreed to accept that.

When Rachael went downstairs to leave the hotel the next morning, the clerk gave her two envelopes.

"What is this?" she asked.

"You must be quite a popular young lady," the clerk said. "They are letters to be delivered to you."

"Thank you," Rachael said. Paying her bill, she walked out into the lobby and sat on one of the circular couches to read her mail. The first was from Mary Buffington.

Rachael opened the envelope and began to read:

Dear Rachael,
  We learned of a train leaving at three o'clock this morning, so we decided to take it. I thought about waking you and telling you good-bye, but given the blow

*we all received yesterday, I thought that sleep might be
better for you.*

*Hugh said he is not going to let J. Garon get away
with stealing our money, and he intends to recover it.
I don't know how he plans to do this, but you know
that Hugh is a very determined man, once he sets his
mind to it.*

*If he is successful in recovering the money, I will try to
see that you receive what is due you, but in order to do
that, you must keep in touch with me, so I will know
where you are.*

*You will always be able to reach us at the Players'
Guild in New York. Good luck to you in your
Western adventure.*

> *Love,*
> *Your friends, Mary and Hugh*

P.S. The rest of the troupe sends their love as well.

Putting that letter aside, Rachael opened the other
one.

Dear Miss Kirby,

*My name is Corey Hampton. My brother Prentiss and
I own a saloon in Higbee, Colorado. Let me assure you,
it is a saloon of the highest repute.*

*Last night I attended the performance you and the
others gave, and I enjoyed it very much. But what I
enjoyed most was your piano playing. It was beautiful,
and it held me spellbound for the entire evening.*

*Then, later, I enjoyed a late dinner, only to discover
that you and the other players were at a table very near
mine. I intended to come introduce myself to you, but I*

*overheard your conversation, and realized that you had
been stranded by an unscrupulous thief who took all your
money.*

*As I understood the conversation (and I beg you to
forgive me for my eavesdropping), you and the others are
now without employment. Also, if I understood correctly,
the others are returning, but you plan to say out here.*

*I would be very pleased to offer you a job playing the
piano in the Golden Nugget. If you are interested in such
a position, please meet me for breakfast at Two Tonys'
Restaurant on Santa Fe Avenue. I will stay there until
ten o'clock, at which time I must catch a train to return
to Higbee.*

> *Sincerely,*
> *Corey Hampton*

When Rachael stepped into the restaurant a few minutes later, the maitre d' came up to her.

"Yes, madam, are you alone?"

"No, Mr. Deckert, the lady is with me," a man said, getting up from a nearby table.

"You are Mr. Hampton?" Rachael asked.

"I am."

Rachael smiled. "I am a pianist," she said.

"I beg your pardon?"

"In your letter, you said you wanted to hire me as a
piano player. I am not a piano player, I am a pianist. Do
you still want to hire me?"

Corey Hampton smiled, and nodded. "Oh, yes,
ma'am, I want to hire you, Miss Kirby," he said. "I think
Higbee is ready for a pianist."

MORE FICTION BY
WILLIAM W. JOHNSTONE

More Western Adventures
From Karl Lassiter

First Cherokee Rifles

0-7860-1008-8 ·   **$5.99**US/**$7.99**CAN

The Battle of Lost River

0-7860-1191-2   **$5.99**US/**$7.99**CAN

White River Massacre

0-7860-1436-9   **$5.99**US/**$7.99**CAN

Warriors of the Plains

0-7860-1437-7   **$5.99**US/**$7.99**CAN

Sword and Drum

0-7860-1572-1   **$5.99**US/**$7.99**CAN

Available Wherever Books Are Sold!

Visit our website at **www.kensingtonbooks.com**.